Dedicated to India, with much love.

"In a dark time, the eye begins to see."
Theodore Roethke

Monday 1st March

These hands are ninety-three years old. They belong to Charlotte Marie Bradley Miller. She was so frail that her grand-daughter had to carry her onto the set to take this photo. It's a close-up. Her emaciated arms emerge from the top corners of the photo, and the background is black, maybe velvet, as if we're being protected from seeing the strings. One wrist rests on the other, and her fingers hang loose, close together, a pair of folded wings. And you can see her insides. The bones of her knuckles bulge out of the skin, which sags like plastic that has melted in the sun and is dripping off her, wrinkling and folding. Her veins look as though they're stuck to the outside of her hands. They're a colour that's difficult to describe: blue, but also silver, green; her blood runs through them, close to the surface. The book says she died shortly after they took this picture. Did she even get to see it? Maybe it was the last beautiful thing she left in the world.

I'm trying to decide whether or not I want to carry on living. I'm giving myself three months of this journal to decide. You might think that sounds melodramatic, but I don't think I'm alone in wondering whether it's all worth it. I've seen the look in people's eyes. Stiff suits travelling to work, morning after morning, on the cramped and humid tube. Tarted-up girls and gangs of boys reeking of aftershave, reeling on the pavements on a Friday night, trying to mop up the dreariness of their week with one desperate, fake-happy night. I've heard the weary grief in my dad's voice.

So where do I start with all this? What do you want to know about me? I'm Ruth White, thirty-two years old, going on a hundred. I live alone with no boyfriend and no cat in a tiny flat in central London. In fact, I had a non-relationship with a man at work, Dan, for seven years. I'm sitting in my bedroom-cum-living room right now, looking up every so often at the thin rain slanting across a flat, grey sky. I work in a city hospital lab as a microbiologist. My dad is an accountant and lives with his sensible second wife, Julie, in a sensible second home. Mother finished dying when I was fourteen, three years after her first diagnosis. What else? What else is there?

Charlotte Marie Bradley Miller. I looked at her hands for twelve minutes. It was odd describing what I was seeing in words. Usually the picture just sits inside my head and I swish it around like tasting wine. I have huge books all over my flat — books you have to take in both hands to lift. I've had the photo habit for years. Mother bought me my first book, black and white landscapes by Ansel Adams. When she got really ill, I used to take it to bed with me and look at it for hours, concentrating on the huge trees, the still water, the never-ending skies. I suppose it helped me think about something other than what was happening. I learned to focus on one photo at a time rather than flicking from scene to scene in search of something to hold me. If I concentrate, then everything stands still. Although I use them to escape the world, I also think they bring me closer to it. I've still got that book. When I take it out, I handle the pages as though they might flake into dust.

Mother used to write a journal. When I was small, I sat by her bed in the early mornings on a hard chair and looked at her face as her pen spat out sentences in short bursts. I imagined what she might have been writing about

— princesses dressed in star-patterned silk, talking horses, adventures with pirates. More likely she was writing about what she was going to cook for dinner and how irritating Dad's snoring was.

I've always wanted to write my own journal, and this is my chance. Maybe my last chance. The idea is that every night for three months, I'll take one of these heavy sheets of pure white paper, rough under my fingertips, and fill it up on both sides. If my suicide note is nearly a hundred pages long, then no-one can accuse me of not thinking it through. No-one can say, 'It makes no sense; she was a polite, cheerful girl, had everything to live for,' before adding that I did keep myself to myself. It'll all be here. I'm using a silver fountain pen with purple ink. A bit flamboyant for me, I know. I need these idiosyncratic rituals; they hold things in place. Like the way I make tea, squeezing the tea-bag three times, the exact amount of milk, seven stirs. My writing is small and neat; I'm striping the paper. I'm near the bottom of the page now. Only ninety-one more days to go before I'm allowed to make my decision. That's it for today. It's begun.

Tuesday 2nd March

What an exciting life I lead. Alarm set for 7.35 a.m. Pull on a dressing gown, even though no-one can see into my flat. I hear my grandma's voice: 'What if there's a fire!' Crappy morning TV. Breakfast of bran flakes, semi-skimmed milk, a glass of orange juice (supermarket own). Freshly squeezed is too expensive. Dad's drilled it into me: save money! I'm not sure what I'm saving it for. Shower, get dressed (a white shirt, a black pair of trousers, smart shoes that hurt when I walk). Mascara. I see myself in the mirror and notice that the lines around my eyes stay visible even when I relax my face. I look back at my grey-blue eyes — they're asking me a question but I can't quite hear what they're saying. Pale mushroom skin. Long, straight black hair that always reminds me of those evil-looking ravens, pulled back into a neat pony-tail. There's nothing about my face that should make me ugly, nothing unusual, but I don't quite pull off looking pretty.

Make sandwiches for lunch. Fetch my boring black handbag with its exciting contents – a packet of tissues, my purse, a small first-aid kit, a mirror. Lock the front door and join the river of commuters at the tube. We're always in such a hurry — for what? Get to work, clock in. Say hi to the others — Maggie, John, Khalid, using my best pretend-happy voice. Button up my lab coat, start work. Collect Petri dishes from the hot room. Collect patient report forms. Match them up. Look at what's grown. Look down my microscope. Look at more Petri dishes. Look down my microscope again. Repeat one hundred times.

10.45 tea break. 12.30 lunch, usually spent in Hyde park, alone with my sandwiches. Back to work. 15.30 tea break. Work. 17.30 home. Stop falling asleep at the back there, this is my life. 17.50 get home and open my exciting mail: bills and junk. 18.00 cook dinner, crap telly. 21.30 choose a photo to look at before I go to sleep. I often toss and turn in the middle of the night, so it's good to get into bed early, and what would I be staying up for anyway? Up at 7.35 a.m. Pull on my dressing gown. You get the idea. Nothing that makes any difference to the world.

I thought about my mother this evening. It's what Dad always called her, 'your mother'. 'Ask your mother if she wants a cup of coffee.' 'Fetch a knife for your mother.' Even now when he talks about her to other people, he calls her 'Ruth's mother' or 'my late wife'. I've never heard him say her name. Morden. A beautiful word; it didn't get used enough. I don't even know if it's a real name. Her mother Aggie liked to do things differently, and I can imagine her noticing it on the map one day and liking the sound of it. To me it sounds medieval, mysterious. I was thinking about her dying, like always. About the three things that happened, the three things I witnessed that I'll never forget. They taunted me as they usually do, threatening to take up the space behind my eyes. They spin like a merry-go-round, and I only catch a glimpse of each one before the next appears. If I'm not careful they'll swing into focus. Maybe if I could look at them full on, stare them out, they'd lose some of their power. I will write them down — I'll tell you about them as soon as I feel strong enough. But not yet. Not yet.

Last night I dreamt up her voice, complaining. I was sat in my bedroom in our old house in Maida Vale as a grown-up, doing a jigsaw with a picture on it that I couldn't make out. There were feathers and fur and teeth on different pieces. It sounded like she was just outside my door. She was saying 'Ruthie! Can't you remember some good days? What about when we went to the circus, or when we made fairy cakes? When I was healthy, before I started to shrink! I'm sick of seeing myself like that in your head, Ruthie, sick of it!' It went on and on. I wanted her to shut up, I wanted to get my jigsaw finished. Her voice held me frozen to the spot, squirming.

I've been thinking about getting a special present for Dad, just in case, and wondered about having my portrait painted. I saw an advert in the local paper a couple of weeks ago — I remember reading it and thinking it odd. I rummaged about in the pile of papers waiting to be recycled and found it. It said, 'Portraits. Want to know how others see you? Come and be painted.' Then it had the word 'Red' (was that her name?) and a contact number. I'll give her a ring tomorrow, see what she says. I'm not sure I want to know how others see me.

Wednesday 3rd March

I'm still not sure what to do with this big white space. It's silly, but before I start writing, my heart speeds up. What should I write about? If I'm stuck on the third day, then what are my hopes for getting this finished? I can write about what's outside me, about the pictures I look at, the people I see on the way to work. But I'm meant to be writing about me. Rummaging about in my head, pulling out what I think will be useful for you to see. Hand over hand — a thread of words that comes out like a string of knotted handkerchiefs from a magician's sleeve. I can't find anything to get a grip on. It feels like there's nothing there. Maybe there *isn't* anything, maybe my soul just rattles around inside me, a pea-sized lump of grey that gets me out of bed, into my clothes, into work, back home. That puts food into my mouth, chews and swallows. That flicks the TV from channel to channel, that speaks pretend words with a pretend voice. How dead am I already? Where did I go? When did it happen?

A girl called Mary started at work today. She's spending some time on the main swabs section with me before she goes to our training officer Tony for some 'proper' training. She's tiny, with matchstick arms and legs, short afro hair and a nervous, toothy smile. The training portfolio they have to fill in now was almost bigger than she was. She seems so young, straight out of university and in her first job — she couldn't even look me in the eye when I talked to her. I tried to put her at ease by telling her about my scary first day when I dropped a tray of agar plates all over the floor. Today I showed her round the whole lab and explained things as I went — the prep room, the TB cabinet, the blood culture room... she was anxious to commit everything I said to memory. I suppose I'm responsible for her for the time being. I felt sorry for her. I wasn't sure what to say to make it any easier for her.

I called the portrait painter from the advert this evening. When a man answered I asked if I could speak to Red and he said, 'This is Red.' His accent was strong, Russian or Eastern European, his voice deep. I'd written down a list of questions so I wouldn't get flustered, and he answered them all quite brusquely — he didn't seem bothered about persuading me to hire him. He charges two hundred pounds for a painting, and he needs you to sit for him twice a week for six or seven sessions. That's quite a lot of time and the price sounded reasonable to me. He works from his house near Hyde Park and has an afternoon slot free at two on Tuesdays and Thursdays. My line manager at work should be OK about that. He wanted me to see some of his paintings before I came round and gave me two internet addresses. I'm seeing him for an initial meeting next Tuesday. When I'd put the phone down I felt a short bloom of excitement — I don't usually do things like that. It pushed aside the usual background sadness for a while, the sadness that I'm so used to I hardly notice any more. Like looking through dirty windows — it's only when a fly lands on the glass that you notice how filthy they are, how much they're obscuring your view.

Speaking to Red reminded me of a book of photos I have of Russia. I looked at a frozen Lake Baikal tonight. The water reaches more than halfway up the page, where it meets a thin strip of land hung with mist, and above is the sky, full of fluffy white and blue-grey clouds that look as if they're made out of something you could touch — marshmallow or whipped cream. The book said that this lake is four hundred miles long and holds twenty percent of the world's fresh water. Three hundred and thirty six rivers flow into it. In the middle of the picture are a few blocks of ice, crumbled onto the water like lumps of icing sugar, balancing the whiteness of the clouds above. In the foreground, you can see pieces of ice floating on the surface in the shape of those scissor-shells I remember picking up from the beach as a child. Underneath the water are big rocks, mostly hidden by the sunlight colouring the surface silver. Further off is a blanket of ice, keeping everything underneath it safe. I'd like to take off my clothes and paddle, feeling the large stones against the soles of my feet. Just before I'm out of my depth I'd take a last, deep breath and submerge — swimming under the ice, my eyes shut and my hair flowing back, feeling the strength of the water as I push past. My skin would tingle as glittering scales pushed up through it and my legs would join together into a strong flat muscle designed for moving fast through water. I'd like to find a home for myself under that ice-covering.

Thursday 4th March

I suppose I'd better start on the story of my life. But where do I begin? I'd rather not start at all — I don't want to drag it all up again (as Dad would say).

I'll start with Abbie, my aunt. I can talk about her — it'll get me warmed up. Abbie is Mother's sister. I only met her a couple of times when I was small. There was some kind of squabble between them, and they hadn't spoken for years. Mother told me she lived 'in the country', and as far as I knew everyone in the country had a farm. I imagined her feeding the chickens and cows every morning, like in a picturebook my dad read to me over and over. I remember being fascinated by the tea she brought to drink — it was light green with no milk and smelt funny. When she let me take a sip, I thought it tasted of grass, and I could even see strands of it floating about at the bottom of the mug. I thought she might have been teasing me but was far too polite to say anything. Whenever I drink green tea now, it takes me back to her dark auburn hair with glints of gold in a thick rope plait, and her crinkly green eyes. It takes me back to her steady, musical voice, which soothed me.

When Mother got really ill, Abbie started coming round again. She used to disappear into Mother's bedroom for hours on end and come out looking grey and drawn. Her clothes were always colourful — patchwork and velvet with tiny stitched-in mirrors — I thought she looked like a hippy. She tried to talk to me in the hallway, using different conversation openers — 'How was school today?' or 'What kind of music do you like?' or 'How are you doing?' I answered in polite monosyllables, and eventually she got the message. I didn't want to talk to anyone by then; it was nothing personal.

Afterwards I stayed with her for a few weeks while Dad tried to gather the pieces of himself together. She didn't have cows or chickens, but she did have a huge tortoise-shell cat, Oscar, who took a liking to me right away and jumped onto my lap whenever I sat down. We'd never had pets at home, and I was a bit wary of him at first — he had massive paws, and I saw his spiked claws come out when he puddened on a cushion. When he washed himself I was amazed at the loudness of the noises he made — sucking and squelching, quite obscene.

Abbie respected my privacy, always offering to spend time with me, and not looking offended when I turned her down (which I inevitably did). She gave me space like a gift. As I write, tears are pricking at my eyes. I'm surprised — I didn't realise how grateful I was. And Oscar became my confidante — I talked to him quietly so no-one else could hear. He was a good listener, except the times when he suddenly decided he'd had enough and trotted outside to stalk the autumn leaves. I couldn't blame him for that. He never answered back. He didn't expect anything from me. And he kept everything that I said to him a secret. In a way, Oscar was more real to me than Abbie during those first few weeks.

I loved her house, too — a wonderful, lived-in house, full of books and mugs with dregs in and lengths of Indian material and small piles of pine cones she was collecting for god-knows-what. There was a real fire in the living room, and one night we cooked chestnuts in the embers. The garden was tangled with weeds and was full of places to crouch in, to hide. I stubbed my toe on a stone fairy once, hidden in the undergrowth. I called her Lila and made a little shrine for her in the broken shed. I surrounded her with fresh flowers, shiny stones and empty snail shells. I talked to her too, when Oscar was busy with other things. I was sorry to leave her behind.

Towards the end of my stay, I thought I might be ready to speak to Abbie as well, but then Dad came to take me home. The strength of her goodbye hug nearly winded me, and after a few startled moments I became terrified that I'd start crying and wouldn't know how to stop. Thankfully she let go just in time, told me to 'go well', and that was that. I didn't go there again — Dad told me that she reminded him of my mother too much, and I was fiercely loyal to him — who else was there to be loyal to?

She lives twenty-three miles away from me now, and I haven't seen her for eighteen years. You think that's odd? It's not that I don't want to see her. It just feels easier to let her slip into the past, with Mother. I haven't even thought about Abbie for ages. Although… that's not strictly true. Whenever I see a woman with dark auburn hair, my stomach does a little flip. I can never decide if I should cross the street to see if it's her, or hide my face and hurry past. It's never been her.

Friday 5th March

Maybe next I can write about the time before Mother got ill. The easy bit.

I've been sat here for ten minutes now, wondering where to start. I was eleven when she first got ill, and when I try to remember her before that, I can't separate her out. It's like the cancer is a part of her personality, the same as her bobbed dark hair or the way she had her coffee milky with three sugars. There, I said the 'c' word. Not 'coffee'. I hate it — I hate the sound of it — like the words mucus or sorrow — they give names to things we'd rather not think about. Without a name, it's harder for things to exist. It was breast cancer to start with, before pieces of it broke off and travelled around her body. I can remember hearing her in the next room arguing with Dad. Mother was saying she wanted to keep it if she could, and Dad was saying she should just have it all taken off, to be safe. I don't think that she ever really believed it would kill her, not until...

I suppose I had a pretty happy childhood until then. We lived in Maida Vale in one of those three-storey houses that are mostly split into flats now, or stupidly expensive. It had high ceilings and was crammed full of a jumble of furniture and pictures and ornaments. It always felt cold. We'd inherited it from my mother's parents — her dad had been quite a successful architect. We moved in when my grandfather died, just after I was born. Grandma Aggie died a few years afterwards — all I can remember of her is seeing her stiff-backed like a statue on her chair in her room.

We had a piano in the front room, where Mother would play jazz. She'd learnt how to improvise from her dad — she never read music. Her playing was infused with energy. When she started, Dad would stop whatever he was doing and go into a stiff pose and then he'd start moving ever so slowly — maybe by tapping a foot, or nodding, or clicking his fingers. I couldn't take my eyes off him, laughter bubbling up inside me. He'd use more and more of his body until he was all over the place, all legs and arms, and he'd dance over to me and sweep me up into his whirlwind, his face still straight as I glowed and giggled. He was usually so sensible, so busy with his work — I loved to see him dance. I'm sure it was one of the reasons that Mother loved to play. Afterwards he'd pretend that nothing had happened.

I can remember Mother baking me rock cakes — I'd had some at my friend's house and had told her I liked them. I took a bite and they were solid, they stuck to the roof of my mouth in a big lump. I made a face and said, 'I don't like it,' and she suddenly swept the cooking bowls and ingredients onto the floor with her forearm. I remember her face as she stormed past me, furious red and dusted with flour. Dad came into the kitchen and said, 'What have you done?' — I still had a lump of cake in my throat and was trying to swallow it. He followed her upstairs. I ate the whole cake and then another one, chewing hard. They sat heavily inside me. We didn't mention it when she came down later, perfumed and smiling.

My room was small, with a single bed and a huge chest of drawers. I loved to collect things and had a whole drawer full of my 'treasures' — coins, packs of playing cards, colouring pencils. I'd show them off proudly to my friend Debbie when she came over, and we'd spend hours counting out the coins or arranging feathers into a pattern on the bedspread. I can remember my wallpaper, covered in leaves. I can remember hiding under the bed during a storm.

What else? What else... why isn't there more? I have to think about different rooms in the house to spark off memories — here's the cooker where Mother made porridge, here's the kitchen cupboard where I get down my favourite blue glass and fill it with apple juice. Here's the worn rug in the sitting room; you can see through to the bones of it. I sit on it cross-legged and play with Suki, my doll. She's tired too. And here's my bedroom, where people read stories to me and where I chose what to wear when I'm old enough not to make mistakes and clash the colours. Where I lie in bed and look up at the ceiling.

What was I thinking back then? I have to look in from the outside and guess. What would a little girl in that house with those parents be thinking? Is she lonely? Does she realise that she can't quite get her teeth into her parents, even before the illness? They skitter away just out of reach. I want to give her something, something special like a musical box or a fairy doll. I feel strange after writing today. Like I have a blackbird in my stomach.

Saturday 6th March

Today was awful. The kind of day that makes me think this whole writing idea is stupid. You don't really give a shit, do you? All these boring, meaningless words. I'm not sure what brought these feelings on. They never seem to be attached to anything; they don't have any reasons. They're like a liquid that gets into me through the soles of my feet and soaks upwards until my whole body is sopping. A cold, grey liquid. Oily. Some days it waits for me — it gets me as soon as my feet touch the carpet. Maybe if I ran really fast, I could shake some of it out of me. Maybe if I lay really still, it would get bored of me and drain away through the floor. Maybe it would go and look for someone else. If only it were that easy.

I didn't get out of bed today. I didn't really see the point — no-one in the world knows if I do or if I don't. There wasn't anything out there that I wanted to go and see or do. I can eat in bed. I can cry here — scattering the duvet with disgusting bits of screwed up tissue. I can feel perfectly sorry for myself here without going through the whole palaver of getting up and washing and Hoovering the flat — and for what? It doesn't last. Dirt and dust is all around us; the air is saturated with it. It's settling right now on my carpet, my TV screen. My skin is excreting small globules of sweat all over my body. Grease is covering my hair from the roots to the tips; I can feel it when I run my fingers through. I'll need to go to sleep again at some point anyway. Why bother with the day? Can you give me a good reason?

I don't think people like to think too hard about the point of their lives. I heard a story once about a man who was on holiday in the Caribbean. He was sitting in a deckchair on a stunning beach — the sky was blue, the sand warm, the sea calm. He was cramming his head full of knowledge from an academic textbook. He looked over at the barman — stood staring at the sky. He felt good about himself — here he was, making the most of his holiday time, learning, doing something productive. There was the barman just idling his time away.

And then he thought again — what difference does it make? What difference does it make if I die with a head full of knowledge? Why not just sit back and enjoy the view? I can't forget this story. I think about it whenever I'm doing something because I feel I ought to and feeling pleased with myself. Like cleaning between the oven and the cupboard. Why do we kid ourselves that it makes any difference?

This crushing sadness weighs on me. It's pressing me down — no — it's pressing me up — to a place where nothing can touch me. I'm in a hot air balloon and sandbag after sandbag are dropping to the ground. Maybe I'll float off so far that I'll never touch down again. I felt the same way when I was fourteen, when Mother was really ill. I remember one night they were arguing about whether Mother should go into a hospice or not. The doctors had recommended it, but Mother didn't want to go. Dad said she never did what she was told; Mother called him a cowardly bastard and worse. Their words were full of needles. I turned the TV up louder and louder and eventually stormed out of the room and ran upstairs to my bedroom, slamming the door shut.

After a while I realised no-one was coming up to see if I was OK. I was in the hot air balloon, getting higher and higher, and I got scared. So I did something I had control over.

I took a safety pin from my drawer. And I made a small hole in the fleshy bit on the back of my hand, between my thumb and index finger. That was the first time. It worked, and so I did it again, whenever the pressure got too great, whenever I started to lose my hold. I let blood out in satisfying bright red spheres that grew from the tiniest spot until the surface tension gave out, and then popped into a drip. Sometimes I'd taste it — touch the tip of my tongue to it, like tasting sherbet. I only ever made three or four holes at a time, just in case someone might notice. Maybe I should have covered myself in them. Maybe I should have made them bigger.

I stopped when Mother died, and I haven't done it since, but when this oily depression enters me I have the familiar urge, a craving. I find a drawing pin or a safety pin and hold the spike close to my skin — teasing, pulling it across the surface. Pushing it in, just underneath, just inside. Never deep enough to bleed. I wasn't going to tell you about that.

Sunday 7th March

Another bad day. I got up, but I may as well not have. I spent the whole day moping about — sitting on the sofa staring at the wall, then crying a bit, then reading a bit, then staring at the wall again. I did do two loads of washing and put the rubbish out, but I don't think I'll get any prizes for that. The oily stuff was still in me. I suppose it never really leaves me altogether; there's always a little bit in the tips of my fingers, or a pool of it at the base of my spine. In fact it seems to be a part of my blood somehow. We've lived together for so long. I'm not sure if it would even be healthy to get rid of it altogether. Am I sounding crazy? Should I start this page again? What are you thinking about me?

I was thinking about Abbie again today. Since writing about her last week, memories of my stay there keep blossoming in my head from nowhere. The smell of the sheets on the bed I slept in — musty, like dried rose petals. The wooden wind-chime in the garden and the hollow, gorgeous noises it made in the breeze as I sat on the porch with cucumber sandwiches with the crusts cut off. The way Oscar used to lie on the rug in front of the fire, all four legs straight up in the air and folded at the knee, eyes shut, belly up. The jam sponge cake Abbie made for me, with dark pink icing and silver balls. She gave me so much.

There's something I haven't told you about Abbie and me. I mucked things up between us. She tried really hard to keep in touch with me after Mother died. There were lots of phone calls — Dad used to say a gruff 'hello' before handing the phone straight to me and I only ever gave her 'yes's and 'no's and 'OK's. She wrote me letters too, saying she understood how my dad felt, respected his feelings. That I should make contact with her when I felt ready. There was even a trip to the cinema, a dreadful film for little kids. I was moody and ungrateful. So it wasn't just because of Dad that she finally stopped calling, stopped writing. I drove her away. I can't remember why I did it, or even whether I did it on purpose. I seem to have the knack.

She's sent me a birthday card every year since then. I got them all out this evening. Eighteen of them — all of them saying happy birthday and, 'You know where I am if you need to talk — I hope this is still the right address for you,' or, 'It'd still be great to hear from you, this is my phone number.' Here's the one she sent me for my thirty-second last May. It's a silk painting of a blue flower, maybe a cornflower. A clear, sunny blue. I think she makes some of them herself. And here's the one I got for my fifteenth, a pencil drawing of a cat; I remember seeing it on our mat before Dad did and taking it up to my room, looking at it quickly before hiding it under my bed.

I didn't tell you about the cards before. It makes me feel worse about myself, knowing that she's made the effort over all these years, and I've given her nothing in return. I can't bear to think about how angry she must be after I've ignored her for all these years. An anger that has built up slowly year on year, piece by tiny piece, filling her up whenever she thinks of me. I wonder if I ought to say thank you to her before... to say thank you and that I'm grateful for everything she did. I am grateful. I've suppose I've nothing to lose any more. That's one advantage of my three-month deadline. Ha ha, deadline. It doesn't really matter any more what I do or don't do. Maybe I could write her a letter. Or send her a card, one with a nice picture. Maybe I'll do it tomorrow.

I looked at a black and white photo of a family of tinkers today. Mathias Oppersdorff took it in County Clare in 1969. I was a toddler in 1969; it wasn't as long ago as you'd think. There are three of them — the father on the left, holding his boy on his knee, and his wife, crouched with her skirt over her knees and her fore-arms resting on the tops of her thighs. Her face is strong and sharp, she has taken the wind and sun like a rock, but there is also a vulnerability to it, leather softened over time. You can imagine her being tender with her child — putting a hand gently on the top of his head, even while she tells him off. He won't have many possessions, no shiny plastic train sets or clean new clothes. Even their cooking pots in the foreground look like old paint pots with handles. But I think he'll be OK, this boy — you can tell by looking at his father's face. You can tell by the way he's holding onto his son. Tight.

Monday 8th March

I'm still looking after the new girl, Mary, at work. She can write up reports on the computer by herself already — she's a quick learner. I'm still worried that she's not enjoying herself. She's so quiet. She goes off on her own every lunchtime with her packed lunch, and she doesn't take any of her breaks with us. None of the others seem to be making much effort to get to know her. I still don't know much about her, either — everything I do know I've had to ask her, and I don't like to prise information out of people. Her family came over from Trinidad in the 60s, and they visit relatives every couple of years. She lives at home with her mother and her mother's elderly cousin — I didn't want to ask about her dad, just in case he'd died. She has two sisters and a brother, all older and already left home. She wants to be a consultant one day. She's a Christian and goes to church every Sunday. She doesn't have a boyfriend. That's about it. It just feels like I'm getting it wrong with her somehow. How can I get her to talk to me a bit more, to relax? I wish there were instruction books for this kind of thing.

I suddenly remembered this evening about the portrait painter. I hadn't had time to look on the internet for his paintings — unlike me to be so unorganised. I looked up the site addresses. One didn't work, so I must have written it down wrong. The other had two painting on it. I read what the site said about the artist with interest — Yevgeniy Nikolayevich, born in 1965, only a few years older than me.

He'd gone to St. Martins Art School, has exhibited at a few small galleries around London;

I hadn't heard of any of them. They described his occupation as 'fine artist and commercial portrait painter'. One of the quotes said, 'Nikolayevich reaches in through his subjects' eyes and pulls out their souls, whether they invite him in or not.' I wasn't sure I liked the sound of that.

I wasn't sure about his paintings either. They were plain, flat, with muted colours. There was something meditative about them. But the ones I saw made me feel uncomfortable. One was of an older woman who sat with her hands folded in front of her, like in the photo of Charlotte Marie Bradley Miller. She looked prim. She was looking just off-camera, smiling a bright, brave smile, but her eyes were tired, watery. In the background, there was a dark shape you couldn't quite make out, maybe a giant hand, pushing down on the top of her head. The other one was of a small, dark-haired boy who was sat on a tall chair, looking down at the floor. In his hand he held a ball, but loosely, like it was about to drop. I looked at them for a long time. I wanted to know more about the people in the paintings. I'll still go and meet him, I said I would, but I feel less hopeful now.

After looking at the paintings, I looked at another photo. It's here in front of me now — I don't know if you want to know what it is. Maybe it's getting boring for me to describe them to you? Or maybe it tells you something about me? It's starting to scare me that I have so little to write about. I want to tell you something exciting, something that'll make you like me. Something amazing happened on the way home from work today... You wouldn't believe what my friend told me last night... I can't wait to tell you about what I'm doing next weekend... other people have conversations like this. I hear them on the street sometimes, or sitting in the park, the rich juicy things that happen to other people. I wonder if you'd believe me if I slipped in a couple of stories I'd borrowed from them, if I promised to give them back as soon as I'd used them? What has happened to me in my life? What is there to tell you?

nothing nothing

Tuesday 9th March

I went to meet the portrait painter today. I was there twenty minutes early and wandered the streets for a while. I came back at 1.57, my nerves growling. I found his place easily enough, a small, ordinary-looking terrace in a row of ordinary-looking terraces. The house next door had a pile of gravel and sacks of cement in their front garden. The door's faded, light blue paint was peeling off in places. The heavy velvet purple curtains in the front room were shut. He had a brass doorknocker in the shape of a lion, and it made a sharp explosive bang that caused me to jump. I heard a deep voice shout 'maaam' from inside the house and waited for a while to see if he came to the door. He didn't, so I turned the handle, pushed the door open and peered inside.

I was looking down a narrow, dingy hallway, and there were paintings everywhere. The colours were all rich, yet somehow muted, like the ones I'd seen on the web. The flowered wallpaper was tatty, and the dark red carpets were worn through to the underlay in places. It still felt sumptuous somehow, faded majesty, as if the person who lived here had money and style but was more concerned with other matters. I said 'hello?' and followed the 'come!' down along the hall to a room off to the right. I poked my head around the door.

He was standing over by a canvas next to the window, washing brushes. He turned round and looked at me for a few seconds without saying anything, not smiling. I felt the blood rush to my cheeks and was annoyed at myself. I'm not sure what he was thinking. Then he nodded and said I should sit down in a battered red and gold armchair, one of those antique stiff-backed ones, and asked me to give him a few seconds while he 'gave attention to his brushes'. He was huge — not fat, but not muscles either, really, not like those pumped up ridiculous gym-boys. His face was pale, flat, and freckled. Pale blue eyes. He had a scar that ran from the outside of his right eye towards his right ear, as if someone had drawn it on with a pink felt tip. And he had the reddest hair I'd ever seen. If his eyebrows weren't the same colour, I would have wondered if he'd got it out of a packet. The sky was dull behind him. But as I watched, the sun moved out from behind a cloud, and he lit up like a match.

Eventually he turned and gave me his full attention. He said 'Ruth?' and waited for me to speak. He said it 'Root' — the 'r' rolled, the vowel sound short and guttural. I nodded and told him my prepared white lie — that it would be my dad's sixtieth soon and that I wanted to give him something special. He nodded and walked towards me, moving his face in towards mine. I couldn't help it — I flinched. He backed off slightly, raising his eyebrows a tiny fraction, and continued to walk around me, looking at me as if I were a bowl of fruit. He towered above me. I felt as if he was deciding whether I were worth painting or not. I sat still, hardly breathing. Then he said 'OK' and pulled a chair over from near the window to sit on. With a nod he said, 'I will paint you.'

'Would you like me to give you some money...?' I asked. He interrupted with a dismissive flick of his hand. 'Later. First I tell you how I work.' He told me about his 'method' — he didn't want me to stay still, he wanted me to 'wriggle and jiggle' if I felt like it, he wanted me to just be myself. Privately I smiled at this — if only I knew who I was! He said he might ask me questions which I could answer or not answer, either was fine. That way he'd get the 'bigger part' of me onto the canvas. I felt a short burst of excitement and fear rise up in me. And I felt safe for no reason. I felt that he'd look after me, this strange, huge, red-haired man. He knew what he was doing. He was an artist.

He asked for my commitment by saying 'so?' and picking up his brush, squinting his eyes into a question. I smiled, embarrassed, and said, 'Yes please, thank you, thanks.' I didn't say it, I gibbered it. He said we'd begin on Thursday. He nodded again, and then walked back over to his canvas and stood there looking at it. I sat there awkwardly for a minute or so, and when I said in a small voice, 'Shall I go now?' he started and looked surprised that I was still there. He nodded and winked, and I thanked him again (stupidly) and saw myself out. All afternoon I thought about his studio, heard his voice in my head. I wonder what it will be like to be painted. When I think about it, a small smile lights up inside me.

Wednesday 10th March

I sent a card to Abbie this evening. I was going to write her a letter, tell her about what I've been doing. But I started it six times, and it kept going wrong. A few stunted sentences, and I just ran out of things to say, like getting beached halfway down these pieces of white paper. It was still only seven, so I got up, put on my coat and went straight out into the bustling, dark street. I walked to a shop I know that stocks beautiful cards. I don't look at them very often, as there isn't often anyone to send one too (altogether now… *aaaah, poor Ruth*).

It took me ages to choose — I couldn't decide between a charcoal drawing of a cat on a rug that reminded me of Oscar, and a photo of violently red poppies. I bought both in the end. I flipped a coin, but when the poppies won I was disappointed, so I pulled the one with the cat out of its rustling cellophane covering. After practising a few sentences on a rough bit of paper I decided on "For Abbie and Oscar, from your terrible niece Ruth — I'm so sorry I've not been in touch. I hope you're well." I put my telephone number in too; it took all my resolve. I licked and sealed the envelope quickly before I could change my mind and rushed out into the street again to post it. It was only when I heard the small thud as it fell onto the pile of letters inside the post box that I thought 'What have I done?' I'd carried out the whole thing as if I were holding my breath. It's gone now, too late to change my mind.

The poppies reminded me of making calendars at my primary school in Maida Vale, using those little booklets with every day of the year printed on them in tiny writing. A whole year in a flipbook the size of a teabag. We used to divide up a big piece of paper into quarters with each section being a season. The teachers had collected small treasures for us to stick in the different corners — acorns and brown leaves for autumn, cotton wool and silver glitter for winter, red and orange tissue paper for making spring flowers, bright yellow sheet plastic for a wonky sun.

I can remember the heady excitement of making these calendars — every season this year would be different! And they'd change back and forth over and over! Back then it made me happy knowing I'd see them change. Knowing I might get to make an occasional snowball. Knowing I would plant bulbs at school and then see the green shoots emerge from the cold dark earth for the first time. Alive! I've lost the magic somewhere along the way.

I can't remember having many friends when I was in primary school. When the whole class went on walks, we were asked to get into a crocodile and most children had the same partner every time. Even the unpopular kids knew who to pair up with so they didn't get left out. I usually ended up with our teacher, Miss Large, who had sweaty hands. Everyone else seemed to know the rules for making friends. I'd watch them approach each other during break time, and suddenly they were running off to play ghosts or mummies and daddies. What did they say to each other? I'd put on my nicest voice and go up to the girls and say, 'Will you please play with me?' and they just shook their heads so hard that their hair flew up into the air.

Maybe they smelt the desperation on me. I'd get to join in most of the time by hanging about at the back, not drawing attention to myself. Most of them were OK, really. We didn't fight or anything. The worst they could come up with was 'Boring Ruth' — not the most original of nicknames. I pretended I didn't care.

I dreamt about our old house last night. I was alone in the house in my bedroom, and I heard someone come in downstairs. I knew it was an intruder and felt strangely calm as I heard them come up the stairs towards my room. They weren't bothering to be quiet, so I guessed they didn't know I was there. I shut my eyes and pretended to be asleep as I heard the bedroom door opening. I held my breath and kept my eyes shut for ages before opening one of them a slit. The door was wide open, and there was no-one there. Eventually I got out of bed and tiptoed downstairs.

When I looked into the living room, the TV was on with no sound. There was a black and white programme on about the war, with planes and wasteland and bodies. Someone was sat on the sofa watching it — I could see the back of their head. It was almost bald, with wisps of white hair like dandelion fluff. I slowly walked round the sofa so I could see who it was. Just as their face was about to come into view, I woke up.

Thursday 11th March

I visited the painter today for my first sitting. He came to meet me at the door this time and actually smiled — mostly with his eyes, but his mouth moved up a little at the corners. He seemed less distracted. He took me through to his studio and asked me to sit down, and did I want tea? I said no thanks, and he left the room. I noticed four photos amongst all of the paintings and blank canvasses. They were all of a little girl, maybe two years old, with green eyes, olive skin and black hair. She was grinning in every photo, her tiny new teeth like sweets. Her smile flew out at you — pure pleasure, nothing held back. How wonderful to be able to let your face do what it wants to like that, rather than having to rein it in, keep an eye on it (or two, ha ha). In one of the photos there was a woman with the child, pale like Red, but with darker auburn hair. Not pretty exactly, but she looked sure of herself, as if she'd have interesting things to say. My favourite was a close-up of the little girl cracking her wonderful grin. There was a swathe of light in the top left hand corner where the sun had got into the shot, and her whole face was beaming.

I didn't see him come back in, and it took me by surprise when he spoke. He said he wanted to ask me a couple of questions first to give him a 'head-start'. I didn't have to answer them if I didn't want to; it was up to me. The first question was 'Who are you?' I said, 'I'm Ruth.' I couldn't think of anything else to say, nothing that didn't seem silly.

Things like 'a woman' or 'someone who loves photos' or 'a microbiologist' didn't seem to add much. They didn't seem to bear any relation to who I really am. I sat there in silence and felt more and more embarrassed as he looked over my face, as if he was searching for clues. 'Is that enough?' I asked after a while, sounding childlike. He nodded, and then asked his second question. 'For what do you live?'

And then something terrible happened. I heard a word come out of my mouth. It was as if something in his question had hooked it out of me without my consent, and there it was squirming on the end of the line trying to get away. 'Nothing.' It floated in the air between us, ugly. He narrowed his eyes, and I thought he might say something, but after a few agonising seconds he just nodded again and turned back to his paints. My god, my god — what was he thinking of me now? He chose a crumpled dirty tube and squeezed out a beautiful blue colour, the deep end of a swimming pool. And then he said 'Now, I paint. You, think what you want, say what you want, move your face if you want. I paint what you show me.' I sat there and felt the redness blooming in my cheeks, the blood pulsing in my temples. Staring straight ahead. I had never felt so naked in my entire life.

After a while, I realised that the sky hadn't caved in, and I started to relax. I noticed the head of a plastic doll on a shelf and thought about my Tiny Tears doll, Mabel. Mother had given her to me for my seventh birthday. She cried real tears after drinking water from a bottle, and she had eyes that closed gradually as she was rocked to sleep. It was the most amazing thing I'd ever seen. I took her into school every day, and at first the other girls all gathered round me, clucking and fussing as if she were a real baby. They quickly lost interest, but a skinny girl with dark blond hair like straw called Debbie didn't, and Mabel was the start of our friendship. Mother had always asked hopefully if there were any 'little friends' I wanted to invite to tea, and I can remember her surprise and pleasure the day I asked her if Debbie could come round.

The sitting went quickly until he interrupted by saying 'time up now'. Before I left he fixed me with a strange look, and I felt, stupidly, that he cared about me.

As I walked through my front door, I felt sadness fall on me like snow. Once it's got into me, there's no going back. I've tried all sorts of different things in the past — junk food, seeing a film, photos, going to the park. Whatever I'm doing and however much pleasure it usually gives me, I'm doing it from inside the sadness. I'd be just as happy lying on my back in the middle of a busy pavement, people stepping over me and cursing me for getting in their way. It does something strange to my senses, blunts them — like eating ice-cream when you have a cold. You're vaguely aware that you usually enjoy mint choc chip more, but you carry on eating it just the same. What else could you do?

Friday 12th March

She called. Abbie called! Just after I got in today — I was thinking about Dan and the phone interrupted. When I answered she said, 'Ruth?' I said, 'Yes?' — guarded, something about her voice sounding familiar. She said, 'Ruth, it's me…' and before she'd even said her name I placed her voice. She said it had been wonderful to get my card; she sounded bright, breezy. She didn't sound angry at all; maybe she's clever at hiding her emotions too. We exchanged a few awkward pleasantries — where I was working, how my dad was. Then she asked me round to dinner on Sunday, just me and her. The thought terrified me, but I couldn't think of an excuse quickly enough and so I said yes. I've been thinking about her ever since, about her and Oscar. About whether I can trust her. I don't even know why I wrote that last bit.

I've been thinking about this weird portrait thing too, wondering what I'll look like in my painting. I hope I'll look OK — the whole point of this exercise is that it'll be something for Dad to keep, something for him to remember me by. I don't want to look sad in it — that might depress him even more. I thought about making sure that I smile a lot, but I suspect that the portrait painter will see through that, and maybe it'll make it worse — like the other woman he painted.

I don't think Dad has a clue about the way I really feel, the way I live my life. I'm a great performer by now. I learnt years ago — for Mother, so she wouldn't feel she'd failed, but even more for Dad — he could barely cope with things as they were. Especially when Mother had gone, how could he possibly cope with me? I always made sure I was a low-maintenance daughter for him — not too happy, I think even he would have seen through that. I fooled him into thinking that I could handle my own life, that when he helped out it was a bonus, not something I was relying on. So maybe even if Red did paint me with a stupid smiling face and sad eyes, he'd probably see me as 'cheerful Ruth' anyway — it's too hard for him to see me any other way. Sometimes I wonder if I ought to get angry about that. Anger seems to take so much energy.

I'm going to have to try and hide all of this from Abbie too I suppose. How do people do it? Strike that balance between letting people know 'the real you', and not scaring people off? It reminds me of a friend I had at University, Judy. We spent quite a lot of time together in the first year, sitting in her room when my boyfriend Tom was at lectures. We drank a lot of coffee — neither of us liked the taste to start with, and it gave us the jitters, but it made us feel grown-up, and that was important. Then she met another girl on her course who was really into some kind of heavy metal music, and she started playing it to me all the time. It just sounded like noise to me. At the same time she was using more eye-liner, wearing black, eating less. I could cope with all of that, but I couldn't cope with the things she started telling me, fantasies about hurting people, about being violent.

To begin with she was angry at politicians, people on TV, and gradually it got closer to home. She said things about her tutor, a boy next door, even her mother. I don't know where it all came from but I couldn't handle it, started making excuses, spending more time with Tom, finding other people to hang out with. I lost touch with her in the second year. By that time she was hanging around with a really druggy crowd, and she didn't look very well at all. I don't know what happened to her. She should have kept some of that stuff to herself. It pushed me away.

It just started to thunder outside. I love thunder, especially when I'm inside and warm. Here under my duvet, it almost feels like home. This evening I looked at a photo taken by Imogen Cunningham. It is of a naked young woman who is curled up into a ball, crouched on the floor — there is a curve from her elbow up to her left shoulder and round along the top of her back, then it plunges down to the full globes of her buttocks. The dark background sets off the white of her skin. Her head is out of sight, hung down and hidden by the top of her back. You can see a sliver of one of her breasts, and her legs seem to be tucked up underneath her, as if she is squatting. The fat on her waist is crumpled. Her spine is scored in as if by the thumb of a sculptor. She is all curve and smooth skin. She looks like a seed or a bulb; if you planted her in dark compost and waited patiently, she'd burst into flower.

Saturday 13th March

Another lazy, blank Saturday. What is there to write about today? It's getting harder and harder, these hundreds and hundreds of purple words. I try to tell myself that it doesn't matter what I write as long as the words are here to prove that I've made an effort. But the only things left to write about are too boring. Or too hard. March 13th — at least ten weeks to go. Today I thought about cheating. Does it really matter if I make it to the end? But it feels like breaking the rules, and I've never been very good at that. The rules are all I've ever had.

Dad called today. I haven't talked about Dad much yet, have I? You know he used to dance when my mother played the piano. You know he's an accountant. That he's married to Julie. Here are some more facts. He walks with a limp; he came off his bike when he was little, and a car ran over him. His voice is dry and clipped. His mother was a housewife and his father was a banker. There's something missing from him, something to do with his emotions. I'm not sure exactly what it is, whether he lost it when mother died, or if never had it to start with. He likes to be the expert. He's got a moustache. That's just about everything I know about him anyway.

I hadn't spoken to him in weeks. He was just calling to tell me how much he loved me... ha ha, that'd be the day. He wanted to talk to me about his investments. Well, my investments really — it's my money, but it doesn't feel like it.

He invests money as a kind of hobby and gets a disgusting amount of pleasure from watching his shares go up. Years ago I'd mentioned I had a bit of spare money every month with my quite good job, my quite small flat and my not-having-a-life (I didn't say about the last bit). He offered to start a portfolio for me and has been looking after it ever since.

He's always elusive when I ask him what it's all worth, says it's 'not doing badly, not doing badly at all'. I suppose I need to decide what to do with it, just in case... 'Dad, if anything were to happen to me...' But maybe he'd remember our conversation once it was all over, blame himself for not picking up the signs, go over and over it? I'll write something about it in the final letter I write to him, sign it — that should be legal. Sometimes I wish there were someone to talk to about all of this.

He also said that he and Julie were going to be over my side of the city next weekend and could they 'pop in to the old flaterooney'. Yes, my dad really did say that, just like that man in the Simpsons cartoon. When I first saw Flanders, I couldn't stop laughing at how similar they were. My dad's cheerfulness is more transparent, though — the Simpsons man seems genuinely happy, but Dad has grief running through him like a stick of rock. He puts on a good show, though, and Julie is his 'little ray of sunshine' as he often likes to say to people in front of her. All that jolliness is really exhausting. But I haven't seen him for a couple of months, so I resisted the temptation to make an excuse and said of course it'd be great to see them.

Maybe you're wondering how I usually manage to fit everything into my weekends, with my wide social circle and my exciting hobbies. It's hard, believe me... I'm forced to turn down several invitations from dashing men every

Friday night. Ha ha. I've always been jealous of couples at weekends; the whole concept seems designed for people who live in twos or fours, so they can spend some quality time at home together or take the kids to the zoo. I've never been very good at weekends. It was fine while I was studying at University for my microbiology degree or for my state registration qualification at work. I'd spend all Saturday and most of Sunday in the library. Now I have two whole days to fill.

Saturdays are usually spent catching up on housework — I admit I'm a bit obsessed with things being tidy and clean, so there's always plenty to do. The oven and fridge get cleaned, the sheets and cushion covers get washed... you get the idea. I often have errands to run too — put some dry-cleaning in, buy some new tights. On a good day I might even go to a gallery, or walk in the park. On a bad day I'll sit at home and stare at the walls. Sundays are harder. I'll look at photos, or get the papers and spread them out over the floor, trying not to think about how lonely I am. I should make more of an effort to use my weekends differently, I know. See some people, do some things I enjoy. I wouldn't know where to start.

Sunday 14th March

I'm back after seeing Abbie. I messed it up.

I nearly didn't go — I was looking through the clothes I have and thinking how boring they were, all navy or black or cream. None of them make me feel good; none of them say anything about me. Or maybe they describe me perfectly. In the end, I put on jeans and a white T-shirt and tried to make my hair look nice. I'd decided to take a bottle of non-alcoholic drink with me, the sort with lots of herbal ingredients; I couldn't remember if she drank or not. On the tube I started feeling a bit sick. It might have been the heat and all the people. I was glad to get out into the air.

When she opened the door to me she looked old, as if she'd done a lot of living since I saw her last. Her hair was short and a bit spiky, peppered with grey. She looked really pleased to see me, and she knew not to hug me but put a hand onto my upper arm and pressed. I thought back to the hug that had nearly dissolved me all those years ago, and I had to blink hard. And look at the plants. From the front, her house looks like all the others, standard Georgian brick, all in a row. But when I stepped inside it was more like a greenhouse than a front room. There were plants everywhere — not many flowers, mostly frothy ferns, glossy dark leaves and long grasses. I gabbled something about them as she led me into the kitchen and sat me at the table. I looked out through a glass door into the garden so I wouldn't have to look into her eyes.

So there I was, sipping my Earl Grey. She didn't have any green tea and was surprised that I'd remembered it. The first thing I asked was, 'Where's Oscar?' and she put on a 'concerned-for-me' face and said, 'Ruth, darling, he died.' I said, 'Oh,' and sat in a shocked silence, willing her to change the subject. Oscar, dead. Of course he would be, how stupid of me. It was years ago. Eventually she asked me about my work, and I told her what I did — she seemed impressed, so I must have managed to fool her into thinking it was anything other than donkey work. She gave a good impression of being interested, but as I spoke a terrible sadness came over me as I scrabbled around for things to say and realised again how little I had achieved, how pale and insubstantial my life is. Work, tidy flat, empty routines. A few work colleagues who persuade me to go out for pizza with them a couple of times a month, so we can talk about bacteria and office politics in a different setting for a change. Botched relationships and friendships littering the path behind me like road-kill. I didn't say these things, of course. I wittered on about easy, surface things, told her about how I was getting on with Mary at work, and described a novel I was reading. I was conscious of her working me out, could imagine what she was thinking.

She told me about her life in London and her work as an illustrator. I'd forgotten what she did for a living — I never saw her working when I stayed with her that time, she just seemed to read and buy fresh bread and potter about the garden. She told me she was working on a book for children at the moment, about a little boy called Malcolm. I wanted to ask if I could see her illustrations, but didn't. And later she told me about Oscar, that he'd disappeared soon after she moved to London. At least three years ago now. She'd hoped he might come back for weeks and weeks. She said he was old; he'd had a long and happy life. The evening before he'd disappeared, she'd given him tuna as a treat, and he'd sat on her lap for an hour afterwards and purred and purred. Oscar had been alive for me until tonight, and now when I think of him I see him stretched out under a bush at the side of the road, cold and alone.

Conversation struggled on. The silences got longer. And then I said something stupid — it's usually only a matter of time. She said I reminded her of Morden when I flicked my hair back from my face, and I asked, 'Do you regret abandoning Mother for all that time when I was younger, now that you can't see her anymore?' Anger leaked into my voice, I didn't know I felt it until I heard it. I saw something in Abbie's face collapse, and for a few awful seconds I thought she might cry. She said that she'd rather not speak to me about that just yet, and her voice was cold. I didn't even apologise. I just said I should go; I was in such a hurry to be out she hardly had a chance to say goodbye. She didn't ask me to stay longer. Then at the door she looked right at me and said it was good to see me, she'd like to see me again. She put on a good act.

Monday 15th March

I went out for lunch with Zoë today. That's my friend — yes — you're a little surprised I have one aren't you? Don't worry — we both manage to keep things pretty superficial. It's one of the unspoken rules of our friendship — don't get too close! I met her at University in the third year. I decided to study for my finals as if I had a day-job, and for a few months I took work to the library from nine until five every day. I'm a creature of habit and found a table that suited me (view out of the window, near the microbiology books) and sat there every day. Zoë's a creature of habit too and happened to choose the seat opposite me. After a few days' build-up of smiling, she asked me if I fancied a coffee with her one morning. We graduated to lunch and were soon study-buddies. We never saw each other during the evenings, but when we left Uni we swapped phone numbers and we're still in touch.

Zoë lives with her partner Jules now, and they have quite a 'traditional' relationship. By traditional, I mean that she does all the cleaning, and he goes out drinking with his friends most nights. And he's allowed to 'see' other women, but she's not allowed to see other men. By 'see', I mean fuck. (Where did that come from? I don't say words like fuck. Fuck fuck fuck!) She's glamorous and confident — I always admire the way she complains in restaurants — so I've never really worked out why she's such a wimp at home. I don't think many people know much about what goes on, and I only know a little bit. She has other friends, but I get the impression that they're 'dinner party friends'; they don't talk about anything too personal. They keep to 'safe' subjects like religion and politics.

We usually meet once a month or so at a small Italian place near where we both work — she has a job as an editor now. As she kissed me on both cheeks today, I was struck again by how good she looked. Her highlighted hair was immaculate, and she looked really chic (is chic what they're saying nowadays? Am I out of date?) in strappy heels, charcoal trousers and a peppermint coloured top. I wish I could dress like that. Underneath it all she looked a little pale, a little tired.

We went through our usual ritual of talking about our respective office politics… we'd got to know all of the characters in each other's workplaces and liked to keep up to date with the latest goings on. It also meant we didn't need to talk about ourselves too much. One of her colleagues has just started an affair with her boss. I told her about Mary. When the coffee arrived, something alarming happened. I saw a single tear roll down her cheek. I wondered for a moment if it really was a tear — maybe she'd just got something in her eye. But when I said 'Zoë?' and she looked up at me, I knew it was something terrible. She fixed her eyes onto her coffee again. And in a very small voice she said, 'I don't really know who I am any more.' After ten seconds of frozen silence, her pain weighing on me as I struggled to stay afloat, she wiped away the tear with her fingers and took a slow breath in. She took a sip of her coffee and smiled me an 'I'm not OK, but I want you to pretend with me' smile, and said, 'Sorry, Ruth. Just ignore me,' and got up to go to the toilet.

As I waited for her to come back, I struggled to understand why things were that awful for her — I had no idea. And I felt scared about what she might expect from me now this had happened. And I also felt — it's stupid to even write it down — hope. A feeling of anticipation. I don't know why. She came back, and we said our usual goodbyes. I said she could call me at home if she needed to and tried to catch her eye, but she wouldn't look at me. Then we went back to our lives.

As soon as I got home after work, I wrote the second card for Abbie. I just wrote, 'Thanks for having me, sorry I left so soon.' When I was in her kitchen yesterday, I could see through into her living room, and my card with the cat was on top of her TV. I liked to think of it there, and hoped the poppies card would end up there too. That's two cards I've sent her; I only owe her sixteen now. I'll send her one a week, one every Monday. I'll find the sixteen most beautiful cards in London for her. Oh — but I haven't got sixteen weeks. And it's a silly idea anyway — why would she want all those cards? Where would she put them all? I wonder if I'll ever see her again.

Tuesday 16th March

When I woke up this morning, I thought about Zoë instead of poor old me and how awful my life is. It surprised me. It's easier to feel sorry for myself because I don't have to do anything about it — I can just lie here and feel numb. I wondered how she felt this morning when she woke up after crying in front of me yesterday. I'm not sure how to be a proper friend — what can I do to make her feel better? Maybe I should phone — we never have conversations over the phone. Or should I just avoid her until she seems happier?

That's what Dad does. If I ever let negative emotions slip out, he just closes up and rushes backwards, like a reversed film I saw once of a train disappearing into a tunnel, smoke billowing inwards. I learnt that lesson pretty quickly after Mother died. One day at dinner he asked how had my day at school been and I'd said, 'Terrible, it's all terrible at the moment.' He'd been furious and had given me a lecture about how we needed to stick together and make the most of things. That's what I learnt — show emotion and your remaining parent won't be there for you either. Push it down, sit on it, like a bulging suitcase. No more room in mine. Oh look, I ended up feeling sorry for myself, after all.

Abbie called again today. I was shocked. She said it'd been good to see me after all this time. Why would she keep saying that? Especially after what I said about Mother. She said she realised she hadn't shown me her drawings and wondered if I might want to see them. I'm not sure what to do now. I didn't really think about the consequences when I sent that first card off. My god, if she wants to carry on seeing me... if she starts expecting things from me... I can't bear the thought of letting her down all over again. I should never have got in touch in the first place. She asked if I were free tomorrow after work. I said I was.

With everything happening with Abbie and Zoë, I'd totally forgotten about my sitting today. It feels like weeks ago that I went there last. I felt strange knocking on the door, like I was in the wrong place When he answered the door, he looked annoyed. He said, 'Come in, sit down,' as if I'd better do it quickly. I sat in the stiff-backed chair and felt more than usually apprehensive as he clattered about. I looked around the room — there was so much stuff; bottles of turps, rags, canvases… and all the bits of junk he had lying around — a shrunken, half-eaten orange, a garden gnome, a buckled bicycle wheel. Did he use these objects in his art? Or was he just cluttered and messy? I couldn't bear to live in the middle of all this *stuff.* I pictured my own flat, and I couldn't even summon up a single surplus-to-requirements object.

Red interrupted my thoughts by saying, 'What you like to say today?' I looked over at his face, and he was looking right at me. I felt burnt. I looked around the room again, making a 'thinking about it' face. It was quiet for a while as he started mixing paint, preparing the brushes. And so to puncture the silence before it got too thick, I started to talk about work. Whenever I looked up at him he looked away from his painting or his palette and nodded at me, a small upwards jerk of his chin. Whenever I used a technical word he didn't recognise, he repeated the word as a question so I could explain it. I told him about the agar plates I'd looked at that morning. Told him about the people I worked with, about Mary.

When he said that our time was up, I was astonished — surely it could only have been fifteen minutes? I felt mortified that I'd talked so much. He'd only wanted me to say a few words to get him in the mood, and I'd wittered on for the whole hour. I picked up my bag without looking at him, said a quiet, 'See you on Thursday,' and slipped out of the door. I heard him shout, 'Goodbye, Ruth,' as I closed the door behind me. I like the way he says my name. He makes it sound exotic, exciting. I said it over and over to myself on the way back to work, trying to get it right.

Things are going a bit better with Mary. For the first couple of weeks, she hardly said a word to me or anyone else. I tried to keep quiet, as I know how horrible it is when someone gets louder and louder to compensate for your lack of noise. It seems to be paying off — yesterday she asked me a few questions about the cold room without me prompting her, and then today she actually made a joke about the dye around the sink looking like blood. She has a lovely shy smile. I notice the way she listens to me sometimes; I think she looks up to me. It's silly, but I feel like her older sister..

Wednesday 17th March

I went round to Abbie's again tonight and enjoyed myself. I know — it's not like me to have a good time, is it? I still feel awkward with her — with anyone I suppose — but she's good at filling the silences, or making me feel like they don't matter. We chatted as she cooked — work, the news, the latest gossip from a soap opera we both watch. All safe. We ate roasted butternut squash with courgettes and brown rice; it was creamy and sweet. And apple crumble with blackberries; she'd made it herself. I haven't eaten so much in ages.

After dinner she took me into the room where she works. It was quite small, with a big window and a large wooden desk like a kitchen table. The walls were brilliant blue, and there were inks and paper everywhere. She took down a large black leather portfolio and got out her drawings.

She draws in thin spidery black ink and fills in the spaces with watercolour. I loved the look of the naked ink drawings she showed me; they looked like you couldn't improve on them. But then I saw the finished ones, bursting with vibrant splodges of colour — bright pink, aquamarine, purple — she made them come alive. She took me through the story she's illustrating at the moment — 'Malcolm's Bubbles'. It's about Malcolm (funnily enough), a nine-year-old boy whose mother works for a fashion designer. Abbie had drawn him with a yellow mess of scribbles for his hair and a tiny button nose.

Malcolm had grown up surrounded by beautiful clothes, playing with bright buttons and rainbow ribbons ever since he could remember. One summer his mother is asked to help out at a show in a different country, far away. She says it is up to him whether she should go or not. He feels very grown up to be asked and says yes, and as there was no-one else to look after him, it is arranged that he'll stay with his great uncle. He gets to his uncles' house and it's grey, all grey. The pictures that Abbie had finished were so clever — they still had the same colours in them as the other pictures, but they were paler, lifeless. At first Malcolm doesn't know what to do. He looks for buttons to play with, or things to distract him, but there is nothing in the house – only grown up things. He cries a few times before he goes to sleep, without letting his great uncle hear. He tries hard to be enthusiastic about the games of Patience his great uncle teaches him, but it seems a bit pointless — even the cards seem grey and bored.

And then one morning something happens. Malcolm looks out into the garden (a lawn and a couple of straggly bushes), and a picture of a flower skips into his head like a door opening. Abbie had drawn it in a tiny thought bubble above his head, a drop of violent orange on the dull page. So he asks his uncle if he can plant some flowers. They go to a garden centre together and plant them out the same day, even though it's dark by the time they finish. On the next page, he has a thought about a picture for his uncle's kitchen, to put on the fridge. So he draws a bright yellow aeroplane in felt tips, soaring through the blue. One day he takes his great uncle out shopping, so he can choose him some new ties and suits, all coloured polka-dots and stripes. As the pages go on, his thought bubbles get bigger, and the edges get blurrier. When his mother comes to pick him up, he carries his new thought bubbles home with him, packed up into his suitcase.

Not all of the pictures were finished, and I couldn't wait to see how Abbie would draw the uncle's new suits, and the thought bubbles getting packed away. I wanted to come back and see them as they progressed and almost asked if I could. But then it was time to go, and I felt I ought to invite Abbie to my flat. I didn't want her to see it; I knew she'd recognise it as the great uncle's house. So I asked if she fancied going to a gallery or something instead. It feels pretty good to be seeing her. I can't quite remember what I was protecting myself from all these years. What a waste.

I plucked up my cowardly courage and called Zoë when I got home. It was late, and I was a bit worried about her boyfriend picking up the phone, but she answered, sounding surprised when I said it was me. I asked her how she was and she said 'yes, fine' — as if she wouldn't be anything else. But she sounded pleased to hear from me. I wasn't sure what to say next, so I asked her if she wanted to come round to mine to watch a video sometime. She's never been to my house before. She said yes — we decided on Friday. What's happening to me?

Thursday 18th March

I sat for Red again today. He was in a different mood when he let me in. He was humming something, a skittering tune with short, low notes. He crinkled his eyes at me — one of his eye-smiles. I blushed a little. He's so big; he makes me feel tiny. But then once I'm in my seat, I find my place again and there's a feeling of power — like when you get into your stride in the middle of cooking a meal you know is going to come out well. He said, 'So Ruth, where will we go today?' I said I didn't know. So after all the meaningless chatter of Tuesday, there was a total absence of words. Wonderful, soothing silence — with the soft crunch of the brushes picking up paint, the clinks and swooshes of them being washed, the occasional low hum from Red. There was a fly whizzing about, trying to escape into the fresh air. There were cars in the distance somewhere. My mind just pottered about lazily. What would I cook for dinner tonight? Would I get a paper on Sunday?

Mostly I thought about Dan. I haven't told you about him yet, have I? Where should I start... Well — I loved him. Or rather, I am in love with him. I haven't actually seen him for a few weeks now — he left work at the end of January. We've worked together for seven years, and for seven years I've carried him around in my head all day like a jewel. I only have to picture the way he raised his eyebrows at me to say hello or imagine the dark hairs on the back of his wrists and happiness gallops through me. No-one knew about it. Maggie might have suspected, but I kept it pretty well hidden. I didn't speak to him very much. Sometimes he'd say hello to me if we went to the coffee machine at the same time, and a few times we needed to speak to each other because of work.

The longest conversation we ever had was at a Christmas party three years ago. He was pretty drunk and ended up talking to me about the problems he was having with his girlfriend. I listened and sympathised for about an hour. I dined off that for months. The next day at work, he pretty much ignored me again.

He didn't have a girlfriend when he first came to work with us. When I first met Parminder at a work function, I was surprised at how ugly she was. They didn't look very happy together. For the first couple of years, I allowed myself fantasies about him sending me anonymous flowers and then sweeping me off my feet. After that, the fantasies had to include getting rid of Parminder first — she'd be involved in a tragic accident and I'd comfort him, or she'd be a secret alcoholic and Dan would finally send her into rehab and come and live with me instead.

I haven't said anything about Dan before because it's kind of embarrassing. I know I'm a grown woman. I should be having real relationships and not ridiculous adolescent crushes. But this was more than that. Dan might not have known I existed, but my love for him was (and is) real. I knew who he really was — I watched him, listened to him... I know he isn't perfect, that he talks in a patronising voice to his mother whenever she calls him at work and that he sometimes lied to his line manager about how much work he'd done. I also know how loyal he is to his friends, and how patient he was with the students we had on work experience. He took up most of the space in my head for seven years. He kept me alive all that time. Don't judge me.

Near to the end of the session I thought about the picture forming of me and wanted to see it, but I knew that Red would make me wait. Then I thought — how do I know he'd make me wait? I don't know anything about him. So I suddenly asked him if I was allowed to ask him questions. 'You did,' he said, and laughed. A loud, deep, bouncing laugh. He said it was only fair that I was allowed to ask him questions. And then I didn't know what to ask him. I'd feel silly asking him any of the big questions he'd asked me. So I asked him who his favourite artist was. He said there were lots and said a few names I didn't recognise. He said that one of them, Jane somebody, had an exhibition on at the Serpentine — I should go and see it. He knew I'd like it. And then for want of a better question I asked who his favourite photographer was. He said the strangest thing — 'Maybe it will be you.' He said it with a smile, and I thought he might be teasing me. I had told him that I loved photographs the first time I saw him. Funny that he'd remembered. I said that I didn't even take photographs, and he said, 'Maybe soon you will start'.

Friday 19th March

Another busy day at work. I'm still enjoying having Mary there. She's getting more and more independent, and she'll be moving on to a different department soon. We have a nice little routine now where she gets coffee for us both in the morning and I get tea for us both in the afternoon. We leave each other alone most of the time, but I make sure I call her over when I'm doing something she hasn't seen before — today I showed her how to use the flow cabinet. Some days she seems brighter than others — today she sang under her breath while she unpacked a new stack of agar plates, so I knew she was having a good day. She told me today about how lonely she was at University until she'd got involved with the Christian Union. I wasn't sure what she'd think about me if she knew I didn't believe in God; maybe she'd be wary of me. So I didn't say anything. It must be nice to believe in something.

Zoë came over earlier to watch the video. I've been deep cleaning the flat for the past few evenings, and it was even more spotless than usual. I looked around in a panic when the doorbell went and thought it looked too sterile. I chucked a cushion on the floor and got a paper out of the magazine rack and spread it over the sofa. At least then it looked like someone had been here recently, although not quite as if anyone were living here.

Zoë stood in the corridor smiling, with a bottle of white wine and a box of mints. Like she was coming to a dinner party. I asked her in and motioned to the sofa. I sat down next to her nervously and then jumped straight up to ask if she'd like a drink, and would she like some music on? And could I take her coat? I caught sight of myself in the mirror and thought of Abigail from that play 'Abigail's Party' — a silly highly strung hostess who ends up collapsing on the stairs in hysterical tears. I smiled to myself, breathed out and felt better. I poured us some wine, put the TV on with the sound muted and took my shoes off so I could sit cross-legged on my sofa.

Zoë started telling me what was happening at home halfway through her third glass of wine. I'd never seen her get tiddly before; she's always so together when she's sober. I quite liked her when she lost her hard edges — it was less tiring to talk to her, somehow. I was telling her about Red and how he worked, and she was teasing me about getting a nice artist boyfriend, hilarious! And then she said she wished she had a nice artist boyfriend, or even a nice boyfriend.

The atmosphere shifted. She didn't cry, which I was relieved about, but she started giving me examples of the things she was unhappy about, as if she were trying to work out how bad the situation really was. She told me about when she'd spent all day cleaning their front room, dry-cleaning the curtains, moving the furniture so she could clean underneath it. When he came in he didn't notice, so she pointed it out. He gave her a withering look, patted her on the head, and said that she only had the other three rooms in the house to do now. Last week her friends had come over for dinner and over the washing up, she'd been talking to her friend about the political situation in Sudan and what she thought about it. He was standing at the door, listening, and made a comment that made her look and feel utterly stupid.

She said that these were only silly examples, that they were 'typical of Jules'. She asked me what I thought. I said I didn't know, but that I was here if she needed to talk about it — I think that's what normal people say to their friends. She said thanks, and then we put the video on. I'd chosen it and worried most of the way through that she was sitting there thinking it was dreadful, waiting for it to finish. And then she went home. Maybe I'd helped her by listening? But I'm still not sure if talking is the best thing to do. Their relationship is fragile already — won't talking too much kill it off for good? Nothing good ever seems to come of talking.

I've just been on the web to look for photography classes after what Red said. More often now I find myself thinking, 'What do I have to lose?' There's one that starts in April on Monday evenings, at a college quite close by. It runs for six weeks, a 'taster' course for beginners. I'd have time to finish it. But I don't have a camera. I'd be useless at knowing what to take a photo of. I've never been any good at technical things either — I'd get the lenses wrong, or forget which button does what. And there'd be other people there too, I bet they would have taken photos before — I'd be the only one weird enough to have never used a camera in my life. Stupid idea.

Saturday 20th March

Well, my daughter duties are over for a while. We didn't get to the restaurant 'til two-ish, as he has to play golf in the morning — it's in his 'rules'. It was the same kind of lunch as usual — full of polite chit-chat and emptiness. He looked tired. Dad and I only spoke a few words to each other, really. There never seems to be anything to say. If you could see relationships hanging between people, I wonder if you'd be able to make ours out. It would be almost transparent, like the flesh of a jellyfish. If you pulled us apart, I don't think it would hold.

We spent most of lunch listening to Julie talk about her new business idea. She wants to start a site on the internet selling her Beanie Babies. You can see why I'm not overcome with excitement about these lunches. She's been collecting these odd hacky-sack animals in a thousand different varieties for five years and they take up an entire room in their small house in Chiswick. They sit on tiny shelves in glass cabinets that completely cover the walls. Dad built them all for her — a labour of love, I suppose. When you walk in you're circled by hundreds of beady eyes; they seemed to be pleading with you... set us free! Let us out of this glass case so we can see the sky and feel the wind riffling our synthetic blue hair! Rabbits, giraffes, bears... if she had more than one of any type then she sat them together, just to really rub it in that they were clones. She's reached a point where she needs to start selling some of them on. Apparently there's a huge market for these things, especially in America. She's done some research, knows a woman from across the street who learnt how to build websites at college and has designed her own.

I looked her neighbour's website up when I got home — it was full of dodgy family photos ('Bob in Hawaii', 'another one of baby Wayne'), and favourite 'poems' with busy flowery borders. Saccharine sweet. Eugh. I watched Dad as Julie spoke. He always wears a slightly glazed look as if he isn't really there with either of us, as if he's a couple of miles away instead, looking into shop windows or practising his golf shots. He caught me looking at him once during the meal, and I smiled a perfunctory smile before turning back to Julie.

Julie is harmless enough, really. She has bulging eyes which she persists in lining with blue eyeliner, pale skin, and baggy shapeless clothes that say nothing about her, except maybe that she doesn't think much of her body. There never seems to be any tenderness between them. I can't imagine them kissing each other, never mind anything else. It's just comfy — comfy and safe. Not what I imagined when I was little and thought about love, being married, romance.

I haven't told you much about my romantic history yet, have I? Apart from Dan. Dan, Dan, Dan. There's not much else to tell… I had a few casual boyfriends at University, but they didn't mean anything to me. I don't want to get into talking about Tom yet. There was another guy, Walt, who was important too. He lived down the hall from me and had dark curly hair and long eye-lashes. He often wore wide purple cord trousers — I always thought they were pretty cool, even if no-one else did. I went to his room a few times and we listened to his music. Music was really important back then; it said something crucial about who we were. He was really into these two bands — I can't remember what they're called now, but the music they made was strange and sad. He had everything they'd ever released, all of the live albums, remixes, everything. We listened together, sitting on his bed, not touching.

I remember one night there was a group of us in someone else's room, and I was sat next to him up against a radiator. I was so aware of him next to me that it hurt. Where the skin of our arms touched, his energy pulsed into me in huge lurching surges. I didn't dare look at him, I didn't think he would be feeling it too, or maybe I was more scared that he was. I sat there for a few minutes, my breathing tight and careful, my heart banging in my chest. Then I left the room, making some excuse about an essay I had to do, not looking at him. I ran away. I avoided him after that evening, never went to his room again, although I lay in my bed and savoured the electricity of our arms touching over and over. He knocked on my door a couple of times and left me confused notes which I still have somewhere.

There was too much fire; I was scared of it burning me. Silly cow, silly cow that I am.

Sunday 21st March

I suggested to Abbie that we go and see the exhibition Red had recommended. My heart always lifts a little when I see the park gates, straining to get inside like a dog on a leash. I love the Serpentine, the way you come across it like a secret in the middle of the park. It's such an odd shape, like a spaceship. As we walked in I could see Jane Barbican's sculptures through a glass door. They were naked figures, life-size, covered in some kind of material. When we got closer, we could see that they were all women, and that the material was thin rope wound round and round. It was difficult to say if the rope was holding them up or holding them back. Or if there was anything inside the rope. The figures were all in positions that were supplicant — is that the right word? One woman was on her knees as if she were scrubbing a floor, but her hands rested on the floor in front of her with their palms to the ceiling and she was looking at them with her blank eyes. Another was lying down on her back with her knees up and open, but her head was twisted away at a horrible angle from where a man's head would be if he were on top of her. There was a fat woman who stood with her stomach sucked in and her hands pressing viciously into her sides as if she was pressing the fat far inside her body.

The one that disturbed me most was of two women side by side. Both of their faces were tilted upwards slightly, looking at the same spot. From the front they looked peaceful, adoring. But when you walked behind them you could see their hands. One of them had pulled a handful of the other woman's flesh away from her back and was pinching it hard. And the other had made her hand into a scooped shape with her long nails pointing into a kind of knife, and was pressing it hard into the other woman's shoulder. I kept walking round to the front and looking into their faces, and then round to the back, but I couldn't see any of the violence in their faces. We are so clever at hiding.

As we walked around we didn't say anything about what we were seeing. I felt a sinking in my stomach as Abbie started to talk about Mother. She called her 'your mum'. She talked about when they were children and holidayed at their aunt and uncle's farm in Suffolk. They used to sweep the yard and muck out the pigs. Mother was older and much more serious about getting the work done. Abbie preferred messing about, sitting and playing with the lambs or making pictures out of straw in the mud. Mother looked down her nose at her and kept on working. She had such 'gusto' for work, Abbie said.

She told me about a fight they'd had — Abbie had left a gate open, and a cow had gone where it wasn't supposed to. She didn't want to tell their aunt and uncle, was terrified, but Mother could hardly wait to go and tell tales. Abbie says she remembers the pleasure on Mother's face more than anything. She started persuading herself there and then that she didn't need Mother, that she'd be better off without her. As Abbie talked, I watched her body grow awkward; she became a little girl.

We came to the end of the exhibition and Abbie stopped talking about Mother. We went to buy a mug of hot chocolate and sat outside next to the lake, even though our breath was white. It felt comfortable to sit there with her. It feels scary too, to be seeing her. It brings the memories of

Mother just a bit closer to the surface, makes it harder to push them down. I wonder how long she'll be able to put up with me once she realises what I'm really like. When I start taking off my mask.

I told her about Red while we sat there warming our fingers on the mugs, using my little white lie that the painting was for Dad's birthday. She sounded interested, even said she'd heard Red's name somewhere before, his proper Russian one. I'd memorised it, Yevgeniy Nikolayevich, and sometimes I found myself saying it in my mind like a mantra. I told her about his studio, how it felt safe. When she asked me if he was good-looking, with a glint in her eye, I changed the subject.

I imagined Dan as my boyfriend in the gallery today. I hooked my arm into his and admired the intelligent things he said. I imagined him offering to buy Abbie her hot chocolate, and later Abbie saying what a gentleman he is. When I write these things down, they lose the sparkle they have in my head. They look pathetic instead.

Monday 22nd March

I met Zoë for lunch again today. We talked some more about Jules and the things he'd done since I saw her last. I think she's still trying to work out how bad things really are. She kept following up her complaints with the nice things he did for her. He cooks for them both, most nights. He speaks kindly of her when he talks to his mum on the phone. He kissed her fondly on the neck last week. But the things he was doing wrong piled up in a sorry mess between us on the table. He stayed out until three in the morning and didn't call her to let her know he'd be late. He said her dress sense was 'criminally misjudged'. He started chatting up 'some tart' at the bar while she was talking with her friends at their table only a few feet away.

When do the scales tip? It reminded me of talking with Maggie about her ex-husband when he wasn't yet her ex, lunchtime after lunchtime of analysis. She picked their relationship apart in front of me until nothing was left. So much of it seemed to depend on how Maggie was feeling that day, whether he had done something small to please her, how brave she'd felt about her future as a single person. In the end he'd made the decision for her and ran off with an 'older, uglier woman'. I'm not sure Maggie ever recovered.

Then Zoë asked me the difficult question I was hoping to avoid — 'what do you think?' I asked her if he made her happy, and she said yes, sometimes. I asked her if he made her sad, and she said yes, often. And I felt hopelessness land on me like a giant grey moth. I knew that there wasn't a 'right' answer for Zoë. She had the choice of staying often-miserable and sometimes-happy, or she could leave and risk everything. What kind of an answer would that have been? So I just said, 'It's hard. I don't know Zoë,' which probably didn't help her much, but was the truth. She half-grinned at me, a tight grin, keeping the tears in. We finished our coffee and paid the bill, and I left her to her difficult life, her difficult choice.

Dad called last night to say it was good to see me at the weekend. I waited to see what else he wanted; he never calls just to say hello. He told me that he wanted to move some of my savings, that he'd been doing some research and wanted to head off a slump before it hit. He always checks things with me before he does anything. I told him about the exhibition I'd been to, said I went with someone from work. I felt weary when I put down the phone. He never asks me how I am.

I thought about doing photography classes again today. I've been thinking that I ought to just take a deep breath and sign up. It's weird, living as if I'm going to die. Or rather, living as if I'm going to die soon. It kind of makes things matter a bit less — what other people will think of me, or whether I'll be any good or not. Either I will do the course, or I won't. It won't make any difference in the end, so I may as well do it and see. It certainly has benefits, this new way of life, but it has drawbacks too. I seem to be getting myself into situations that'll be difficult to get out of — with Abbie, with Zoë…

And I've thought about death every single day, every single hour, every single minute since the beginning of March. Maybe you don't believe me. I've never believed that men could think about sex once every eight seconds, or whatever the ridiculous statistic is, but now I do — it almost feels as if it would be easier to count the seconds I'm not aware of my life running out, the weight of the decision ahead of me. I don't think about the process of dying, not that much. Mostly I think about actually being dead. What it means to be dead, to be 'not-here'. It's not too bad a thought — peaceful — no relationships, no absent mothers, no safety-pins. Being dead. What a relief.

I looked at another photo of an old lady today, but not Charlotte Marie Bradley Miller. Maybe I've got a thing for old women. This was Nettie Harris. She was seventy-nine in this photo. The photographer, Donigan Cumming, used her as a model for nearly ten years. He must have seen her wrinkle and shrink in that time. She is lying curled up on her side on a stained mattress, faded blue with white ornate swirls. We are above her, a bird's eye view. Behind her, a blue dress still on its hanger drapes an empty arm over her bare waist. There is a framed picture of a baby between her knees. Her eyes are shut, her black hair is thick and fuzzy. I spent a long time looking at her skin. The folds at her neck, her armpit. The way it stretches over her bones, tight, her hipbone jutting out, her sunken cheeks.

I didn't feel anything.

Tuesday 23rd March

I signed up to do the photography class this morning. Can you believe it? I haven't got a camera or anything. It starts in a couple of weeks. I was quite excited when I put the phone down, looking forward to creating something of my own. Then I looked over at my photography books stacked up on the shelves, laden with perfect pictures. How could I possibly add anything of value to a sea of such beautiful images? I just read that back. For goodness sakes Ruth, you don't have to be the next Ansel Adams. It might be fun, and maybe I'll meet some new people. Pull yourself together! I sound like my own mother now. I suppose I am in a way.

I met with Red today. This time I was looking forward to talking. I had a few things I'd stored up in my head to tell him, things that happened at the weekend, and questions I wanted to ask him. I found out some things about him today. He talked slowly, easily. He'd only come over to England four years ago, when he was thirty-one, to study art at St. Martins. He'd come from quite a wealthy family in Russia and he'd been under a lot of pressure from his father to do something 'worthwhile', not this 'arty-farty shit' (he said this in Russian first and then translated for me). He'd planned his escape for years, saving money, working in the corporate jobs his dad had set up for him, pretending that he wanted to work his way up into management and then going home to paint into the night. I was impressed by his determination and also felt guilty — I was failing at my life, and I'd had it all pretty easy in comparison.

When the money was saved, he'd got a place on the art course and booked his plane ticket before he told his parents. His dad hadn't spoken to him for a whole six months — when he called his mum she would make excuses for him, he wasn't in, he was sleeping upstairs, he was busy at work. In the end Red had sent a letter to his dad, telling him that he loved him, but that he had to let him go. His father recognised something of himself in Red's tone and called him, saying in a strangled voice that he was proud to have raised such a stubborn son.

They'd visited him in the UK a couple of times now. They had a great time doing all the tourist attractions — the wax museum was their favourite, his dad tutting disapproval at some of the politicians, his mum shrieking as she recognised celebrities. His mum sounded a bit eccentric; she also had 'hair like flames' and 'a hot head to match'. He mimed how she covered him in kisses whenever she saw him, and how she slapped her husband's cheeks affectionately or swept her hand over his forehead and then flicked her fingers as if shaking off something nasty if he had done something to frustrate her. He stopped painting to make these movements for me, and I giggled, holding my hand over my mouth. He told me that the photos of the little girl on the wall were his sister's daughter. They were still in Russia, and he visited them whenever he could. The little girl was called Oksana, I asked him to spell it so I could write it down here. He pronounced it ahk-SAH-nah. Her nickname was hard to say, KSYU-shah. I practised, and he laughed his rumbling laugh at me. I said it was a pretty name. He said 'yes'.

We talked about my family too — I described Julie and her Beanie Babies, trying to be funny, but mostly he was amused at my attempts to describe the words that he didn't understand. I told him about Abbie too, and that we'd seen the exhibition together. We talked about what I'd thought — he seemed interested in my opinion, which made me feel important and also self-conscious. I told him a bit about Oscar and Lila the stone fairy in Abbie's garden.

Finally I told him about Mother dying. He stopped what he was doing and looked at me, waiting. I was pleased to see that the time had run out — we were a couple of minutes over. It meant I could say I had to go, that I didn't want to be late back. He hadn't said anything about a girlfriend. He probably has his pick of cool young artists with bright hair and interesting clothes. The type of girl who doesn't put a stupid smile on all the time, the type of girl everyone wants to talk to. The type of girl who would make me feel twelve years old. It doesn't matter. It's good to get to know him a bit, I enjoyed making him laugh. He makes me feel funny.

Wednesday 24th March

Thursday 25th March

Dad's been in a car crash.

Friday 26th March

I'm still here. Will try and write tomorrow.

Saturday 27th March

Right, I'm here. I've been too — what? — too numb, I suppose, to write.

Dad popped out to get some ice-cream on Tuesday night at eleven o'clock. Julie had baked an apple pie. He bought posh vanilla, didn't spare any expense, Julie told me this more than once. On his way home, a man driving on the other side of the road suffered a minor stroke and lost control of his car. He swerved onto Dad's side of the road, and a car in front of Dad ploughed straight into the side of him. It was a seven-car pile-up by the time it had finished, and two people died. Died!

At a quarter to one in the morning Julie called me from the hospital. I answered the phone with my heart pumping, mouth dry, expecting a death. She sounded like she'd been crying; her voice was thick, but she was calm, and careful to reassure me straight away that he wasn't in 'any immediate danger'. She had already arranged a taxi for me — it was due to pick me up in fifteen minutes. She told me what I should bring — a warm jumper, my address book, money for the taxi. She asked me to write it down. I sat on my bed for twelve of those minutes and watched the second hand go round on my watch. Some of the words that she'd said repeated on me — immediate danger, crash, your dad, hospital. Immediate danger.

I gathered my stuff together in a daze, nearly forgetting my house keys. I didn't remember what hospital she said she was calling from, but luckily the taxi driver had been told where to go. I was deposited outside the hospital and felt like an unwanted dog that'd been driven out into the countryside and dumped. I was queuing to see the receptionist when Julie came round the corner. I'd never been so pleased to see her before. She opened her arms to me and I fell into them. Her face was red and creased, but she was smiling, reassuring. I was so grateful for that. We had to wait for a while before we could see him, and she told me what to expect — he'd lost one of his fingers (lost!), his legs were fractured, and he had bad whiplash. There was a lot of bruising. She said he looked quite poorly but he was going to be OK.

I wasn't sure I could do it. Julie would look after him. 'Can I just…' 'What, Ruth?' What? I want to wait here? I don't have the guts to see my own dad? Instead I asked if she'd come with me. She said of course and kept a hand on the small of my back while we went through, as if she knew I felt like bolting. It felt good to have it there. It anchored me. The doctor said we could have five minutes and then they'd need to do some more tests.

I caught sight of him round the corner of the door and thought at first that it couldn't be him. This man was purple and hugely swollen. My dad wasn't purple. I looked at Julie, afraid, and she was still there, reassuring, her eyes welling up. I went over to his bedside and looked down. It was as if I was in someone else's life. A moment ago my dad was in my head, pink, awake, buying posh vanilla ice-cream, and now he was this lump of bruised and broken body. He had one of those machines to help him breathe, and it was whooshing in and out. His eyes were shut; I knew he was unconscious. I wanted to say something anyway. It was just me and him — nothing else was there — the room, Julie, the nurses.

I said 'Dad, don't go.' It was what I had said to Mother, a few weeks before she'd died, when I went in one day and she seemed to be struggling for breath. Tiny breaths, each one hardly seeming to contain enough oxygen to keep her alive for a few seconds more. 'Please.' It didn't do any good last time, but what else could I say? I didn't want him to go. Not yet.

The next minutes, hours, days went by painfully slowly. Like sitting in the dentists' waiting room, or waiting for an exam to start. It went on and on, cups of coffee from the machine, phone-calls to distant relatives, people in uniform moving about the hospital like ants. It was mostly Julie and me - we took it in turns to sit with him. I went home for a change of clothes, to sleep. My elderly neighbour Margaret asked me for updates when she met me in the hall and patted me on the shoulder. Julie went to fetch pyjamas for Dad, to buy magazines for us. We sat. We dozed. We didn't cry much, we didn't talk much. It reminded me of sitting with Mother, those last days. I tried not to think about that.

Abbie came to visit me at the hospital and brought me some good food — a wedge of vegetable pie, fruit, cheese, bread parcelled into tin foil packages. She didn't go in to see Dad, said it would be 'unfair of her'. I left a message for Zoë on her answer phone and she left messages for me, asking what she could do to help. I cancelled my sitting with Red, I cancelled work. Everyone treated me as if I might break at any moment. And still Dad didn't wake up. The doctors told us what was happening but it was confusing. They said 'possible brain damage'. We waited.

Yesterday afternoon we were both sitting with him. I was reading another trashy magazine and looking at his purple face every so often. The colours were changing every day, the shape too. I got lost in it. It wasn't like looking at a face. Julie was doing cross-stitch, a 'home sweet home' design with kittens and balls of string. And there was a strange noise, a gurgle, and I looked at Dad and his eyes were opening. He looked right at me and smiled. And I said, 'Julie's here too,' and he looked over at her, nodded, and shut his eyes again. The tears slid out of me easily then, sweet tears of relief, dripping onto Julie's jumper as I held on to her. I knew that he was still there, that he was still Dad. We called the nurse, who seemed pleased, went off to fetch somebody. She reminded us that it was still early days, early days. But I think he's going to be OK.

I've felt things that I'd rather not have felt over the past few days. I've felt... resentful. There, I've said it. Resentful of Dad, for getting himself into an accident, for messing up my days. I don't trust my colleagues to look after my work properly. Mary might be needing me. I've missed a programme on TV I really wanted to watch, one I'd been looking forward to. I've had to spend money on taxis, on expensive plastic food. I've got behind with my housework. I missed my sitting. You see what a terrible person I am? To think about these things, these pointless, stupid, insignificant details of my life, when my own father is lying in hospital? Sometimes I really wonder how screwed up I am, how many broken connections there are. It doesn't add up, does it? One minute I'm crying into Julie's jumper and the next I'm wishing he'd just get on with his healing without me, leave me to get on with my life. It's not that I don't care about him. But how can I have both sets of feelings at the same time? I don't really know who I am either, I suppose, just like Zoë. Maybe it's easier to pretend that we know who we are, maybe it's safer to pretend that we are cohesive, that we make sense. I don't know.

I left the hospital a few hours ago to come home and write this. I'm looking forward to going to bed soon, my first proper rest since Tuesday. I can sleep now; he's going to be

OK. He said something to me today, just before I left. Julie was outside getting us some tea. He felt for my arm on the bed and squeezed it, his eyes still shut, and told me that he was sorry. He called me Ruthie, like he did when I was little. Like Mother did. Repeated it over and over. *I'm sorry Ruthie, so sorry, so sorry.* Now he's sorry.

Sunday 28th March

I called Zoë half an hour ago. Her voice was strained; she said she couldn't talk. I don't know if I'm doing very well as 'concerned friend', but I am trying. Dad is going to be OK. I'm going back to work tomorrow. Back to my ordered life. He'll be in hospital for another week or so, and then Julie can take him home. Until then she'll take time off work and will stay with him during the day — I'll visit in the evenings so she can go home and rest.

She's surprised me. I'm starting to understand what Dad sees in her. I've thought a lot about him, especially when I was waiting at hospital. What kind of a man is he? I've been remembering family outings to the woods, or to the beach. Mother would look out into the distance and her whole body smiled. Dad was the one who worried about getting me home before bedtime or fussing when I got ice-cream on my T-shirt. He never just sat, never just soaked it up. I always wanted to be like Mother, running into the sea squealing, or gathering shells in huge bucketfuls to take home and decorate the rock garden. I've just realised with a horrible judder that I've turned out like my dad after all. My predictable Monet prints (why not photos for goodness sakes?) and a gingham duvet cover that matches the bloody curtains. My neat desk, everything tidied away. My boring beige and navy clothes.

Fuck it. I shouldn't feel like this; I should feel happy, now that Dad is alive. But what does it matter anyway, if I'm not sticking around for much longer? Wouldn't it be better if he were dead? And now I know that he loves me. I heard him say it, tonight. He beckoned me closer and whispered it into my ear. I didn't believe he did before tonight, not really. He's never said it. It makes this whole thing harder. I'll have to be colder now, stronger, remembering that it'll be better for him in the long run. Because I'll only disappoint him. Just like he's disappointed me. Over and over. Like when he chose to finish the wall-papering rather than watch me in my biggest ever part in a school play as a lion-tamer (he said it was at a 'critical stage'). Like when I painted a special painting for him at school and he threw it away the next day by mistake and I found it crumpled in the bin under bits of egg-shell and cut-off crusts. And the worst disappointment, the one I'll never forgive. I was at my friend Debbie's house — we were about eleven. We hadn't been getting on very well; she kept telling me to leave her alone, and I was trying harder and harder to please her, but it didn't seem to be working. We'd had a fight because I'd torn one of her favourite Barbie's dresses by mistake when I pulled it over the doll's head. I was mortified and apologised, but she just seemed to get angrier and angrier. I even offered to let her give me a Chinese burn if it'd make her feel better.

We were sitting in stony silence in the living room at five o'clock, the time I was due to be picked up. Mother was out with her friend all evening and had asked Dad to fetch me. He was late. Half an hour went by, and half an hour more... Debbie's mum tried to call my house and eventually set an extra place at the table while Debbie glowered and ignored me. My sausages looked like fingers, rubbery, swollen. I cut them up small and tried to swallow a few mouthfuls. It was after nine o'clock when he arrived, he didn't even bother to think up an excuse, just apologised to Debbie's mum and said it'd 'totally slipped his mind'. I just slipped out of his mind. On the car journey home I imagined us crashing and him going through the windscreen in slow motion. The blood.

Fuck it. There's just a black hole ahead of me, nothing more to write. A black hole. Black. Bloody black. Black and blue. Like I was, the time that Dad beat me. Black and bloody blue. I hadn't really expected him to do it, even when he was getting up from his chair, even when he had raised his hand, even when his palm made contact with my cheek. That sharp crack, the noise of his skin meeting mine, and I kept going even then, saying he killed her with his nagging, saying he suffocated her, saying that I would have been better off if he'd died. He took my right arm in his fist, squeezed it, lifted me by it. Shook me. Used his other hand to slap me again. Then he made a fist and pushed it into my stomach. I was winded, I stopped talking then, stopped wounding him with the words that had been growing inside me all the time that Mother had been ill. Great, ugly growths of words, black and bulging. And when I stopped talking, while I struggled for my breath, my eyes wide, he dropped me into a heap on the floor. And left me.

Monday 29th March

I'm not sure where to go after yesterday. I didn't mean to tell you about Dad hitting me. After he left the room I heard him slam the front door and then drive off. I lay still for half an hour, but when I realised he wasn't coming back I picked myself up, aching all over. I went to the bathroom to examine myself — my eye was bloodshot, my cheek was still red. My stomach hurt when I touched it, but it seemed OK when I carefully prodded it. My arm was throbbing, a slow shoosh shoosh as the pain climaxed and then faded. I felt a bit sick, a bit light-headed. I fetched myself a glass of water and two aspirin, the pills choking me as they stuck in a lump in my throat. I picked the chair back up — it had happened in the kitchen, and I'd knocked it when I fell over. A glass had been broken, so I swept it up, wrapped it in newspaper and put it carefully in the bin. I wrote 'sorry' on a bit of paper and left it on the kitchen table under a cup. And then I went to bed, turned off the light and fell asleep.

When I woke up, sore, it took several shocked seconds to remember what had happened. I looked out the window and saw that the car was back and that it was morning. I went downstairs and Dad smiled at me. It was a bigger smile than he'd usually give me in the morning, there was pleading in it. I answered by smiling back, sheepishly, and he asked me if I wanted a cup of tea. I told everyone at school that I'd fallen over in the bathroom and caught my face on the sink. The skin went purple and lots of colours in between as it slowly faded into green. He'd put a lot of force into it. I tried not to wince when anyone brushed up against my arm. A bruise encircled it like a bracelet, and I watched it blossom and fade for three and a half weeks before all traces of it disappeared. I was glad that I'd said those things to him, and, even worse, I was glad that he had hit me. I knew he was feeling guilty. I had won. He'd hurt me because he knew I was right. I hated him. That's all I want to say about it.

It was strange being back at work. I hadn't been away for very long but it felt like things had moved on without me. Maggie had been helping Mary out, and they seemed to be getting on quite well. I felt a bit disappointed, left out... jealous I suppose. Silly. But when Mary went off to eat her lunch on her own as usual, Maggie asked if she could have a word.

She said she was worried about Mary. Last week she'd left her alone in the prep room for half an hour, and when she popped back to remind her about something, she saw tears on Mary's cheeks. She asked her if everything was OK and Mary said 'yes, fine' and wouldn't say anything else, just looked embarrassed and wouldn't look at Maggie for the rest of the day. Maggie said I was good with her, that maybe I could try and find out what was wrong. It was good to hear her say that. Maggie suggested I invite her for a cup of tea so we could talk about how she was getting on.

So I took Mary to the canteen. I asked her some general questions to start with, about work. And then I asked if she was getting on OK outside work as well The question came out clumsily. Mary looked down at her tea. Her eyes filled up, and she sat there in silence for ages. I just waited. Eventually she looked up and said, 'Not really.' And then she told me things, in a quiet voice and not looking up until the end.

Her mum had a new boyfriend — Mary said she

seemed happy for the first time since her dad had divorced her and moved out several years ago. Mary didn't like him — he seemed too charming, too 'showy', but she made an effort for her mum's sake. Then she started noticing the way he looked at her, sure at first that she must be imagining it. One day last week she had been alone in the house with him. They were watching TV, and he patted the sofa beside him and asked her to come over and sit next to him, to keep him company. Then he started unzipping his flies and raised his eyebrows at her. She quickly said she was feeling tired and went up to her bedroom. The next day he winked at her when her mum's back was turned. As she talked to me she seemed most worried about whether she'd given him the wrong signals — he must have become interested in her because of the way she'd behaved, the way she dressed. She felt she couldn't tell her mum, since she was so happy. But she was scared to be in the house on her own with him. I wasn't sure what to say. I said she should stop blaming herself. And that maybe she should try and speak to her mum. Also that she should let me know if anything else happened. When we stood up to go back to work she said 'thank you', but I don't think I really helped her at all.

Tuesday 30th March

Julie was busy today so I took the morning off work and visited Dad. When I went in, he was sleeping, so I got out a novel. I was pulled from the story ten minutes later, when he said my name, his voice cracking. I made a silly joke about the new pyjamas Julie had bought for him (they were covered in sheep), and he smiled, but his eyes were already filling with tears. I've only ever seen him cry once before, when Mother was ill. I wished Julie were there with me. He said he'd been thinking; he was glad I was there. And he started saying things that were difficult for me to hear.

How he'd never really known how to be a proper father. That I reminded him of Mother, and he knew he'd kept his distance since she died. That he'd managed to keep going by pressing it all down, pulling the cotton wool around him, going out with a woman he felt safe with. But when the car impacted, the moment before the pain kicked in, he'd known with sudden clarity that he'd been getting it wrong. That if he died, he wouldn't regret the financial decision he made for me last week, but that he'd never told me he loved me. He'd regret not letting Julie in, even though she'd waited for him patiently.

I squirmed, tried to believe him. Didn't say anything. When it was time to go I let him hug me goodbye. I squeezed my eyes shut when he was hugging me and I thought about my childhood friend Debbie again. I remembered how we used to braid each other's hair and she'd make me shut my eyes tight when she was doing mine, so it was more of a 'surprise' when I opened them. I loved sitting there cross-legged on her floor in the semi-dark, with her tugging at my scalp. After that night when Dad forgot me, she didn't speak to me the next day at school. I followed her round at a distance, turning suddenly away and pretending to be doing something else whenever she turned her head towards me. We made up a few days later, but things were never quite the same. I didn't know how to fix it. Eventually a new girl called Emma joined our class and took Debbie away from me — I couldn't compete with her stories or her long blond hair. I had other girls back to my house, but they weren't proper friends. They didn't know me like Debbie did.

I'd arranged to go to Red's house that afternoon and went straight there from the hospital. We talked for a few minutes about what had happened to Dad, how he was doing, what the doctors had said. Red listened in the way he does, dipping his head and smacking his lips every so often in a gesture of disbelief or disgust. And then silence settled. Red noticed that I was quiet, looked into my face for a moment and said, 'Something is haunting you?'

To my shame my eyes filled with tears, and one or two rolled down my cheeks, huge, warm. I caught them with my tongue and tasted the salt, staring straight ahead, not daring to catch his eyes. 'It is difficult for you.' I nodded mutely, another tear escaping, and I was afraid that the dam would break, and they'd all come at once, flooding the studio. I kept absolutely still and tried to think about something else, but it was difficult to hold back the pressure in my throat, the hot pain tugging at me inside. I wasn't even sure what I was crying about. 'You British, you have tea for crying?' Red asked, and I smiled and half cried-laughed, taking the paint-stained rag he was offering me. It smelt of turpentine.

After I'd blown my nose, I wasn't sure what to do with the rag — would Red want it back? He'd gone off into another room to make tea so I slipped it into my handbag. I took some deep breaths, and by the time he reappeared with a purple mug of steaming tea, I'd pushed the tears back again. He'd put sugar in it — I don't usually take sugar, but it tasted perfect. I said thank you and he nodded. He doesn't need to say much. He motioned with his brush to ask if he could carry on, and I said yes, feeling less and less silly, taking wonderful sips of hot, sweet tea and wanting to sit there forever.

On the way back to work I noticed that crocuses were starting to push out of the ground, bright yellow crumbs, and that the leaves on the trees were getting ready to unfurl. I looked down into an alleyway and saw a boy; he must have been about twelve, sat with his back against the wall. He was playing on a Game Boy. He was surrounded by bits of cardboard and rubbish. His hair looked dirty, and he had a pretty face, frozen in concentration. And suddenly I knew that it would make a good photo. My first. All I need now is a camera.

Wednesday 31st March

I washed the bit of rag that Red gave me to blow my nose on. It still smells faintly of turpentine. I'm going to keep it — I've put it under my pillow. Rather than thinking about Dan, I thought about Red's eyelashes as I was going to sleep last night. They are long and pale; they frame his blue eyes like flakes of snow. Then I thought about his arms, his huge, fleshy arms. He has freckles on the back of his hands that run up his arms as if they were sprinkled on, disappearing underneath his shirt sleeves. I imagined what it would be like to be held by those arms. I could curl up and be small; he would encircle me completely. I'd come in cold from walking through the rustling autumn leaves. He'd be there in his usual seat, welcoming me back with his heat. I could warm my hands on the glow of his hair. I could sleep in the glow of his body.

It's time to write about the first thing that happened. Remember? I said there were three things that haunted me from Mother's dying. I'm a third of the way through this journal now — it's time to tell you the first. I must have been about thirteen. Mother had been ill on and off for years, so we'd got pretty used to her being a bit slower than me and Dad, more often tired, weaker. But it felt like she'd reached a kind of plateau — for the past few months, things had just seemed the same. And then early one evening, I left my bedroom to get a glass of water. I walked past the bathroom and the door was ajar; I could hear the soft sound of splashing. We always kept the door just pushed to — something our family has always done. It seems a bit weird now, not very private. So the door was ajar, and this time I stopped, keeping quiet, and looked inside.

Mother was in the bath. The first thing that shocked me was how thin she'd got. How hadn't I seen it? I hadn't seen her without any clothes on for a long time, and although I'd noticed her legs getting thinner and her face hollowing out, the sight of her bony chest made me feel like I'd swallowed some lead. Her bones were all showing, poking out through her stretched skin like they wanted to escape — she was wasting away. I wondered how she'd been able to hide it from me so well, or if I'd just been refusing to look.

She hadn't seen me. She was trying to get up out of the bath. She pushed her hands down onto the sides of the bath, and when she was halfway up she slipped back down, with a splash and a look of mild amusement. She pushed and slipped back again, and as she tried and tried, the look on her face changed into annoyance, exasperation, anxiousness, and as the water splashed onto the floor and she put as much strength into her stick-thin arms as she could, her face twisted into a shape that few of us are familiar with. She collapsed back into the bath and put a hand over her eyes.

And then she let out a horrible soft moaning noise, an animal sound. It came from right inside of her, right inside the cancer. And it went on and on. I put my fingers half into my ears to muffle it, like watching a horror film from behind an open hand, and waited. Eventually she grew quiet, and I turned away from her and tiptoed downstairs to find Dad. I casually told him that I thought Mother had called for him. And as he went upstairs I caught sight of myself in the big gold mirror in the living room. I remember thinking, 'My hair looks awful.' I felt sorry for myself for having such a horrible, pudding-basin haircut, for being such a misfit. Then I remembered what I'd just seen and was stabbed with guilt, right through the chest. What a selfish cow. What a bitch. I went out into the garden then, sat down under a tree at the bottom and hugged my knees. There were some clumps of bedraggled daffodils and I stared at them as hard as I could. Tried to drink in the yellow, to let it seep in to my brain, hoping it would wash everything away.

I wonder what was going through her mind. I wonder if it was the exact moment, the tipping of the scales, when she realised that she was going to die. Not in forty years, sat in a comfy armchair with a glass of wine in her hand and photos of her great-grandchildren surrounding her, but soon. That her failing arm muscles were as strong as they'd ever be again. I wonder if she raged against it. Or if she were already tired by then, if that quiet horrible moaning was all she could manage. It wasn't fair. She didn't want to die. And there — I've told you. Don't think it was easy. I don't want to get my journal pages wet - I keep having to turn away so the tears drop onto the duvet. And yet I feel a little emptier now. I feel a little lighter.

Thursday 1st April

I felt a bit apprehensive about seeing Red today after Tuesday and all that silly crying, but it was fine. We had a chatty session about photography and art and how things were different in Russia. It feels more and more comfortable, our conversation, our being in the same room. It helps that he's there to paint me, so if the talk dries up it doesn't matter — we're still there for a purpose. But even if he weren't painting me, I think it would feel OK to just sit there in silence. We just think our own thoughts, and I wait for a topic of conversation to emerge when it wants to — it doesn't need forcing out to stem the bleeding silence.

He told me about another exhibition I should see, in a small gallery near Docklands. I'm dying to see how the painting is coming along. He said we only have two more sessions to go after today — maybe I should try to confuse him about the dates so he has to spend longer looking at me!

Things are going OK for Dad. He's awake for most of the day now. Which makes it harder to visit him! He keeps making jokes about his missing finger, pretending he's mislaid it and searching under the pillows ('Have you seen it?'), or asking if I'm hungry and fancy any 'fish fingerless or maybe a fingerless of fudge?' He still keeps getting emotional and clingy, which I'm sure is normal after what happened to him, but it makes me really uncomfortable. I preferred it when we just played at father and daughter.

I should be pleased, I know. It's just weird that he suddenly wants to know things about me after all this time.

Where was he when I was sixteen and didn't know which A-levels to choose? Where was he when I got depressed a couple of summers ago and he didn't even call me for two months, and when he did it was to ask if he could borrow my laptop? It'll take a bit of getting used to.

He asked me today if I was happy. What a question! I said yes, of course, but he just looked at me hard and said, 'Are you?' I said I was sometimes, which might even be true. So he asked me what made me happy. I said 'Dad' in that whining embarrassed voice I haven't had to use for years, and he shrugged his shoulders and looked annoyed. It's making me uneasy to discover how much it suits me that we don't know anything about each other. Safer that way. Less to lose.

Julie seems to be in her element. She brings him financial magazines to read and fresh fruit every day. Often when I come in, they seem to be talking. I haven't really heard them talking before. I'm still not sure how I feel about the whole thing. I remember the strength of feeling in me when I thought he might be dead, the sudden stab of loss, but that's gone now I know he's going to be OK. Maybe it's not that easy to fall back in love with your father after years and years of keeping each other at arm's length. I've talked to Abbie about it a bit. I think she understands.

It's already April. Today at work, someone made an April fool of a colleague, John, by gluing his pen biro top on with super-glue. He sat there for ages trying to pull it off, looking at it with a confused look on his face as we all tried not to giggle. Maybe even scientists can have fun every so often! It made Mary laugh too, a tinkling, childlike laugh, and when I heard it, I realised what a rare sound it was. I've been worrying about her since she told me what's going on at home. We haven't mentioned it since Monday, although when I ask her how she is in the morning I've had a different tone in my voice, and she knows what I mean. She says 'fine' and I say 'really?' and she says 'just the same'.

I talked to Maggie about it, and we agreed that I can't really do anything about it for now. Maggie said I should just try and make sure she has plenty of opportunities to talk to me. Mary's moving out of our department onto the enteric lab tomorrow. We talked about it this morning, and she said she didn't want to go, that she liked to learn from me. I said I'd keep an eye on her, and she smiled her shy smile.

There's still white space on my page today. They're really starting to pile up, these pieces of paper covered in neat purple words. I keep them in a tidy sheaf in a brilliant blue pocket folder. The writing isn't turning out how I thought it would. I read small bits of it back to myself sometimes. I'm still not being very convincing about how tough my life is. If I were reading this, I wouldn't give this whining, selfish girl permission to kill herself. Or maybe I'd think she deserved to die. I don't like the sound of myself. Are you still reading? Are you hanging on in there with me? If you are, thank you. I appreciate it, I really do. It's good to be listened to.

Friday 2nd April

Just as I was about to start writing tonight there was a soft knock at my door. It was late, nearly midnight. I immediately pictured a stripy cartoon robber, complete with a swag bag and shifty eyes. They knocked a little louder. I picked up a heavy metal candlestick from my bedside table, feeling slightly foolish, and went to the front door to look through the peephole. It was Zoë. She was standing in the corridor with a duffel bag, looking small and nervous. She had a big grey smudge of mascara under one eye.

I opened the door and smiled a smile that was meant to reassure her. She looked at me with red, raw eyes and said 'sorry' in a small voice. I told her to sit down and I put on the tall lamp. She wouldn't want too much light on her. I wasn't sure if I should hug her or not — we don't do hugging, just that little kiss on both cheeks that means you can get away with hardly touching each other. Instead I asked her if she wanted a cup of tea. Red was right, there's something about tea that softens a disaster, brings you back to the practical, the everyday. It gives you both something to do. She said yes please, so I left her there and went to make it — I remembered how she took it from last time she was here. I smiled as I handed her the mug, and she thanked me — her eyes were wide; there was wildness there.

I sat down next to her, and she started talking. She told me they'd been arguing a lot recently. It had started when she'd refused to do the washing up one night, her usual job. She was tired, said she'd do it in the morning. He said he wanted the kitchen to be clean in the morning when he got up — she should do it now. She wouldn't. And then she thought she might as well bring up a few other things she wasn't happy about — the way she did all the housework, the way he patronised her. He reacted by talking to her as if she were a child having a tantrum. After a while she felt like she was having a tantrum and went to do the washing up. But she thought about it all night, lying there, staring at the ceiling. Was it worth it? How long was it since she'd been happy?

The next evening when he slumped on the sofa after work, she just started pouring stuff out to him. That he'd never ever changed their sheets. That he never asked how her work was going, even though she always asked him. That he hadn't supported her when she'd wanted a promotion (he'd said he doubted she'd be able to cope, especially as she was already 'struggling to keep up at home'). Each thing he dismissed as if it were nothing. Each time this made her even more determined to find an instance when he'd indisputably treated her badly. She wanted a small apology from him. She became obsessed — if she could get this, then maybe there'd be a future for them. She wrote lists of things that had happened between them, examined them objectively. Left him letters. Sent him emails, texts. But everything she said was dismissed by him as female, obsessive, hormonal — however calmly she delivered it, however aggressively, however logically.

She'd given him one last chance tonight. She said to him, if you don't want me to leave, just say. Give me something. This is your last chance. Tell me you want me. He sat there, watching football, and didn't even turn round to look at her. Just carried on watching. She'd gone to pack a bag; she was furious, trembling. She said she can't even remember what she packed, she could hardly see straight. She wanted to smash a plate or punch a hole in the wall. And then she just walked out and sat on her front step for about twenty minutes, listening to the noise of the TV inside. He didn't come out to see if she'd really gone.

So she came to my flat; she didn't know where else to go. She said she was sorry again. She looked so pathetic curled up on my sofa, she hadn't touched her tea. I wanted to say something comforting, but there was nothing. So I fetched her a spare duvet and pillows and lent her a pair of pyjamas. She settled down on the sofa and dropped off almost immediately; I could hear her breathing change. I washed up the mugs quietly in the kitchen and wondered what she would do now.

And now I'm writing my pages for today and it's really late, but I'm wide awake. I can hear the occasional shoosh of cars on the wet roads, the ticking of my clock. And a new sound — Zoë's gentle steady breathing across the room. I feel tenderly towards her, as if she's my responsibility now. I suppose she needs some space. Maybe that's something that I can give her. Something I've got plenty of.

Saturday 3rd April

When I woke up today, Zoë was still sleeping. I left her a note and slipped out to get some breakfast for us — proper fresh bread from Tesco and some Brie as a treat. I got some jam too; I wasn't sure what other people liked for breakfast — I hadn't eaten breakfast with anyone since — God — since University. Unless you count a couple of breakfast meetings with my line manager in the hospital canteen at work. When I got back, she was dressed, and the duvet and pillows were piled up tidily. She didn't look quite as pristine as usual. I liked her looking ruffled; she looked more human. She said she'd be off soon, but when I asked her where she was going, she couldn't think of anywhere, and her face crumpled. I said she should stay for tonight at least, and then she could decide what she wanted to do, and that she was welcome to stay as long as she liked. She did cry a bit then; it always happens when someone is nice to you — you're holding it together, and then someone touches you on the shoulder, asks how you are in a concerned voice. She said that she'd stay, but only if I didn't mind; she didn't want to get in the way. I made a joke about how tidy I was and that I'd try not to tidy her away as well, and she laughed that full-of-tears, choked laughter, and that was that.

So we had breakfast — she had some Brie, and the bread was crusty and fresh and white inside like snow. Pale butter. A glass of cold milk. A white breakfast. Zoë ate a lot, seemed surprised at her appetite, slightly apologetic. And then we drank milky coffee and talked about how weird it was that she was here, eating breakfast with me.

I visited Dad at hospital in the morning and while I was talking to him I thought about Zoë watching TV back at my flat. It was a nice thought. I told Dad about her. There were still awkward questions and confessions from Dad, but I'd discovered that if I kept talking, I could keep him quiet. He seemed interested in Zoë, was pleased that I'd been able to help her out. We almost had a normal conversation about it. I thought about food again on the way back — how strange to suddenly have someone else to eat with.

I wanted to make something tasty for Zoë — we had pizza and salad, but I made fresh salad dressing and put extra ham and mushrooms on the pizza to make it nicer. In the afternoon I had planned to buy a camera, so Zoë came too. I told her about the research I'd done about different makes and models. It was down to a choice between two, and I wanted to see them both before I decided. I weighed them in my hands in the shop, getting a proper feel for them, and just as I was about to make a sensible decision, I caught sight of a different model in the next case. I'd heard good things about it, but it was out of my budget. Zoë encouraged me to have a proper look it anyway — it was beautiful — gun-metal grey, lighter, smooth edges. I had to have it! I might as well use my money while I can. So I bought it! I couldn't wait to get it home, take it out of its box, read the instructions from cover to cover.

I felt like I wanted to celebrate, and so we went to Harvey Nichols and bought six expensive chocolates each for later. Zoë wanted a new skirt and suggested we try on some clothes together. At first I picked out cheaper stuff, even though I wasn't planning on buying anything, as if morally I should be able to afford whatever I tried on. But

Zoë told me to stop looking at the tags. So I did — I felt braver with her there; I picked out what I liked. We did turns for each other in the changing rooms. And I fell in love again, with a deep pink cardigan, soft and fitted.

It was eighty-nine pounds. I'd already spent several hundred, so with Zoë spurring me on, I thought 'why not', and bought it too! It felt naughty, but at the same time, I felt like a proper grown-up, buying quality clothes with my own money. I can see it now from where I'm writing, draped over a chair. It looks gorgeous. I can't wait to wear it on Tuesday when I see Red.

I've persuaded Zoë to stay here for at least a few days to give her some space to think — she's decided to call in sick on Monday so she can have a bit of time to herself. She can start looking for somewhere to rent, if that's what she decides. I said I'd help her. She's being very brave. I like having her here. I showed her today how to use the washing machine, where the sugar was, how to work the shower. We watched TV together this evening, and I enjoyed her company, even though we didn't say much. I hope we don't fall out. I don't want to get it wrong.

Sunday 4th April

Zoë went to see her mum this morning, in Hampshire somewhere. When she opened the front door to leave, the grey, oily liquid was out there waiting for me. I ducked under my duvet in a vague attempt to avoid it, but it was too late. Sundays are always difficult days. It's easier to fill Saturdays with other things — errands, cleaning. I usually run out of things to do by the evening, when normal people are out in bars and clubs, drinking and laughing. Zoë said she'd be back by seven, so that meant a whole nine hours to fill. Even my cardigan didn't look exciting this morning. I just looked at it and thought 'eighty-nine pounds'.

I spent half an hour trying to gee myself up. I even wrote a list of things I could do with the day: go to see the exhibition Red recommended, visit the park, read, bake a cake, work out how to use my camera. It all sounded quite convincing — the kind of things I'd look forward to doing on another day. But this morning they were dead on the page. If I started thinking myself into doing something, like going to the gallery, I thought about having to decide what to wear, then getting there, then having to walk round on my own, and by then I'd talked myself out of it being any fun at all. So I just sat and watched the clock's hands moving round.

Thoughts eddied through my head — my dad, Zoë, photography classes, Red, my decision. And I started feeling an odd pressure, the helplessness became sharper, turning into desperation. I recognised the particular flavour of these feelings; I'd felt them before. They always led me to get out my safety pins and think about drawing blood. It felt like it was only a matter of time before I let some of the feelings out by watching the beads of red escaping. The trouble with feeling like this was that you wanted to carry on, like when you get a craving for chocolate. Imagine someone coming along and saying, 'Look, I've got this pill here that would instantly take away your craving for chocolate, or instead you could have this box of expensive Belgium truffles. Choose.'

I don't know many people who would choose the pill. It's not that I couldn't stop myself doing it, it was that I wanted to do it. And today was the same. I wanted to go further, to see what would happen. Once I knew that, the panicking melted away and I became calm — calmer than I've been since I can remember. Since last time. I thought I'd do it a bit differently this time. Using a safety pin would have been going backwards, wouldn't it? So I took a knife from the kitchen drawer. I have a small one that I use for cutting vegetables — it's thin and beautiful, slices mushrooms like moving through fog.

I locked the front door from inside, drew all the curtains and turned the lights on. Took all my clothes off, put them in a neat pile. Studied my body in the bathroom mirror. Considered my stomach, my thighs, my breasts. The skin looked so smooth, so unblemished, innocent. I was worried about the blood supply in these fleshy areas, I didn't want to make too much of a mess, wanted to be neat. Upper arms seemed like the best place. But on the inside, where it was pale and smooth, where I could see the blue veins running underneath the skin? Or outside, the bit covered with freckles? I decided outside, because then I could look at myself in the mirror and see the marks more easily. I always wore long sleeves until it got warmer, and I didn't have to see the summer in if I didn't want to. I took my time.

I made three short lines using the side of one of my bookmarks as a ruler. Each one was above the other, the same length, about half a centimetre apart. It was quite awkward, and I thought a pen-knife might have been easier. I could buy one if I wanted. I almost forget to breathe with the concentration. And then afterwards I washed the ruler and the knife using disinfectant — Zoë was here, and I didn't want her to use the knife if it wasn't properly clean. The lines bled quite a lot, more than I expected. But they didn't hurt too much. It was a good hurt, it reminded me of what I'd done, of my secret, and I felt proud. The oily liquid started seeping out of me. By the time I was walking down the street I almost felt cheerful. I browsed in a bookshop for nearly an hour and bought a blue book by Gretel Ehrlich, This Cold Heaven. I loved the title. It's about her travels through Greenland; the cover called it an '...unforgettable tribute to the realm of the great dark, of ice pavilions, polar bears and Eskimo nomads.' I flicked through it, and it was full of shining words. Snow. Clear. Hunter. Sun. Iceberg. Stars.

Monday 5th April

My first photography class! I came home from work feeling really sick, and if Zoë hadn't been there, I wouldn't have gone. She said it was only nerves and offered to walk me there if it'd help. She went on and on, and I gave in eventually. I thought it might be something interesting to tell Red about. I'd already sussed out where the class was, so I arrived exactly twenty minutes before it started. There were quite a few teenagers wandering about the corridors — some wearing bandanas, others with pierced noses or lips.

I got to the right door and looked in through the reinforced glass at the top. There was a woman at the front of the room with short feathery hair and a wiry body. I waited in the corridor, leaning against the wall, trying to look nonchalant. An older woman with a crinkly face came along and asked if she was in the right place for the photography. I love the way you turn into the expert on something if you arrive a few minutes before anyone else. We chatted for a couple of minutes — she was Susan; she'd never done anything like this before. We plucked up courage to go in, and the tutor shook our hands with a firm grip and told us she was Milly. She seemed a bit intense, but I liked her.

The class slowly filled up with other students. I looked round at everyone, trying to figure them out. Milly said it was a very interactive course, and that after some theory we would take a whole film of photographs and have these developed ready for the next lesson. We'd then discuss 'as a class' which photos from the previous week were more successful. When she said this, my stomach lurched, but I looked round the class and saw a few more people trying to catch each other's eyes in a pantomime of looking worried, so that made me feel better.

Our first project was to pair up with someone and take photos of each other. I worked with Susan — I apologised to her for getting my face, and she said the same about hers. But I thought her wrinkles were great, and I took photos where I tried to exaggerate them. I talked to other people too, and smiled at a girl with coffee coloured skin who seemed to be about my age. It was easier than I thought it would be. I was just myself.

I feel embarrassed about what I wrote about yesterday. I didn't tell you the truth when I said I hadn't hurt myself since the safety-pins at fourteen. During my first year at University, I had the only 'proper' boyfriend I've ever had, Tom. Tom was a bony archaeology student from Scotland, with the greenest eyes I've ever seen. We met at a hideous party in halls during the first week. He used to come to my room and talk about his family.

I didn't think I fancied him, but one night he leaned over and kissed me on the lips and it sent a shiver of pleasure down to my toes. We started walking each other to our lectures, went to arty films and snogged in the dark. After a few weeks, I couldn't bear to hold on to the hot itch of my virginity anymore and handed it over to him willingly. We tried to be serious, that first time, but there was too much hilarity — re-reading the instructions on the condom packet to be sure, the embarrassing noises, the sudden surprise on his face when he came inside me after only a few clumsy thrusts.

After that we spent a lot of our time naked in my tiny room with the curtains drawn. We got better at sex. We got to know the nooks and crannies of each other's bodies; we got to like them. Afterwards he liked to lie on his back with me resting my head on his shoulder and cupping his penis softly in one of my hands. We talked about our most embarrassing moments and named our future children. When he dumped me, by leaving me a terse note in my pigeon-hole, I didn't believe him. I arranged my face into 'aren't you funny!' and went straight to his room, where I burst in to find him sitting cross-legged on his floor and leaning against the legs of a pretty girl from the next block. She was stroking his hair.

I felt so ashamed, so stupid. I couldn't understand it. I analysed the whole situation to death, boring a few fledgling friends away in the process. Eventually I did something else instead and used nail scissors to cut into little pinched flaps of skin on my hands and ankles. It only happened a few times. After we left halls I only saw him from a distance. I still hate him. I still love him. My arm hurts now from yesterday, and when the pain throbs, I feel a little throb of shame. It's not normal, is it? You don't need to worry though — I'm not going to do it again. I won't hurt myself again. Not like that anyway.

Tuesday 6th April

Before he started painting today, Red came over and sat in a chair close to mine. I hadn't sat that close to him before; he's always over by his easel. I could have reached out and touched his face. I could smell him — a spicy, warm smell: cinnamon, cloves. He said that he had an offer — if I carried on sitting for him so he could paint another portrait, he'd give me my first painting for free.

He wants to paint me again! I said yes, of course. Then I asked him if makes this offer to everyone, wanting to be special, and he said, 'Sometimes, if there is more to paint.' I joked that he hadn't quite worked me out yet; he took me seriously and agreed he hadn't. I was surprised at how pleased I was that I could keep on coming. I feel I've got more to say to him.

We had a good chat today — it's usually hard to get much out of him, but he can certainly talk about art. He said most artists thought that doing portraits for money was 'cheap', but he feels privileged to have had some 'critical' acclaim as well as making his living. He also told me about a theory he has — he called it his 'thought structure'. He said that people's faces are often trying to hide things, but in the very act of hiding, they give the game away. He said it's the same with what people say and do.

He told me a story about a woman he'd painted a few years ago. She started telling him about how happy she was in her life and listed all of the things she had to be thankful for — two beautiful children, a loving husband, a cottage in France, an interesting part-time job. She spent so long explaining her happiness to him that he believed her less and less. He painted what he saw. When she saw her portrait she burst into tears and cried for ten minutes straight. He described her crying by doing it himself, great shuddering sobs, awful to hear. She said she couldn't keep it but she was happy to pay him, was there somewhere he could hang it in his house maybe? A small corner somewhere? And then she said thank you. 'We want people to know, yes?' he said. 'Even if just one person'.

He took me to see her painting, which was in his kitchen. She was blonde, middle-aged, ordinary looking. And she did look sad, desperately sad, but there was a beauty about her too, a sense of defiance. On his sink I noticed a single plate, knife and fork waiting to be washed up, a single cut-glass tumbler holding a few last drops of purple wine. Not two plates. Not two glasses. I wanted to have a better look around his kitchen, but it felt rude to stare. When he said goodbye to me, he said, 'See you again, Ruth! You are not escaping me!' My cheeks burned as I walked off down the street.

The woman he talked about reminded me of someone. Outside, inside. If you took a cross-section of my body, you could study the colours running through me like a piece of rock. You'd find a lot of blue and grey, and fiery streaks of red, although I keep them pushed down where they're safe. It's all surface, the cheerful yellow that people see. It's a thin layer. If you look closely, you can see the other colours moving underneath. The blue-grey grief is always there in the background, like the seagull cries you no longer notice when you've lived near the beach all your life.

Hurting myself has helped me to keep my yellow nice and pure. I look at my cuts whenever I shower and feel strangely proud of how symmetrical they are. I know some people scar themselves on purpose for the pattern it makes on their body. Scarification. I've seen pictures. Maybe I could be one of those people. Am I so different from them?

This photo is famous. It's by Diane Arbus, who killed herself in 1971. It's of a boy — he's 'child' in the title, but he looks like a Martin or a Charles. He's stood centre frame, and the first thing you notice about him is his mouth — it's in a bizarre grimace, reaching straight across from cheek to cheek, his chin a thin line underneath. The bottom part of his face is all tight and pulled back. If you cover his mouth with your hand his eyes stare at you, not really seeing, wide. Asking for help.

And then his hands — his arms are stiff against his body, and his hands are like claws, mummified, so tight you can see the tendons. In one hand he holds a toy grenade. He's so prickly, so brittle. If you picked him up he would stay in the same position, like a stiffened corpse. When I look at him, I want to hold him, just hold him until he starts to soften, becomes flexible in places, maybe starting with his belly, so he could bend in the middle, and then his knees, and then last of all his hands and mouth. And then we would hold hands and skip through the playground, looking for fallen leaves.

Wednesday 7th April

Zoë and I are settling into a nice little routine. She's been getting up early and is first in the bathroom while I'm still dozing. I enjoy lying there, hearing the shower trickling; there's someone else in my flat! We eat breakfast together without speaking much. I make the toast, and she makes the tea. She has peanut butter; I have marmite. I used to have bran flakes before she came — I'm not sure why; maybe Dad drummed into me once how healthy they are, and I'm still trying to keep him happy. I like toast better, the gorgeous smell of it turning golden. In the evenings we sit around watching TV, chatting about our days. Today there was a moment when I wanted to get into work early, and Zoë was slow in the bathroom and I wanted her gone, but it was only fleeting. All things considered, I don't think I'm doing too badly.

She started asking me about boyfriends tonight, said she'd not known me go on a date for years. She was right. I'm not sure how I've got away with not talking about it for all this time. So I gave her a potted history of my love life. I told her about the boys at school, the ones who liked me (who I didn't like), the ones I liked (who didn't like me). I told her about green-eyed Tom, and how he broke my heart without even knowing it, as effortlessly as he took my virginity. And how after him I was wary of getting too close to anyone, like having to step into seawater that's deep and murky, and you're not sure what creatures are swimming around your ankles and whether any of them have teeth.

I made friends with a girl called George in the second year who was also anti-boys. We called them 'immature' and 'testosterone-ridden', and reassured each other about the benefits of being single. Last year I saw on Friends Reunited that she is living with her partner Sally in Middlesex, so that explains why she wasn't very keen. I told Zoë about lovely Walt. And about the few fumbled relationships after Tom, especially in my third year when I went through a phase of drinking too much Bacardi. They mainly featured drunken slobbery kisses on other people's stairs at other people's parties, and mornings full of regret.

Romantic opportunities started drying up once I left University — there was a spotty guy from work and a short bizarre fling with my 'gay' hairdresser, but nothing worth writing home about. They all left me untouched. Zoë was a good listener; she seemed genuinely interested, and so I confessed about Dan too. The way I felt the first time I saw him. The time he spoke to me at the Christmas party. I described the way he used to fiddle with his hair when he was thinking. I even got out the single photo I have of him. Maggie had taken a dodgy one of me at another Christmas party, and she'd offered to get a copy for me. When she showed it to me he was in the background, looking off to the right and laughing — I couldn't believe my luck.

When I'd finished talking, Zoë said she could see how much I cared about him. Then she hesitated and said, 'Do you think Dan might have got in the way of a real boyfriend, Ruth?' I winced when she said 'real'. She's right, of course. I didn't want to hear it. I'm not quite ready to admit it to myself.

I've been thinking about Dad. I can't work out how I feel about him anymore. It was much easier before his accident. He's changed the rules. He's still being nice to me — well, not just nice, but more honest, I suppose. He reminds me of a little boy sometimes, who just says what he thinks. I spoke to Julie about it today on the phone; she says he's different with her as well, and mostly it feels like an improvement, but she gets frustrated with him too sometimes. A couple of days ago he decided he wanted to leave half of his money to Childline. Out of nowhere. And when she tried to rationalise with him, he got angry and then upset that he'd been angry. It's weird, but the nicer he is to me, the more interested, the more I want to turn my back on him. You'd think it'd be the other way round.

When he came to the phone, I told him on the spur of the moment that I'd been seeing Abbie. He was shocked but said he was glad — not for himself, but for me. I was quite impressed. He continues to impress me, in little ways. I asked him if she could go and visit him in hospital, she'd said she wanted to see him again. He said no 'for now', but to thank her for her concern. That sounded hopeful.

Sometimes when I catch sight him out of the corner of my eye I feel a jolt of love for him. For all his faults. My dad.

Thursday 8th April

Red said that my painting was almost ready when I got there, but that he wanted ten more minutes. I got more and more nervous. I couldn't think of anything to talk about, so I ended up just looking around the room at all the things I've seen before, seeing if anything was out of place, like that parlour game with a tray full of objects. What's missing? The china mug with an olive green glaze that sat on the shelf up there. Maybe it finally got washed up. What's new? A photo of Red's niece, Oksana, looking a little older, her face a little less round, grinning her dazzling grin.

I was about to ask after her when he said he was finished and that he was 'anxious' about me seeing it, that he always was. He said he'd leave me in the room for five minutes with my painting. He shut the door behind him, and I was alone with it. I walked slowly over to the easel. My body coiled as if expecting the painting to bite me.

I was so disappointed. Not in the painting, but in myself. There was pain in my face, horrible, twisted pain. And there was something about my eyes — they didn't seem to connect with anything, like someone was looking at me and I wasn't looking back properly. I looked pretty in the painting, and that was nice, and surprising. But I realised with a sinking heart that I could never show it to my father.

I realised how stupid I'd been to choose Red to paint me. I should have known what he'd do from the other paintings I'd seen. He'd done what he said he would, he'd painted me exactly as I am. I could feel the tears prickling, and I didn't want to cry again. I could keep them in for a while, but then Red would ask me what I really thought and I'd cry. Fuck it. For a couple of minutes I just stood there transfixed, looking at me looking back at me, or rather avoiding my gaze. And then I found a bit of paper in my bag and wrote, 'Thanks, need some time to think, see you on Tuesday.' I walked out like a complete coward, not looking round, shutting the door behind me. The tears started streaming before I even reached the end of his road. I went to a private place I know in Regent's Park, a quiet corner with a bench, and just sobbed. That was me. That face all contorted with pain, those unfocussed eyes.

When I got back to work, I went into the toilets to splash water on my face, and I could hear someone crying softly in the cubicle next to me. I stood at the sinks for a while to see who would come out and it was Mary. When I asked her if she was OK she just said, 'Yes, fine thank you.' I felt nervous in my stomach, but I asked her to come and sit in the hospital garden with me. We sat on a bench, and I said she should tell me what had happened. After a second of silence she said, 'He's touching me.'

Last week her mum had been out shopping again, and he'd followed her into the kitchen when she was making tea. He came and stood behind her and pressed into her, breathing hotly into her ear and whispering 'dirty bitch'. She could feel 'his thing' sticking into her bottom. She pulled away from him, feeling too weak to let any sound out of her mouth, and went upstairs to her bedroom, leaving the tea half-made on the counter. And then last night when she passed him on the stairs, he'd caught one of her wrists roughly in his hand and circled it like a band of cold metal while he touched her 'in two bad places' before she was able to squirm away.

There were huge empty silences in between her words, and she spoke so quietly I had to read her lips. I didn't have any answers for her. She sat there with her head bowed, tears dripping onto her skirt, and I felt utterly useless.

And then a perfect finish to a perfect day, I had an argument with Zoë. My own stupid fault. I just wanted some space and rather than telling her about what had happened with Red, I was just in an awkward mood with her all evening, making snipes about her cooking, how much space she took up on the sofa, how much time she took in the shower in the morning. In the end she looked at me and said bitterly, 'Well, if you want me to go, why don't you just spit it out?' She threw some things into a bag and left. I didn't even look at her when she was doing it. I thought about how Jules had just carried on watching the football when she left him, how hard it was to believe he hadn't said anything. What a bitch I am. I don't know where she went; she's not back yet. She's probably wandering around London in the cold and dark. I've texted her 'sorry' and then later 'Come home Zoë, I'm sorry I didn't mean it,' but I'm too chicken to phone her. Some friend I am. Some friend.

Friday 9th April

I heard Zoë come back late last night, and in the morning she'd left before I got up. I found a note saying that she was coming home from work early to pack and then she was going to stay with her cousin for the weekend to give me (and her) some space. On the bottom she'd written, 'Don't worry, it's OK.' I feel like a total bitch. I always screw it up in the end.

And work was dreadful too. Mary was quieter than ever, and it was as if we'd never had our conversation yesterday. I said to her in the morning that she could always speak to me if she wanted, and let me know if it got worse or if there was anything I could do. I know she still blames herself for everything; I can't seem to persuade her otherwise. I worry that she won't say anything to me. I worry that she won't come in to work one day and her mum will find her crumpled up and crying in a stone cold bath.

And it got worse. Much worse. Julie invited me round for dinner tonight, and I thought it would be better to be out than sitting in with only my awful self for company. So I made myself look respectable, put on my happy face and went over with a bottle of red. I thought all the way there about what I was going to do about the painting. Maybe I could get Dad something different, a golf club or something, but it wouldn't be the same; I wanted it to be something he could remember me by. I wondered if Red could paint me again and make me look happier, but I'm sure he'd laugh at that. So when I got there, I was even more miserable.

Julie annoyed me from the moment I saw her. She started wittering on about her bloody Beanie Babies and how the website was coming on. She insisted on showing me everything she'd done so far, going into excruciating detail about the decisions she'd made. Dad was hovering about in the background on his crutches, grimacing and making a fuss. I started gulping wine as soon as I was offered it. By the time we sat down for dinner, I'd had a few glasses and was feeling a bit giddy. Dad had already made a sarcastic comment about how I must have eaten too many salty crisps, and I smiled back sweetly.

The conversation somehow turned to bringing up children. I think Julie started it by talking about one of her friends and her monster child. Dad started explaining his philosophy on how to be a good parent. He said discipline didn't matter — the main thing was that children felt they were loved, were given enough attention. I couldn't believe it! I asked him through a clenched jaw when he'd changed his mind. He ignored me completely and carried on, spouting all this rubbish about how children should have permission to be wrong, that they should just concentrate on being children.

Julie noticed my face, started to look worried and fiddle with her napkin. Whenever I felt like telling him he was talking shit I swallowed more wine instead. But I could feel all these poisonous words boiling up inside, it scared me. It also felt powerful. And then I heard myself speaking, and I heard the fury in my voice. I said I'd never fucking felt like I was allowed to be a fucking child. And that he'd disciplined me like I was a disobedient puppy, like I was a piece of shit. And when he finally looked at me, when he finally stopped talking, I said the worst thing. Just like last time. I said that if he'd died instead of Mother, then I wouldn't be so fucked up and so fucking miserable all the time.

It was as if someone had pressed pause — I realised I was standing up and glaring at him over the salad bowl, the salt and pepper pots. The look of anger drained from him and he reeled. After a while he put his head into his hands, and after what felt like minutes more I felt Julie touch me on the arm and gently say my name. Ruth. I unfroze then, moving my body as if it were brittle and might snap. I thought I might throw up. And guess what? I bolted again. Straight out of the front door. Slamming it so hard that I smashed one of the panes of glass, leaving shards of it all over their front doorstep.

When I got home, I didn't know what to do with myself. I wanted to go out and walk, just walk, but then people might see me looking crazy, someone from work might see me. I didn't want to answer any questions. So I looked at a photograph. I looked at a photograph of a dead child, half buried in the earth. Her face was like a doll's face. I looked at it for too long. I didn't feel anything. And then I cut myself again, on my other arm. I didn't feel anything. I didn't feel anything. My decision is getting easier.

Saturday 10th April

How am I going to fill two whole pages today? There's nothing to write. Nothing in my life that's worth the ink. I didn't eat today, and my stomach hurts now, but at least it's taking my mind off the hurt in the rest of me — dull, aching, wrenching hurt. There are three messages on my phone. One from Julie, checking I am OK and asking me to call her. The second from her again, seven hours later, telling me to just call and tell her I'm OK. I texted 'I'm OK' to stop her from calling again. I'm such a bitch. Why is she bothering with me? And one from Abbie, saying she hadn't seen me for a while and was wondering how I am. She sounded sunny and chatty, speaking to me from a different world. It's alright for her. Her mother didn't die on her. Her mother didn't slowly desert her, bit by bit, no matter what I did to encourage her to stay. However well I behaved, whatever marks I got at school, however much I loved her. What is the point of anything, if we can't stop people leaving us? I'm sick, I can't write any more.

Sunday 11th April

I want it to come early. I want it to finish now.

Monday 12th April

I hardly moved the whole weekend and I didn't get up for work this morning. I've never missed work before like this. I feel I'm letting Mary down terribly — what if something happened at the weekend? I called in and said I've got a bad stomach. It's true: I feel all screwed up inside, can't eat. I put the phone down and just carried on crying. I slept pretty much all day, couldn't even stomach daytime TV — it all seemed stupid, pointless. Designed for bored pensioners and housewives with no lives.

And then in the afternoon there was a knock on the door, and it was Zoë and I had to face her after being so horrible to her. My face was all puffed up, my hair was greasy and I was still in my nightclothes. She looked shocked and asked me if I were ill, and I said I didn't know, before bursting into tears again. And she hugged me. I can't remember the last time someone hugged me like that. I just dissolved, and sobbed into her shoulder, feeling self-conscious about my dirty hair and my snotty nose. And then I sat down and told her what had happened, between the catches of my sobs, how I'd messed up our friendship, and ran out on Red, and totally obliterated my dad.

Then I felt a bit stupid and looked around at the mess in my flat, my rumpled duvet, the tissues all over the sofa. Zoë went all efficient on me. She said that I hadn't ruined anything, I'd just said what I felt for once, and that it's about time I started doing that a bit more. And that my dad would forgive me because that's what parents do. And that she knows that I care about her and that I've been a good friend to her (I cried again at that bit). And that what I needed to do now was have a hot bath, have something to eat, and then go to my photography class.

I hadn't even remembered I was due to go until she said. I started protesting, but she said she'd sort everything out, did I want bubbles in my bath, and what did I want in my sandwich? The nicer she was the more weepy I felt, but it was wonderful, wonderful. I said maybe someone from work would see me, but she wasn't budging; she said she'd walk me there and pick me up afterwards, that I could wear a pair of false glasses-and-nose and a frizzy wig if I wanted. She said we'd both take a day off work tomorrow and we'd spend a lazy, girly day together and make me feel better. Where did she learn how to do that stuff? I can't remember ever being looked after like this.

Over our sandwiches, I told Zoë how worried I was about Mary, how out of my depth I felt. She was really helpful. She said it sounded like Mary had told me things that she probably hadn't told anyone else. That it was a good sign that she was talking to me. She made some good suggestions — that I give her my mobile number in case she needed to get in touch when I wasn't around, and also that I give her the number for the local Women's Aid group; they were trained to deal with abuse, and she could phone their helpline or arrange to meet with one of their workers if she wanted to. She could even go to one of their refuges if she needed. We talked about how I could force her to tell her mum what was happening, and Zoë agreed with me that there probably wasn't anything I could do about that — people have to make their own decisions about these things. The important thing was that I let Mary know I was there for her if she needed me. I felt better after we'd talked.

So I managed it with her help — I went to the second class. It was like a miracle — once I'd emerged from the rose-smelling bubbles and hot water, I felt almost human. I kept remembering the bad stuff I'd done on the way to the class, but once I got there I forgot it all for a while. I sat with Susan again and talked to a few more people. I'd forgotten to pick up my photos from the developers last week with everything that's happened, but I wasn't the only one so that wasn't too embarrassing. And something good happened too — a couple of the photos Susan had taken of me were pretty good, they really were. She was flattered to be asked for copies, and I thought I could choose one and put it into a really good frame, wooden maybe, for Dad. The painting seems a bit of a waste now, but if I keep going for a while, then at least I won't have to pay for it. And meeting Red hasn't been a waste. So that's sorted. I'm still here.

Zoë was asleep when I got home. I felt like I ought to have been scared — about facing Dad, about facing Red, but more than anything I just felt sad. Sad and tired. But also a little bit hopeful, like maybe I can survive if I want to.

Tuesday 13th April

I wanted Zoë to call Red today and tell him I was ill, but she refused; she said it would be better for me to talk to him. She can be a real bully! So I called early in the morning when I thought I might get the answer phone, but he answered, sounding even more gruff than usual. I said it was me, and his voice brightened, and he asked if I was OK. I said I wasn't feeling too good and that I'd be in on Thursday — I tried to say goodbye, but he interrupted and asked me if I'd been 'hurt' by my painting. I thought I might as well tell the truth and said it had made me sad. He said, 'Yes, it would,' and asked me if I'd definitely be there on Thursday; he wanted to ask me something. I said he could ask me now instead, but he said he'd rather see me to ask. What can it be? Maybe he's changed his mind about using me as a model for more paintings.

I sent a card to Dad and Julie too, with a blank cheque so they could fill it in to pay for some new glass. I know you shouldn't send blank cheques in the post. I wasn't sure what to write in the card, so just put, 'I'll be in touch soon, sorry.'

So Zoë and I spent the day together, and you know what? It was fun! She had this idea that we should do a 'tourists in London' trip, and when she came out of the shower while I was making breakfast, she said, 'Gud mah-ning, Rooth, today vee are going to see ze Lah-ndon, no?' in the worst French accent you've ever heard. Or maybe it was German.

We went to the Tower of London and saw the glossy ravens. We did an open-topped bus tour with Zoë talking at the top of her voice in her terrible accent. We went to the waxworks museum (I thought about Red's mum and dad as we walked round), and we laughed at all the tacky celebrities, especially the ones that moved. We ate cheap burgers and onions, and candy floss, luminously pink and sticky. She made me join her in buying a T-shirt with a Union Jack on it, and we both changed into them behind some bins down an alley-way, giggling like teenagers.

I caught site of my reflection in a glass window at one point, and I looked happy, laughing — I wished that Dan could have seen me. He only ever saw the neat microbiologist, not this funny person out for the day with a good friend. I brought him along with us in my head for a while, imagining us exchanging high-eye-browed looks and laughing at Zoë's clowning, holding hands on the open-topped bus. But then I remembered what Zoë had said about Dan. Having him in my head is something I take for granted now — seven years is a long time, and he's served me well. He never disapproves of me, is always enchanted by my sparkling conversation, even thinks I have a cute nose. But I imagined what Zoë would say if she knew what I was thinking.

It's not right, is it? Dan came along with us for a while longer, but it wasn't quite the same, and in my fantasy he suddenly remembered he had some work to finish and said he'd wait for me at home. I felt guilty about not needing him, sending him away — ridiculous! Maybe it's time to start making space in my head for something (someone?) else. When we got home, we were exhausted and both dropped off watching a dodgy detective programme on TV. I woke up later feeling groggy and looked over at her and thought how lucky I am, how lucky.

In the evening, I called Abbie and told her some of the stuff that's been happening, and what I'd said to Dad. She said, 'Oh, Ruth,' in a sad, quiet voice. It brought home to me again what I'd done like a stab in the side. Ouch. I told him I'd rather he were dead. But that's how I feel. It's not his fault that Mother died. But that's how I feel. What do we do with those feelings that have the power to slice into others? I've always thought it was a better idea to keep them hidden, and what happened with Dad has proved that. But I said this to Abbie, and she wasn't sure; she said that maybe now 'you and your dad can move on'. I didn't ask her where she thought we'd be moving on to. To not speaking? To never seeing each other again? Anyway, it was good to talk to her — I care about what she thinks. How did I get here? To a place where there's more going on in my life since — well, forever? With Abbie and Zoë and Red and the classes and Dad… It's making my decision so much more complicated. With all these people around me I feel more happiness, but more sadness too. What sums do you do to find out whether it's worth it in the long run, all the hurt? How do you work out whether it's worth making friends with the snowman before he melts?

Wednesday 14th April

Zoë has decided to leave Jules and find somewhere to live on her own. We've talked about it quite a bit. She'll rent, to start with. The two of them have been talking on and off while she's been here, but their conversations often end in arguments. She met him for a drink at the weekend and said it upset her, as he'd been really nice to her. But he said he'd call her the next evening and then didn't, while Zoë sat around pretending that she wasn't waiting for the phone to ring. He said when he spoke to her the next day that he'd been playing on the Playstation and got carried away and then it was too late. Playing a game! She's more important than that, surely.

She called a couple of estate agents today and arranged to look round a few places. She's been really apologetic about how long she's stayed and keeps trying to offer me money. Since I blew up at her last Thursday, it's been better — I've been making a conscious effort to talk about the things that annoy me before they build up into huge deals in my head. I was quite proud of myself today. It sounds really silly, but I like butter to be spread smoothly from the tub, and she kind of digs in with her knife, as if she's looking for treasure in there. I asked if she'd be able to indulge my eccentricity, and she was fine; she laughed at me, but I know she'll remember. The weird thing is that even if she did carry on digging into the butter, I don't think I'd mind. As if saying it was all I needed to do. Look at me, learning about relationships at the age of thirty-three.

We watched a holiday programme this evening. I never usually watch them; they're too depressing — look at all the wonderful places you could go and visit and be alone in! Look at all the exciting experiences you could have with no-one to talk to them about! I've never handled holidays very well — it's a real struggle to take all of my allotted days from work by the end of the year. When I've got studying to do I've been able to take a 'working holiday' and spend most of the week in the library, and a couple of disastrous times I've gone to stay with Dad for a few nights. Once I was even brave enough to go and stay in a B&B in the Lake District on my own for three nights — it mostly rained. I didn't know how to handle eating dinner on my own, and once an old woman I bumped into when I was out walking asked me where was my boyfriend, and was I sensible to be out on my own? I couldn't wait to get back to London.

Zoë asked me why I'd never tried a holiday designed for single people like me, with activities already arranged for you. I said they always sounded a bit sad, and also that you might be expected to talk to people. She laughed and said we should book a cheap sun, sea and sand holiday in a few months' time and go together. Someone to go on holiday with! I felt like she'd just casually offered me a million pounds.

I got my photos back from the developers and I looked at the ones of Susan first. Most of them looked like holiday snaps. But a couple of them were OK, they really were. In one of them there had been a loud noise at the moment the photo had been taken, and she'd flicked her eyes over towards it. I'd caught her eyes as they moved, and there was a look of threat or defence on her face. I liked that one. And in another one, she was looking straight at me, but I think I had just told her I liked her face. A shudder of something crossed from her mouth upwards, a grimace, self-consciousness, denial, pleasure. It was interesting. The second batch, of the college garden, were disappointing. What I'd hoped would appear in the photos had got lost somewhere; I hadn't managed to capture it. But I'm still learning. I'll see what Milly has to say. I'm still learning, and I like it.

I still feel heavy inside about Dad. The whole scene plays out in my head in slow motion several times a day. I just can't take my eyes off his face when I throw that final rock at him. I wonder what was worse — hearing what I said, or knowing that I still hate him enough to say it — to damage him with it. He's definitely been different since the accident — I don't trust it. But maybe I want to trust it, maybe what I want more than anything is for him to just hug me, to say it's alright. I could lie there against his chest forever, if he did that. I could.

Thursday 15th April

I went to sit for Red today, and something amazing happened. I'll tell you from the beginning.

Being there after I'd run out wasn't as awkward as I thought it would be. Red did ask me how I was feeling about my painting, and I couldn't give him a proper answer — I looked at it again and couldn't even decide if I wanted it or not. I couldn't take my eyes off it — there was something compelling about it, like the smell of your own skin, or when you're listening to other people talking about you. He said that if I wanted, I could have the other painting he did of me — my choice. I don't know if the next one will be any different, but I asked if I could choose at the end, to buy me more time.

We chatted about silly things; I did most of the talking. I had noticed that he always looked out of the window before he picked up his brush for the first time and joked that he was checking that the sky wasn't falling in. He explained that he needed to remind himself how small he was, how insignificant, before he started. He said if he 'got out the way' then the painting was better. It was as if someone else was creating the painting, and he was just a channel. Not God exactly, but maybe some kind of universal force, or his subconscious even. And then he started to tease me a bit, about silly stuff, how I always asked him if he understood me when I was talking (I hadn't noticed I did this), and how he couldn't shut me up now after the first few meetings. I liked it — he teased and I protested, and the more I protested, the more his eyes twinkled.

When he'd finished, he put his paint brushes down and said casually, 'An exhibition is arriving at the weekend, photographs, Alex Taylor. I think you like it. We go together?' I said, 'Me?' stupidly, like he might be talking to his clock instead, or to the picture of his sister. He smiled and nodded. 'Umm... I don't know Taylor. Is he any good?' 'Yes — and he is not he, but she.' 'OK — thanks.' I got up and started fiddling with my bag, ready to make my escape. 'Bye.' 'Wait, Ruth. I will meet you here? At eleven on Saturday?' 'Yes, OK.' I practically ran out. He must have laughed at me after I'd gone. Silly Ruth. When will she start acting like a grown-up?

So now I've got that to look forward to/to dread... Oh my God! What shall I wear? I keep imagining the conversation drying up and having to sit in that awful silence... It also feels naughty somehow, like he's my doctor, and we shouldn't be socialising. But also... Oh, I'm so happy! He wants to spend time with me, even after all he's heard, after all he's seen. I can't make any sense of it, but I don't care! I don't care!

Zoë is even more excited than me, if that's possible. I told her before she went out; she's staying with her friend tonight. She said it was our first date, but I don't think it is. Is it? She wants us to go shopping tomorrow after work to find me something nice to wear. It's good to have her here. I almost wished I could tell Dad about it. I had a text message from Julie saying, 'Get in touch when you're ready, don't leave it too long,' but I'm too angry still, too sad. Too ashamed.

I did the things Zoë suggested with Mary at work today. I gave her my mobile number and my home number, and also a Women's Aid leaflet I'd got from the library. She felt awkward about accepting my numbers but said it was 'a relief' to know she could call if she needed to. She said she'd managed to avoid being alone with him since last time, but he still winked at her behind her mum's back and mouthed rude words at her and she felt it was only a matter of time. She'd asked her mum how she was getting on with him, to see if anything had changed, but her mum had said it was all wonderful. These things are so difficult. How do you find out what the 'right' thing is?

Mary is in a different department now, but we've got into the habit of meeting up for our morning break in the hospital garden for ten minutes and catching up. I've started to tell her a bit about my life too, about Red, about Zoë. Work is going fine in general — we're still pretty busy. Today I used a grouping kit for a streptococcus. I noticed the colours as if for the first time — the straw colour of the first reagent, the pink of the second, the blue of the third. And then the positive test agglutinating into blue clumps on the test card, the background fluid becoming clear. The blue clumps are the deepest of royal blues. The colour of a cloudless sky in late evening. I found myself wondering what it would look like as a photo, in extreme close-up with a silver frame.

Friday 16th April

I met Zoë at a potential new flat after work. She looked round one yesterday and said it was horrible, poky and dark. This one is only fifteen minutes walk from mine, so I really wanted it to be nice. The estate agent met us outside — he would have been quite good looking if it hadn't been for his plastic hair and dodgy, spotted tie. When he started talking, it was as if someone had written a script for him and he was reading it from an autocue at the back of his eyes. I wondered how he sounded when he was chatting with his friends in the pub, if he could possibly be as fake in real life. He introduced himself as Jules, and Zoë made a 'yuk!' face at me when he wasn't looking.

The flat was on the first floor, and the corridors and staircase looked newly decorated. The previous owner had painted the whole flat white in preparation for selling, and it smelt fresh. A clean slate. I could tell that Zoë was impressed. It was at the higher end of what she could pay, so she said she'd think about it, and we both shook the agent's hot, clammy hand goodbye. As soon as he'd driven away I said, 'You have to have it!' and she said I was right and called him on is mobile. They arranged to go through all the papers on Monday. She's really excited. I can see myself there too, helping her arrange her furniture, having a cup of tea, chatting about work. We talked about paint colours all the way home. Maybe new beginnings are possible.

Then we hit the shops. I took Zoë to my usual shops this time, but we had a deal that I would try on three things she chose from each shop, whether I liked the look of them or not. She kept choosing stuff I would never wear in a million years — a suede mid-length skirt, a top the colour of poppies, a white linen shirt — clothes for someone much cooler, much more adventurous than me. When I looked at myself in the mirror I thought I looked like a fake, someone who'd been on a daytime TV makeover programme. No point in looking great if you're not yourself. I tried to explain this to Zoë as she whooped and crooned about how gorgeous I looked, but she didn't really understand; she said that I could change how I looked without becoming someone else. Maybe I can.

I ended up letting her choose my entire outfit. There was a baby-pink woollen top that wrapped around and tied — as soon as I felt the material I knew I'd have to have it; it felt like baby bunny rabbits. Sorry to be so girly. And she gave me a really long A-line skirt to try, in charcoal grey. Plain white T-shirt. And I chose my shoes, plain black with a single flash of pink on them. They cost more money than I've ever spent on shoes before, but I loved them, and Zoë thoroughly agreed, which made things easier. Then she took me to a jewellery shop to find a necklace to finish the outfit off. So strange having to think about a whole outfit, to pay such attention to it. But also fun! So I bought a thin, black leather necklace with a single pink stone, holding it up to my neck to try it out. We got stuck on the bag, the final bit of the puzzle. I really liked a brown one, but Zoë said it didn't go with my black trainers and necklace. So I thought of myself as a photograph, a composition, and was drawn to a bright bluey-green colour, a splash of deep-sea water. I held it against the colours of the clothes in the bags, and Zoë cried, 'You genius!'

I tried it all on together when I got home, and I felt pretty good in it. If only it were so easy to put my character together in the same way. I think I'll take along a big dose of sense-of-humour, a scoop of intellectual-thinking, a large portion of being-interesting. And a pinch of *je-ne-sais-quois* to finish me off.

I'm terrified. Terrified!

This evening I looked at a photo called 'Girl on a Spacehopper'. She has her back to us, so it's difficult to work out how old she might be — maybe seven or eight? The photographer has caught her mid-bounce, suspended above the empty concrete and brick streets. She's wearing a long, sequined dress with a big bow on the back under her pale woollen jumper, and the full skirt has swallowed the Spacehopper whole, you can only see a thin slice of circle poking out beneath it. Her head has moved too quickly for her hair and it floats around her as if the air were water. Strands of it are clumped together into rat-tails and point in different directions. It could do with a brush, but she doesn't seem to care what she looks like, doesn't care if a dress-strap has fallen from one of her shoulders. She's bang in the middle of her experience of bouncing. She's jumping for joy.

Saturday 17th April

He kissed me! He kissed me! He kissed me… Did I tell you he kissed me? He kissed me! I'm floating. Up in the clouds, up above a lake somewhere, looking down at the clear water, watching the silvery fish twist and glide. I'm zooming up towards the stars. I keep remembering it with a jolt, while I'm making a cup of tea or taking out the rubbish. It's a strange feeling, a swoop of fear and joy all mixed up together. I stop whatever I'm doing and just smile. He kissed me!

Let me start at the beginning. I got ready as soon as I got up, glad that my outfit was already decided on. I wasn't hungry for breakfast, but Zoë made me have some toast and butter or she said I'd feel even worse. I put mascara on, which I don't usually do and borrowed some of Zoë's clear lip balm that smelt of strawberries. I spent most of the morning trying to calm myself down, laughing at how silly I was being. Zoë told me I looked beautiful as I left the flat, and I carried her words in my head for the rest of my journey. So there I was on his doorstop at exactly eleven, full of not just butterflies, but moths and dragonflies and small birds as well. He opened the door and grinned at me, and said, 'You look delicious.' I blushed, much pinker than my new top, probably, but he didn't seem to notice and disappeared into the hall to get his jacket. And I felt another surge of panic then — maybe he was taking me on a date. He'd had a twinkle in his eye.

So we walked and talked. It was so strange being out of the studio with him, like we knew each other as people, like we were friends. I talked about Zoë and our trip to London and my photography class. The simple stuff. I tried to make some of it funny, impersonating Zoë impersonating tourists, and he laughed his easy laugh. He told me a funny story about one of his artist friends who'd needed to find some empty snail shells for an 'installation' she was putting together and some recent news about his sister and Oksana. There were a couple of silences, but they were just gaps in the conversation, that's all. I was aware of the physical distance between us as we walked.

We got to the gallery and spent an hour looking at the photos. It was nice to be with someone who wasn't in a hurry. I went to a gallery with Maggie once during our lunch hour, and she couldn't stay still — she was always off looking at the next thing. But Red took his time. The photos were of mountains and landscapes, a bit like Ansel Adams, but less idealistic somehow, less beautiful. There was a sense of fear in some of them, a sense of overwhelm, if that's a word. We didn't talk about them when we were there, moved round in silence. We signalled to each other with a look when we wanted to move on.

And then we drank strong coffee and ate carrot cake in the little café and talked. We talked about ordinary things again, but as we talked, I felt as if I were moving towards him imperceptibly, getting closer. His flaming hair. His icy blue eyes with their pale lashes. I was conscious of my breathing. When our eyes met they locked, reluctant to let go, holding on a little bit longer. By the end of the conversation something was different between us.

We stopped to buy an ice cream afterwards, and he insisted on buying me a double-scoop of sticky toffee and chocolate chip. We glanced at each other every so often, sometimes smiling, sometimes not. When he asked me if I'd come back to his house, I suddenly felt a need to go home, and he said that was fine. And then he asked me if we could do it again. Next Saturday. He wanted to see me again! I felt like I was losing my hold on the pavement, that I might need to grab onto him to keep myself tethered. And I smiled and nodded and said, 'Bye then,' making to go.

He caught me by the arm — maybe he noticed me starting to lift up off the ground. And before I even knew what was happening, he moved towards me, fast, and landed the lightest kiss on my lips. It was like a small insect touching down. And pulled his face back a little way, hovered there. And so I kissed him back, sucking on his lips so gently I'm not even sure he felt it, before I got scared and pulled away. He took my chin in his finger and thumb as if we were in some Mills and Boon novel then said his goodbye and started walking away. He spoilt the Mills and Boon effect slightly by jumping up and kicking both his feet together, then turning around and grinning. And I'm still remembering that first kiss, it's like he's still here, kissing me, every time I started to forget. There. There.

Sunday 18th April

Red called this morning; he woke me up and I felt caught out, unprepared. My heart pounded through the whole call as I waited for him to let me down gently, to tell me how mixing business with pleasure was never a good idea… He didn't say any of that, just chatted about yesterday and told me what he was going to do with his Sunday, asked me about mine. After he'd rung off, I couldn't make sense of why he'd called.

I spent the whole morning reading back what I've written here so far. I've passed the half-way mark without noticing. Looking at the pile of paper covered with my handwriting reminded me of when I was fifteen and I went through a phase of letter writing. I hadn't got any proper friends at school and the weekends were a bit lonely. One day our French teacher offered us the opportunity to be matched up with a pen-friend in France. I loved the idea and was given the name and address of Mirabelle Jacquemin — I remember thinking how beautiful her name was. I sent her a long letter in dreadful French with useful information about me including my favourite colour (blue), animal (panda) and TV programme (Newsround). When I got my first letter back a week later, I was on a high for days.

I asked my French teacher if I was allowed more than one pen-friend, and she took pity on me and gave me two more. Then I discovered English pen-pals in Jackie magazine and there was no stopping me. At the height of pen-pal madness, I had seventeen and was writing at least a letter a day. After a while, the buzz of seeing letters addressed to Ruth White on the doormat began to wear off. Mirabelle lasted another year, and then even she stopped writing. All those words flying back and forth. Dissolving into the air.

So I went through my journal, suicide note… whatever it is. I tried to imagine from the beginning what kind of a person would write these things. I couldn't work her out. She seemed distant from me somehow — I wanted to pull her closer, squeeze her on the arm and say 'hey!' to get some kind of reaction. The thing that I did decide about her was that she lived safely. Even when she did things that were risky, through choice or through necessity, she did them in a way that left her protected. It was quite convincing, the way she wrote about yesterday and Red's kiss. It sounded like she was happy. But I know (because I do have extra information about this person, not like you) that she also thought, at exactly the same time as every whoosh of joy, that Red would probably tire of her soon, so she should make the most of it while it lasted. He would find out how empty she really was, how screwed up, how mean. And then she'd be left again, and it would be worse than before, because she would have tasted what it feels like to be wanted. And it tasted sweet.

It makes me think about William, a colleague at work. He's crazy about model cars. I know that people laugh at him behind his back, calling him Model Car Willie — one of the histologists even does impressions of him, stuttering about Morris Minors from behind his hand. I ended up sitting next to William one lunchtime, and I asked him lots of questions about his hobby — his face lit up when he talked about it. He said he spends all of his free time going to junk shops and auctions, making records of what models he has, restoring them, spending time in specialist internet chat rooms. He said he 'hardly had time for a social life'.

We're not so different, William and me. I can understand the attraction of model cars. They're not going to do impressions of him behind his back; they're not going to decide they don't like the way he sniffs when he's making a point. They won't expect anything from him. They won't stab him in the heart with sharp words when he tries to do the right thing.

So how do I break into myself after all these years? Maybe it's too late for this person I've read about to become anyone different. Think about what it would take. It would mean a total restructure — not just a new coat of paint, or a mended roof, but different rooms, fresh foundations. That old building would have to be rooted up from the ground, and the thought of having nothing in the earth, nothing to hold me steady, is terrifying beyond words.

In my new book Gretel Ehrlich is in the middle of a polar winter. Her days are the same as her nights. She writes, "I don't know where I am. Wind comes through the wall. Maybe the walls have fallen away and merged with the walls of the galaxy." And then, "…I look into indigo space, and indigo space, like an eyeless eye, looks back at me."

Monday 19th April

When I woke up this morning, the thing with Red felt like a dream. Did he really call me yesterday morning? Did he really kiss me? I lay in bed and tried to remember exactly what he'd worn, what we said while we ate cake. It all felt a bit fuzzy. I gave up and got up, deciding that I needed to sort things out with Dad. I've had enough of waking up every morning with a sinking feeling in my stomach. I spoke to Julie a few days ago, and she said he's not really angry, just deflated, and still shocked, even after a week and a half. I need to keep the end of May in mind, just in case — I need to give us time to be OK with each other again. So I called him this evening. I hate making calls like that — if he were just a friend, I'd never speak to him again, easier that way. I said hi to Julie, and then I could hear her trying to persuade him to talk to me in the background, 'Go on, you'll have to speak to her sometime. Just for a bit.' I stood there with the phone pressed to my ear and tried to keep breathing.

His first hello sounded like it came from a little boy. I started the call cheerfully to try and get a conversation going, said something inane about the weather, but he didn't reply. I asked him how he was getting on with his physio. 'Slow.' I asked him about my investments, a subject that always gets him going. 'They're fine.' So in the end I just had to ask him round for dinner. He said he'd check with Julie, see if they were free. The conversation ended awkwardly, and as I put down the phone I noticed that my hands were shaking.

At least I've spoken to him, got the ball rolling. I wonder if he would ever have got in touch with me again if I hadn't made the first move. Would it matter? I don't know. I didn't say I was sorry.

Photography class was good tonight. Milly agreed with me about which photos of Susan were the better ones. She said I had a 'natural flair for portraits'. It doesn't really make sense for me to be good at taking portraits — I'm not very good at people. I suppose I am good at looking at them, because if you're not involved in a conversation you get a lot of practise just observing. I can sit at the back of the room and spend my time sussing things out. Susan wasn't there, so I sat with Sara, the girl who smiled at me the first week. I felt comfortable with her. She has lovely skin, smooth and glowing, and her hair is in narrow braids. She wears comfortable looking clothes — wide trousers, loose tops, has a neat figure, big eyes. We chatted about a film we'd both seen on TV the night before about a national dog show — 'Best in Show'. I thought it was hilarious, but Zoë hadn't found it funny at all, and after a while I stopped laughing so hard and wondered if I'd got it wrong. But Sara loved it too and said she'd seen it several times — we laughed about it together. At the end of the class she asked me if I fancied coffee sometime. Am I giving out 'come and make friends with me' vibes or something? I said I was busy tonight, and she suggested next week so I said yes. I can't work out if I'm pleased about it or not.

Our assignment today was taking photos of the sky. We were allowed to take the sky 'through' something — a tree or anything else we could get underneath. There was a box of props in the corner of the classroom. The sky was grey and miserable looking, so I had the idea of an umbrella and tried a few with half-umbrella half-sky. Then I took a few with my hand above me, the back of it facing down as if I were shielding my eyes. Sara and I helped each other out. I'm halfway through the whole course now. I'm starting to feel more comfortable with my camera — knowing what all the buttons do, what I can expect from it. I might try another roll of film myself this week, just buy one and go out and see what I can see. That feels pretty exciting!

Zoë is all signed up for her new flat. She'll move out of here on Saturday, has got the new keys already, so she can pop back and forth with bits and bobs. She hasn't picked up the rest of her stuff from Jules yet. I offered to go with her, and she was really grateful. I don't have to think so hard now about what a good friend would do, I just do what I think at the time. She's been a bit weepy this week; maybe the reality is hitting home. I'm looking forward to having my own space back again, being able to watch what I want on TV without worrying about whether she's enjoying it, being able to look at my photographs in peace. But I'll miss her too. The way she says, 'Wouldya like a cuppa tea, chuck?' in a bad Northern accent when she's making one for herself, and having someone to pull soap operas to pieces with. I will miss her.

Tuesday 20th April

Abbie has met a man! I popped in to see her after work today. I feel at home in her house now, I know where the sugar is kept and how many she takes in her tea. I knew that something had happened as soon as I saw her; she looked like I felt. He was one of her clients' colleagues, and they'd had dinner on Thursday. I was really pleased for her.

She hasn't told me much about her past, but from what I can gather she hasn't had the easiest of times, romantically. She was briefly married to a Swedish guy called Torvald when she was quite young — they'd met through friends and she said they'd happened to share a love of 'mild recreational drugs'. They became serious very quickly but when she introduced him to her family, none of them had approved. She was most furious with her mother, who when pressed could only confess to disapproving of his 'shifty eyes'.

Abbie being Abbie, this catapulted her into proposing to him and everything happened very fast. Her parents didn't go to the wedding. The marriage lasted a couple of years, which Abbie felt was 'quite good going' for a partnership based mainly on doing the opposite of what her parents wanted her to. There'd been a few longer relationships since then, but Abbie said she was a 'free spirit' and had found that most men ended up wanting to tie her down or own her. She'd already had a conversation about this with her new man, and she said that early signs were 'promising'.

Work went slowly in the morning. Nothing much exciting is happening. Things have been OK at home for

Mary, as far as I know. I've been telling her about my new photography classes. I'd like to photograph her; she has such an interesting face, all closed down and private, unless you catch her smiling. She has huge eyes and delicate little hands. Maybe I'll ask her if she'd mind. In the afternoon I felt more nervous about the sitting than I did about seeing Red on Saturday, if that's possible. I took ages deciding between all my rubbish clothes and then spent a good while longer in the bathroom than usual, plucking my eyebrows. I've never bothered before, didn't really understand the point, but Zoë has introduced me to phenomena such as eyebrow plucking and glossy lip salve. Nothing over the top, you realise. Just basic grooming, the kind of things that make me feel better about myself. I suppose I never had anyone to teach me before. My body almost wouldn't let me travel the usual journey to Red's house. It got more and more unruly the closer to his house I got, and I had to keep it under tight control so it didn't bolt. The energy it was producing in readiness for running away all ended up in my stomach, tightening it, and it was hard to breathe properly. I had to give myself a good talking to before I knocked on the door. And there he was. He always shocks me with his sheer size, even though I keep thinking that I make him taller in my mind. He looked pleased to see me. I blushed immediately, deeply, and walked straight in behind him to try and hide until it faded. I saw him notice. Sometimes I wish he wouldn't pay such close attention to me.

It was kind of a normal session, but different too. I felt like he wasn't just my portrait painter any more, he was Red, the man who worshipped his older sister, who liked scrambled eggs for his breakfast, who had put black boot polish in his hair when he was five to try and get rid of the ginger. I teased him about this, asking if he'd stocked up on polish for the weekend. We had more to talk about now — he knew about what was happening at work, about Zoë, about Abbie. I knew that his parents were visiting in a couple of month's time, and the preparations he was already making in readiness for his mother's critical eye. I teased him about the studio looking tidier. It felt good to tease him — it gave me power somehow, helped me feel less nervous.

I'm not sure he got much painting done today, as he kept stopping to threaten me with his cup of paint-stained water or to stretch out his finger and thumb, rest them on his chin and look to the ceiling in a parody of being a serious artist in thought. I grimaced and rolled my eyes whenever he looked at me, hoping to confuse his painting. Eventually he came over to me and put a large flat hand on each of my cheeks, trying to hold my face in a normal position. There was a moment when we both stopped laughing, and I thought he might lean in and kiss me, but then our time was up — it had gone so quickly. All the way back to work I thought about what he'd said when he let me in — I hadn't paid attention when he said it, I was too busy being embarrassed. It seemed a strange thing to say. He said, 'You're melting, Ruth.'

Wednesday 21st April

Ernest James Bellocq took photos of prostitutes. They found a pile in his desk drawer when he died — eighty-nine of them. This one has a beautiful bottom. I know that doesn't sound like something I'd say, but she does. The curve of it undulates from her waist in a perfect outward sweep, the cheeks are plump and pert. There's a crude tattoo of a heart on the right cheek. Her left arm is by her side; the right arm is out at a right angle from her body, and in her hand is a piece of white chalk. She's drawing a butterfly on the wall — a fat butterfly with a stocky body and compact wings. Like her. Her dark hair is draped over her left shoulder. She is looking up towards the butterfly, and her face has been scratched out, showing as a series of grainy jet black marks.

He found her beautiful, Bellocq, but did he see her as a real woman? Was it easier for him if he didn't have to look at her face? There is something too perfect about her. I wonder what happened when she changed back from being a butterfly to a woman who leaked blood once a month and was hairy and sweated just like a man. Who had her own needs, her own mind. I don't think men like those things about us. I'm certain that Dad doesn't. He hated having to be more involved in Mother's body — seeing it as a messy living package of blood and bones rather than a tidy, smooth-skinned object to have sex with. Sometimes when she was in pain, he reacted as if she were doing it on purpose to disturb him, as if it were her choice. Sometimes she'd let out a small moan when she sat down or stood up, and he actually used to roll his eyes. She never seemed to get angry with him; I couldn't understand why — I was furious. I always regret not saying something to him about it.

I started my periods really late — it was after Mother had died. When I told him, he was astonished I hadn't already started. I don't know why Mother hadn't told him — I suppose she was preoccupied with dying. I nearly didn't tell him at all, and I wish I hadn't. He went straight out to the shops and bought sanitary towels and came into my bedroom and threw them on my bed, saying, 'There you are.' He sounded disgusted. After he left, I just cried and cried into my pillow for Mother. He never mentioned it again. But I do want him to phone now. I just want him to phone.

I'm thinking about Red a lot. We've arranged to meet up again on Saturday afternoon, go to the park or something. There are so many things I want to know about him; they're queuing up in my head. Yesterday I asked him what his favourite food was. He told me it was a salad, 'olivye'. He said it's made of a mixture of little chunks of sausage, boiled potatoes, pickles and peas, with mayonnaise mixed in as dressing. He wants to make it for me. I want to taste it. And I want to know what his favourite animal is, his favourite colour, his favourite day of the week. I want to know if he prefers brown or white bread. Whether he sleeps on the left or the right side of the bed. I want to know his language. I've also been trying to guess at what he wants from me. Trying to understand why he wants to see me again. But I am happy. Don't think I'm not grateful for this. Every so often I just give myself a break and think, 'It doesn't matter why. He just does!' He just does.

It's past the middle of April. I'm feeling panicky about the time moving on.

I couldn't have imagined that my life would be so full of people by now; some of them even care about me. It makes me feel like a jumpy horse, half wild. The more people get their fingers into me, the more people I get tangled up with, the dirtier it feels, in a way — no — not dirty, but just… I don't know how to explain it. I don't feel myself. People don't know about me, and I've always liked it that way. It just feels dangerous having them so close to me. What happens if I drop them, and they smash all over the floor? What happens if they drop me?

I was a naughty girl today. Zoë was out for the evening with a friend from work, and I opened up my wounds. It felt like sitting at home with a huge cream cake, eating it, and then feeling really sick. Not even enjoying it, really. I made a mess of my top. Sloppy, unlike me. I felt stupid afterwards, not better. I felt uncomfortable about this part of me, this bit that I don't show anyone. Maybe I should get some help? But it's not like it's actually affecting my life; it's under control. I could stop if I wanted to — I'm just playing around with it, really. It feels like an exciting secret to have at the same time as being a shameful one, a kind of a dirty pleasure. How does it make you feel about me? I imagine you're curling your lip in disgust.

Thursday 22nd April

Red and I just talk and talk when I see him now. I keep forgetting that he's painting me. I still have to fish information out of him; he still isn't volunteering anything. Is that a problem? Is it that he doesn't have anything to say, or doesn't he trust me? These questions buzz around my head like a cloud of gnats. Today he wasn't feeling very well, had a cold. I made him sit down in the chair I usually sit in and made him hot lemon and honey; he'd never had it before. He told me he's worried about his mother, she's been complaining that his father treats her like an idiot. He says it's hard with them so far away. I wonder if he'll ever move back to Russia. Maybe that'll be how this thing will end. I'll try to enjoy it while it lasts.

I watched a programme on TV tonight about girls who cut themselves. I probably wouldn't have watched it on my own, but Zoë was interested, and I thought it might have been suspicious if I said no. She said it reminded her of someone she'd known at school once, a really geeky know-it-all girl who no-one liked. Things were difficult for her at home — her little brother had muscular dystrophy, her father was out of work. One winter they found her dead in her bedroom. She'd taken Paracetemol, thirty-six of them crushed up into a strawberry milkshake. When they did a post-mortem, they found marks all over her body, scars. Some of them were years old they said. Years. And they found small knives in her bedroom. How could her family not have known? Maybe she always kept her cuts properly hidden, like I do. I suppose I can't blame Dad for not knowing. But maybe he could look a bit harder for the marks on me — surely he realises that there must be some scars somewhere?

I tried to watch the programme with Zoë in a detached way, but I kept recognising things that the girls said. "I cut myself to calm myself down — I'm never trying to kill myself," and, "I self-harm to try and shock my body back into living." It was comforting to know that I wasn't the only one, that those girls at least understood me. I cried at one point, when a girl was talking about how alone she felt, and how she wanted to protect her parents from her pain. But Zoë cried too, so I don't think she suspected anything. It makes me so sad to think about them, those girls, I'm weeping as I write (silently so I don't wake Zoë). Those poor girls.

Julie called this evening, finally — I was glad it was her and not Dad. She said that Dad wasn't ready quite yet, that he'd been doing a lot of thinking, and that he didn't want me to think I didn't love him. He was 'seeing things in a new light' and just wanted to spend some more time 'thinking things through' before he saw me again. I was upset on the phone but I didn't show it, I said I understood. She said she'd call again in a week or so. Dad's being a coward again, just like always. Sending Julie to do his dirty work. He can't hear the truth. Can't face it. I wish I'd told her that I wasn't sure if I wanted to see him either.

It's strange — since that awful night, a part of me has wanted to see him more than ever, and another part of me is even angrier, even more furious about how he failed me after Mother died. Failed to be a parent really — in anything more than name. He didn't have any space for me, he didn't… what exactly? What is it? He didn't want me. That's it — he's never really wanted me. I don't know if he's even capable of it. He wanted Mother, that's for sure. I always felt like I was in the way, getting between them. Maybe he never really wanted children in the first place; maybe Mother talked him round. Then I arrived and he saw how much she loved me and got jealous. Never recovered. Then she goes and dies, leaving me behind. The one he never really wanted anyway. I don't know if we can fix this thing now, maybe it's gone too far. Maybe this was inevitable.

I flicked through a few of my photography books this evening but I couldn't find anything to settle on. I wanted to look at something uplifting, or soothing at least. But the only thing that kept my attention for long was something agonising. It was a photo of a man suspended by hooks on the end of ropes that hung from the ceiling. The hooks went into holes that he'd made himself in his pectoral muscles. I don't know how he made the holes. I don't know where he got the idea from. Triangles of his skin and flesh were being wrenched out away from his body and it was amazing that they didn't rip. I thought — look — here's someone who's more disturbed than me. And also — look what a human body can do before it breaks.

Friday 23rd April

Saturday 24th April

Zoë had arranged with Jules to pick her stuff up from her old flat yesterday while he was out at work. We were both pretty nervous. She'd hired a small van and we joked about being Thelma and Louise, considered roaming the streets to find ourselves a Brad Pitt (each) before riding off into the sunset. We tentatively knocked on her old door, ready to run if anyone answered, and left it a long time before using her key to get in. I wondered how she was feeling, but her face was hard and unreadable. The flat was clean and tidy — Zoë said he'd hired a cleaner a week after she'd gone and we laughed at how easily replaceable she had been. But it also felt oddly bare, barren.

He'd put all of her stuff in the spare room. It was piled up higgledy-piggledy on the bed. One of her photo frames was cracked, and a book was rudely splayed open. Zoë picked it up to smooth out the creased pages. I thought she was going to cry. But she got angry instead, screwing her face up into a threat, calling him a bastard. I wanted to do something to him then, cut out the flies from all of his trousers or pee on his bed. I told Zoë and she laughed. We just got on with it then, carrying loads to the car. A couple more things had been broken — a china dog had one of his legs broken off and a clock had its face smashed. But Zoë didn't mind — the dog was only a 'dodgy present' from her mum, and she could buy a new clock. We took the stuff straight to her new place, puffing and sweating with a couple of heavy pieces of furniture, an easy chair, a table. Zoë looked fragile, but there was a determination too.

When we'd unloaded we drove to my flat and filled the van up again — we couldn't believe how much stuff she'd got at mine; where had it all fitted? When we were finished, my flat looked wrong. She said she wanted to move the last of it in herself as a symbolic gesture. If she were going to live there alone, she'd need to learn how to do things on her own. As she said this, her voice shook. I asked her if she was OK and she said, 'No, I'm fucking terrified,' and I didn't know what to say to that, so just stood there in awkward silence until she smiled and took a deep breath. She thanked me for having her to stay for so long, hugged me tight. I knew I couldn't say anything to make her feel better, really; it's not easy being on your own. No false jollity for a change. So we cheek-kissed goodbye, and she left.

I sat around feeling miserable for a while, flicking around from channel to channel, and decided to call Abbie. She was pleased to hear from me and suggested I come over for a drink — she'd bought a case from one of these wine clubs and needed someone to help her out. So I went round and we drank. We drank and drank — I think she'd been having problems with her new man; she hinted at it but didn't go into details. She's not such an open book, either. I can vaguely remember screeching with laughter about bus conductors; god knows what we found so funny about them. We matched each other glass for glass. But she's had more practise than me, and I started feeling out of control, a bit wonky. At one point I thought I might fall off my chair. But after a few minutes I got my balance again and felt quite clear headed, so I thought it'd be OK to have one more glass. Eugh. And then things went blurry, and I remember being in her bathroom, kneeling in front of the toilet, and then I remember Abbie smoothing my forehead with her hand, her skin was cool.

The next thing I remembered was waking up in a strange bed with a strange nightdress on. I looked around at the dressing gown draped over a chair and the bookmarked novel on the bedside table... it was Abbie's room! It was mortifying. I couldn't remember anything. I could hear someone clattering about in the kitchen — the alarm clock said 11 am — but I was too embarrassed to go down for twenty minutes.

Abbie met in the kitchen with a strange smile. Then she made a joke about it making a change for someone else to be sleeping in her bed. I apologised and she said it was fine; she shouldn't have fed me so much wine. She cooked me a fried breakfast — mushrooms, eggs, bacon, hash browns. I wasn't sure it'd be wise to eat, but it smelt amazing, and I was suddenly ravenous. It seemed to go down OK. She said she was going out in ten minutes, and could she leave me some keys to lock up? I wanted to ask her if I'd said or done anything embarrassing the night before, but she was in a hurry so I thought I'd wait. I wonder if I talked about Mother.

So that's where my missing day went! I saw Red again in the afternoon for our second — date? I'm still reluctant to commit that word to paper, words like 'date' or 'boyfriend', as if I might jinx something. For goodness sakes Ruth — jinx! You need to grow up! I was still feeling a bit rough around the edges, and spent ages looking at myself in the mirror, trying to work out how hungover I looked and whether I'd put Red off. If only I knew how to use make-up as disguise, like most women, but I don't have a clue what to do with blusher or how foundation might help. Is it too late to learn those things?

Luckily he took me to the cinema, where it was dark anyway, and I forgot all about my crumpled face by the time we left. The film was average, a big-budget, American sci-fi film. It didn't have any soul, but there were some good aliens in it. I loved sitting there in the dark knowing I was sat there *with him.* I was ultra-aware of his presence; I swear I could feel the heat rising off him. And every so often our forearms would brush against each other on the arm of the chair, and those tiny touches sent shocks of pleasure through me. I dreaded to think what might happen if more of our skin came into contact at once… I might pass out. We shared the largest sized tub of salty popcorn; he ate most of it, and we groaned at the really naff bits in the film. Before the film had finished, after a particularly cringey part where the evil aliens 'turned good' and saved the life of a small chubby-cheeked boy, Red turned to me and whispered, 'Shall we go now?' I said, 'We can't!' and he asked me why, and I couldn't think of a good reason apart from being embarrassed about people seeing us. So we got up and went! How naughty!

We went to Hyde Park — I wanted to show him the friendly squirrels and we bought peanuts to feed them. And as we stepped over the threshold of the park, he took my hand in his. His hands were massive, but it felt like my hand fitted his perfectly, like it was always meant to be there. He looked at me and smiled, and I just looked away and blushed, giving his hand a tiny squeeze a few seconds later instead. We didn't say much as we walked; I couldn't concentrate on anything. It rang through my head like a peal of bells over and over... he's holding my hand! He's holding my hand! I nearly whispered it out loud at one point and caught myself just in time.

We found some squirrels and fed them peanuts for a while. They were so tame. I couldn't get enough of looking at their soft, strokeable fur and their tiny hands and their liquid eyes. I wished I'd brought my camera with me and told Red — I'd told him about the classes I was doing. I was worried that he wouldn't take my hand again afterwards, that he would have found it too hot or too cold or too small. But he did! He did! I could have walked round and round the park forever.

He dropped me off at my flat. I didn't ask him in, as it was still messy from Zoë moving out and said I'd invite him in next time, feeling bold, implying that there'd be a next time. He said, 'Good,' and I waited for him to kiss me again and he did, just lightly, another feather landing. I felt more confident this time, stayed in close. He put a hand onto the small of my back and pressed a little harder with his lips; I pressed back, parting my mouth and finding his tongue and tasting salt before I pulled away. And he said, 'You are my girlfriend now.' Just like that. Simple. Beautiful. I don't want to think about the implications of that today, the complications, the ramifications, all the other –ations, ha ha. I just want to hear him say it over and over in my head. I am his girlfriend now. I am his girlfriend.

Sunday 25th April

He called this morning! I was sat on the floor with the newspaper spread out around me. He asked what I was doing right now, and then he said he was coming over to read the papers with me. He arrived around twelve, and I spent a mad half hour tidying up and then scattering things about again, just like when Zoë came. I tried to arrange myself on the sofa so that when he looked in from the street he'd see me looking glamorous and sexy. After holding the pose for ten minutes I needed the toilet, and he knocked just at the wrong moment. I made him tea and toast with marmite, and we just sat and read, not talking much. There was only a rustling of paper and a crunching of toast. It felt comfy.

Suddenly he put his paper down with a big crinkly crash and said, 'Ruth, over here!' narrowing his eyes and raising his eyebrows. I smiled and got up from the floor, my poor heart jumping. He raised his arm up and I slipped underneath it. Mmmm. Better than diving under freshly-washed cotton sheets and a feather duvet at the beginning of autumn. I touched as much of his body as I could with mine, tucking my head underneath his chin, my cheek to his chest. And I breathed him in — great sweeping sniffs of him, that warm honey-and-pepper smell. Sugar and spice. I could hear his heart, and as I pressed my ear to his chest it got faster, and I felt my whole body tightening. My breathing got faster, jagged. His hand moved onto the outside of my thigh, holding it gently as if he might lift it up, and his thumb started to make a tiny sweeping motion, back and forth, back and forth. And my head lifted itself up towards him. His face was serious, but his eyes were twinkling. I whispered, 'You have to be careful with me,' and tears came to my eyes. One of them slipped over my bottom eyelid and rolled down my cheek — I was about to stick out the tip of my tongue to catch it when he dived forward and sucked it off with a kiss. Then he smiled at me, his wrinkles crinkling up around his eyes, and said, 'It is hard to melt. We go slowly. OK?'

We went slowly. He waited for me to kiss him, and when our lips pushed up against each other, I didn't really feel anything. Felt clumsy. What next? How did you do this again? I suddenly remembered a gangly boy at University and the way he used to kiss me, his tongue darting in and out of my mouth like a lizard, and a little giggle escaped me. We stopped and Red looked a question at me, but I shook my head, took a deep breath and went back in. This time a sensation came from inside me, a flower blossoming in fast motion. It felt like my entire store of touch receptors had moved through my body and into my lips and they were all perched on the absolute edge of where our skin was touching, jostling for position. I felt wetness, smoothness, the inside of his lips. And then the tip of his tongue, just the tip. There were no thoughts, just a warm, red feeling. Odd not to be thinking of anything. And we snogged for ages. Silly word! Just snogging, and it was wonderful. Wonderful. We stopped sometimes and giggled about something — he'd stick his tongue out at me, or I'd make silly mwah!-mwah! kissing sounds on his neck. And then we carried on. Near the end, his hands started to move about a bit, testing the backs of my legs, settling on my waist. I felt warm and tingly. And then he pulled back and sighed a huge sigh and said that was it, if he carried on, it would be harder to stop.

I was disappointed, wanted to carry on, held on to his ear with my finger and thumb. But he shook me off and got up to go to the kitchen, turning round to shake a finger at me and looking fake-stern. So that was that. I sat there for a few frozen seconds and then got up to help him make the tea. I haven't thought about Dan for days.

Later we decided to go and see Zoë in her new flat. I told Red she wants to meet him and he said, 'Let's go now.' How did we get here? Everything is so simple with him. I wanted to phone first but he said we should, 'Give her a good surprise,' and he was right; she was pleased and shocked to see us — I don't think she expects me to be spur-of-the-moment. Red helped her put up a new flat-pack bookcase, and they laughed together, especially about me and my neatness. When we were leaving and his back was turned, she raised her eyebrows at me and gave me the thumbs-up.

Monday 26th April

I woke up this morning to the phone ringing. I was still lying in a fog of sleep and so let it go to answer-phone. They didn't leave a message, so I checked the number afterwards and it was Red. He hates answer-phones. I wonder what he was going to say? He's my boyfriend. Boyfriend. Girlfriend. I'm happy. *Schastlivyj.* I can't do the Cyrillic alphabet yet; I want to learn Russian.

But also — there's something else. Something inside me that's different from all of this sunshine. Sinister, building up. A bit like the way it feels before I cut myself — panicky, like I can't get comfortable in my own skin. Bugger it — it'll go away. Just ignore it. Concentrate on the happiness, Ruth, for goodness sakes. Concentrate on the sunshine.

Photography again today, and not much to report — it was a bit dull actually. That girl Sara, who wanted to have coffee with me last week, wasn't there. I never realised that doing all these new exciting things might be boring every so often. We took photos of our own bodies without our heads. I couldn't find anything interesting about mine. If only I had hands like Charlotte Marie Bradley Miller.

I know what I can't get out of my head. It's being dead. It feels ridiculous to be thinking about it now at the beginning of something so exciting with Red — if I've ever had a good reason not to die, I've got it now. But along with all that good stuff comes inevitable risk. What ifs. After Red's aborted call this morning, after the first flush of remembering had worn off, I spend half hour thinking about all the things that might go wrong. Most of them were silly — what if I'm not Russian enough for him, or what if his parents don't like me. But some of them were pretty plausible really — how will he like being with a scientist, or what if he's a bit screwed up and gets attracted to people he can't really have, one after the other, and when things get a little deeper, I'll run away and he'll look around for someone else? I feel bad writing these things down, as if I've been given a beautiful toy for Christmas, and now I'm just banging it on the banisters, neglecting it, suspicious of what I have to do to pay someone back for it.

I just realised that it's been a whole month since Dad was in the crash. It feels like even longer since the hole opened up between us. Since I opened up a hole between us. I'm still waiting for Julie to call. What would happen if she never did? What would I do? I've run out of sensible things to say in my journal today — the first time it's happened for a while. That probably means the things I do have to say aren't things I want to hear. My brain has hidden them away from me and pretended that there's just a blank. I think I'm getting to know myself a bit better; at least I recognise that about myself.

What's on the other side of the blankness? If I keep travelling through the whiteness of this paper where will I end up? I feel like Gretel Ehrlich being pulled by dogsled through the white wilderness in Illulissat. Over rock, ice and snow, as the metal edges of the runners spit out sparks into the darkness. I wish I could learn to feel her joy in being lost. I wish I could appreciate the beauty of this place without the gut-wrenching worry of whether I'll get there safely or whether I'm even going in the right direction. I wish I had some stars to guide me home. Maybe I'm not looking hard enough at the sky. Maybe going in the right direction isn't the point, anyway. I'm not making sense today.

I've been looking at a book of aerial photos recently, all taken from different heights. I'm not too sure about them; they all seem too far away. Some of them scare me with their scale. There's one of a flock of flamingos — over on the right hand side of the photo, you can see them as individual birds surrounded by borders of black water, their pink necks separate and sticking straight up. But as you go towards the left they thicken up, until all you can see is a wide strip of solid flamingo. It looks like the skin of some kind of huge pink creature, or a piece of knitting. There's another photo of gannets on Eldey Island in Iceland. The book says that this seventy-metre long piece of rock sticking up out of the sea holds forty thousand birds. Forty thousand! Each one is a white dot smaller than the eye of a needle. They are scattered about on the black water beyond the rock, and they cover the rock like lichen. They fly two hundred miles to get there. No, I read that wrong — two hundred miles a day. We are so small; there are so many of us.

Tuesday 27th April

Mary asked if she could have a chat with me today at work. She's been talking to me recently about how she feels about the situation at home — every week she trusts me with another tiny nugget of information. I hope I've been keeping them safe for her. Last night her mum's boyfriend had touched her again, when her mum was in the room next door. He put his hand right up her skirt and tried to kiss her. He was forceful. Again she managed to struggle away, but in her room later, she decided she had to leave home. She still doesn't want to ruin her mum's life, wants her to make her own decision about him. She's been saving her money and can afford a room in a shared house — she's going to put a notice up on the hospital notice board. I was impressed with her strength. I forget how old she is, think of her as fourteen rather than nearly twenty. Later on, we laughed about what it would be like to live with any of our colleagues. People always seem to be stronger than I think they are.

The darkness and doubt from yesterday feels further away. I think Red pushed it back — we had our sitting this afternoon. When he opened the door to me, he tweaked my nose and kissed me. He didn't get much painting done today. He started fooling around straight away, pretending he couldn't find a colour for my hair. I felt shy for some reason, kept blushing. The more I blushed, the more he teased me, mixing more and more red into my skin colour, coming and holding it next to my cheeks, going back to mix in more red. In the end I went over and took a bit of blue paint on a fingertip and smeared it on his nose. I called him 'blue-nose' in a scornful voice, and for some reason we both found that hilarious; I think you had to be there. He started tickling me, and it was like being tickled by a bear. I collapsed into him, a heap of giggles, and made him knock over a chair. We lay in a tangled mess on the floor for a few minutes, as helpless as babies, the tears streaming down my face.

After we'd calmed down, he got up and lifted me clear off the floor and carried me through to a window-seat in his kitchen. It was piled up high with papers and bills and goodness-knows-what. He gathered the piles up in his arms and put them on the floor, where they tipped and skittered out over the lino. And we just sat there and kissed for ages. I'm getting used to the soft feel of his hair under my fingertips, his stubble against my cheeks, the taste of him. I found myself tracing the line of his scar from the corner of his right eye to where it disappears behind his hairline.

After a while, he told me how he got it. He was sixteen and his friends at school were 'bad people'; they liked to throw their weight around and were making quite a lot of money by taking a small 'protection fee' every week from other boys. They used to go out every weekend and 'drink until they vomited'. One night they got into a fight with a gang of older boys. Red picked out a harmless looking tall gangly boy and tried to punch him, but the boy got out a penknife and held it against his neck. He said he'd never known such pure terror. He said it in Russian too, *strah.* Instead of freezing he started to struggle and pushed the boys hand away from his neck — he felt a cold sensation up near his eye, and his hand came away red. He can still see the look of horror on the other boy's face. He had thirteen stitches and became a kind of hero in his gang until he started getting into art and found different friends a couple of years later. I didn't like the story, didn't like to think of Red fighting, even if he had only been sixteen.

Before I left I wanted to tell him something about me from when I was little. He doesn't know much, not really. So I told him about when I was at school — the first class — and needed the toilet. You were meant to join the queue to see the teacher and ask if you could go. So I did, knowing as I queued that I was pretty desperate. A classmate noticed from my body language that it was an emergency and he urged me to go to the front of the queue, to just push in. What kind of little girl stays in line because it's polite, it's what she's been told to do, and then lets out a stream of urine right there and then in the middle of the room, staining her clothes and the carpet? As I told Red I was laughing, but afterwards I felt so sad inside I thought I might split.

Later at home I picked up the phone and it was Dad. He sounded gruff, but he made an effort to ask me how I was. We didn't say anything about what had happened. He asked if I could come over tomorrow to have dinner; he knew it was short notice. I accepted gratefully. I don't know what it'll be like.

Wednesday 28th April

I remember when I was about nine, Mother had an interview for a promotion at work or something and she wanted to spend a day getting ready. She was a microbiologist too; I don't know if I've told you that. She worked for a big drug company, probably made much more money than I do. She'd asked Dad to take me out for the day — it must have been the school holidays. I overheard them talking in the kitchen about it — Dad was saying, 'What should I do with her all day? You're better at these things,' and Mother was amused, telling him I was his daughter, that I didn't come with instructions. I heard the panic in his voice. And I remember thinking that I needed to make it easy for him. If he thought I was difficult to be with, then I could change. I think we went to the zoo in the end, but I can't remember the animals. What I can remember is telling him all about a project I was doing at school in minute detail in the car on the way there, filling in every awkward silence. As I was telling him, I had the terrible feeling that this wasn't what he wanted either, not really. I wish he'd told me what to do instead.

I've just got back from seeing him. It was difficult — I don't think we're going to mend our relationship overnight. I'm still not sure if it's mend-able; it was never that impressive in the first place. I don't really want to write about it, but feel like I should. Maybe you're not that bothered anyway. I'm glad Julie was there — she kept pretty quiet, but there's something solid about her; she kept things grounded, somehow. It would have been easier if she'd just wittered on, like she usually does, but it was more truthful this way — awkward, but real. I tried to put on my best good daughter act, asking him how he was, keeping the conversation going. I didn't tell him about Red, not yet. I mentioned Abbie and also Zoë — he asks after Zoë now; I think he's still pleased that I have a friend. He also asked me if I'd bring my photos over so he could see them; he seemed genuinely interested in them. That was nice. He was also a bit cold still, as if he were bruised and had to ease himself along. I suppose he is bruised.

You'd like me to tell you that we fell into each other's arms and sobbed, wouldn't you? That we forgave each other everything and vowed that we'd never be apart again? I'm not sure that kind of thing happens in real life. Instead we congratulated Julia on the shepherd's pie and wondered whether it was feeling colder than usual for April. The closest we got to any kind of reconciliation happened just before I left. We were by the door (which had new glass in it) and I went to kiss Dad on the cheek. He grabbed me instead and pulled me into his shoulder, a half-hug. Fierce. He wouldn't look me in the eyes afterwards. Not really your big reunion is it? But enough for me. Enough.

I called Red when I got back, told him how it went. He was pleased. Writing about it all has made me emotional. That seems to be happening a lot these days. Yesterday at work, someone was describing a book they'd read about a boy who'd been adopted by his crazy therapist. I got a lump in my throat for the boy; I had to stop listening. There's something going on in me, a kind of blossoming. When I least expect it I get a huge surge of feeling — anger, joy, loneliness... at least I'm feeling something. That's got to be progress.

I found a photo today that made me feel claustrophobic. It's of two faces in close-up with their eyes shut. They look like fourteen-year-old boys, although they could just as easily be girls. They both have the same colouring — the photo is black and white, but the dappling on their skin and their pale eyebrows give them away as redheads. One lies on his back with his face on the left of the photo, facing the top right corner — you can see a soft nipple, his breastbone. And the other — his brother? — is somehow coming in from the top left, his face parallel with his brother's chest, his mouth tantalisingly close to the other boy's mouth, both of them shut, but gently shut, relaxed. They both look peaceful, but not asleep — they are too perfect. Their faces are so unruffled; there isn't an area of tension anywhere on their skin. Is it about sex? Or brotherhood? Or just being in a relationship with someone? Do we need to get that close to each other, so that our noses are breathing in the same air, fighting for it? So we can hear the rumbles and the creaks and the sighs that each other's bodies are making? Something about that scares me to death. And it also makes me want to look at it more. Makes me want to try it.

Thursday 29th April

Red was busy today, he cancelled our sitting. He was short with me on the phone. He said he had a painting to finish for a commission and was behind after spending Sunday with me. I apologised, but he told me not to. He's probably getting tired of me now he's getting to know me. Every second I'm with him feels like it might be my last — I imagine him pulling away from a kiss and saying, 'OK, enough now, thank you and goodbye.' Whenever the phone rings, I just know it's him, calling to tell me it's over and then hanging up, leaving me holding the dead phone against my head like a gun.

I haven't said anything about my doubts to Zoë or Abbie, because deep down I know they're thinking the same thing. I don't want to put them in an awkward position where they have to lie to reassure me. I can imagine Abbie with her careful tact — 'Yes Ruth, I can see why you're worried...' I've not even let him have sex with me yet. I know he wants it — the way he moves — it's coiled up inside him. There's a bit of me that wants him too, but I'm also terrified of the hugeness of him — the hardness — how is he going to fit in me? I imagine him forcing himself inside me and a tear starting on each side of me that just grows and grows until I split in two and lie there flapping on the bed like two fish, no blood, no noise. There isn't enough space inside me. So it's only a matter of time. I'm sick of this feeling in my stomach; it keeps making me think of Mother. What kind of a future is that, when all of my relationships remind me of death? That's not fair on Red. Enough of that.

He did say he wants me to go out with him tomorrow, to an opening at a gallery. He said it was a kind of party. The last proper party I went to (if you don't count embarrassing work Christmas dos or 'Boxing Day drinks' at Dad's) was years ago. A girl at work invited me, and in a fit of madness I said yes. I spent all Saturday deciding on what to wear — the danger of living alone: small events take on a disproportionate significance. Her small, terraced house was teeming with people — they were standing on the stairs and sat cross-legged on the carpet between the sofas. My bottle of wine and after-dinner mints were sadly out of place. Just like me.

I recognised a man from work and spent most of the night cornering him, wondering how long I needed to stay without seeming rude. I ended up in the kitchen, washing up wine glasses; it was such a relief having something to do. So I thought I'd call Zoë for some advice, being a little out of practise with parties. She said she'd help me with some shopping. I haven't spent so much in years. Zoë seems to be getting on OK — she says she gets lonely in her flat sometimes but being able to do 'whatever the fuck she wants' is keeping her going. She's been going out with a friend from work, clubbing, doing the stuff she was never allowed to do before. It's good to be able to call her when I want to, to know that she'll be happy to hear from me.

I called Abbie today as well. She's still seeing her new man, Bill — it sounded like it's going OK again. She wants me to meet him this weekend. It almost sounded like she wanted my approval. She's been a bit weird with me since that night when I got really drunk. Maybe she thinks I'm a closet alcoholic or something. She keeps saying, "You know you can tell me anything, Ruth, whenever you need to, even if it's in the middle of the night..." What is there to tell? "Hi, Abbie, thought I'd wake you up to tell you that I've never been cut out (ha ha, cut) for this living business and that even with a new boyfriend and proper friends, it's touch and go.... I'm going to think about it for another month, and then I'll probably kill myself; pills will probably be easiest. So how are you?"

It's none of her business, what I do with myself, none of anyone's business. They'd all just interfere. I can imagine how Dad would react. No, actually I can't imagine it — I think he'd just freak out and not get in touch again. Actually, he'd probably get me committed. Then I'd be someone else's responsibility. I don't want to give him the pleasure of final proof that I'm faulty. I heard a couple of women talking about their friend's son once — they were saying, 'He wasn't right — he was never right.' I thought, 'That's me.' I wasn't meant to be here; it's just too hard. I'll fail you. I'll fail you too in the end, you out there. Whoever you are. I know you want a happy ending. It's in our natures — however much we dislike them, we always want the underdog to come out on top. We want the losing team to pull something out of the bag. Just be prepared to be disappointed. That's all I'm going to say.

Friday 30th April

The party was a disaster. I'm a disaster.

The first awful thing was what I wore. I asked Red if it would be posh, and he said I should wear something 'normal'. So I dressed down, wore my new trainers, a denim skirt; I felt OK — quite funky even. But when we got there, the other girls were in short, strappy dresses. On our way in, a few of the girls looked me up and down and then looked away without smiling. I was angry at Red, and whispered that I looked a fool, but he couldn't see what I was worried about. He said I looked delicious and not to be silly, pinching my cheek and winking.

I felt patronised and even angrier. Red saw someone he knew — a skinny blonde girl with amazing blue eyes. She flirted with him shamelessly, hardly acknowledged me. I felt like his country cousin. So I accepted glasses of champagne from the big silver platters floating around with waiters attached and said no to the tiny morsels of fancy food. At least if I were sipping champagne, my mouth couldn't open and tell that girl Suzie to shut the fuck up and fuck off. I just smiled sweetly, drained the glasses. Smile, sip. Hahahaha. You're so funny Suzie, how wonderful you are, isn't this a great party?

It got worse. I think Red had been drinking at home before he came out — he just went on and on about his paintings to anyone who would listen. He didn't pay me any attention at all. When yet another skinny, sparkly girl came over, she dragged him away to look at something and he let her — leaving me standing there like a sore thumb in a room full of slender little fingers. I didn't know what to do — did I smile like an idiot and wait for him to come back? Approach one of the tight little cliques of people standing around, knee deep in their intelligent, arty conversations? The rules are that you're allowed to join these circles if you stand there and wait for a gap and then say something witty, but what would I say? So I just stood in the middle of the room for a while, alone, feeling my whole body tensing up.

I started feeling dizzy. Everyone in the room went fuzzy round the edges. I suddenly needed to get out of there, pushed past people and ran. The next thing I knew, I was outside in the street in the cold drizzle, being buffeted by giggling packs of girls tottering on heels. When I looked down, I was still holding my glass of champagne. I stomped home and slammed the door behind me like a child. The phone rang after twenty minutes, and an hour after that there was a knocking on my door which changed to banging and then shouting. It was angry shouting. I hugged my knees and held my ears and squeezed my eyes shut for ages, and when I opened them again, the banging had stopped.

So I'm here at home in the half-dark, lying on my side and writing slowly, not forming the letters properly. I can't be bothered. It's the end of April. I'm two-thirds of the way through. And here's the truth. The more I enjoy my life, the more people I have around me, the more reason I have to finish it myself before *they leave me*, which is inevitable. Even if Red and I had three children and a dog and a house in the country, I know that he'd go and ruin it all by dying on me and leaving me all alone again. I couldn't bear that. And now it's time to tell you about the second thing that happened. After Mother couldn't get out of the bath. The second of the three things.

It was months later, maybe even a year — the whole thing happened so slowly. I wanted it to speed up sometimes, for the cancer to put her out of her misery, release all of us from our misery. I'd got up in the middle of the night to go to the toilet. I was good at being quiet, knew exactly where every creak in the floorboards was. Mother and Dad had left their door pushed to, and I could hear them talking quietly, a murmur. I paused outside their door and waited to see if they'd heard me or not, holding my breath. Dad sounded like he'd been crying, his voice was thick, guttural. He was saying, 'I can't, I just can't — what will the point be? What will the point be?' He was pleading with her, desperate.

Her voice was reassuring, calm. Why did she always have to be the calm one? Why couldn't the bastard have looked after her, for a change — just once? She was saying, 'Ruthie — you have to do it for Ruthie. If you do anything for me, just do this. Come on, she needs you, she'll need you.' He wouldn't stop — his whining voice, on and on — 'No, no — don't make me. I want to come with you. *I want to come with you.*' I stood there digging my fingernails into the palms of my hands. The terrible knowledge seeping in through my skin like icy water.

Saturday 1st May

I've been ignoring Red's calls all day. He's rung seventeen times. He hasn't left any messages — he hates answer-phones. I think I already told you that. He'll be getting angrier and angrier. I've been flopping around the flat all day like a goldfish out of its bowl. I managed to stare at the floor for eighteen minutes earlier — I timed myself. The less I do, the more I can let everything settle down out of sight in my brain, like those plastic snowstorms filled with white flakes and water. I'm not stupid; I'm sure Red will forgive me for walking out. But sooner or later he'll realise I'm hollow in the middle, like a chocolate Easter bunny. It'll start when he gets annoyed by the sound of my laugh, the way I leave my hair in the bath plug-hole. Then he'll meet a stunning new artist with bright blue hair and vulnerable eyes. She'll make clever comments about his work; she'll understand it in a way I never will. He'll talk to her about his problems with me. One day he'll start crying into his vodka and she'll comfort him and he'll cling on to her and they'll end up at her arty flat, fucking on her tie-die duvet. He'll finally make his choice several months later, and when he comes to move his things out, she'll help him with his boxes, smiling at me with genuine pity.

And Abbie. Abbie will be overwhelmed with love for her new boyfriend Bill. He'll ask her to move to Canada with him, and she'll jump at the chance; all that snow and beauty would suit her perfectly. She'll call me once a year on my birthday but won't think of me very often, being so far away. Me and Zoë will drift apart so slowly that I won't even realise until I look back and can pinpoint moments when I thought about her but didn't pick up the phone, the times she asked me out and I said no, because of Red... We'll start to feel awkward, avoid each other, carry on sending Christmas cards to keep up the pretence. And Dad will die. I know that much. He's nearly died already. It's only a question of when.

Today I started my research on how to do it. The method. I went onto the internet and typed in phrases like 'suicide methods' and 'aspirin overdose'. The first thing I found was a table of the 'LD-50s' of various drugs, which is how much of each drug they had to give to mice or rats for 50% of them to die. You'd have to take one thousand six hundred Valium tablets to be sure of not waking up. Then I found a message board where suicidal people discussed the practical side of doing themselves in. The site was 'pro-choice' and encouraged the sharing of information that would help people die more easily. I spent hours reading what people had written. One asked, 'Has anyone here tried hanging themselves? What does it feel like?' Many wrote to ask about lethal doses of various drugs — others replied with, 'Don't know anything about this drug, but good luck.' One discussion was about the potential of a single stab wound to the heart — some people wondered if the pain would stop you from following through, but another had a story of a man who'd done it, was found in a field with the knife sticking out of his chest.

I couldn't find an easy way anywhere. There was so much to read. I found a long document called the 'Methods File'. If you wanted you could poison yourself with nicotine, water, a huge list of prescribed drugs, iron, various types of mushrooms. You could jump off buildings, slit your wrists (apparently not usually very effective), shoot a bullet into yourself, pump air into your veins, jump in front of a train, drown, electrocute yourself or starve yourself (which can take up to forty days). There was also a table of 'hanging heights' so you could work out how far you needed to drop depending on how heavy you are for your neck to break. And it gave information about what these methods felt like. Dangling on the end of a rope for ten minutes (the most common successful cause of suicide) was 'very painful depending on the rope'. Paracetemol overdoses become fatal after ten to twelve hours, but you live for a couple of weeks after this point of no return, suffering 'horrible side effects' including intra-abdominal bleeding and acute toxic hepatitis. It told you how to take your poison to increase the likelihood of it working — wash it down with vodka, tie a plastic bag over your head. The document was full of 'variable's, 'unreliable's and 'don't know's.

Society would rather not think about those of us who want to die. It would rather not listen, rather not help us out. I want someone to tell me how I should do it. I don't want it to hurt. I don't want to be saved.

Sunday 2nd May

Another bad day. You probably don't want to read about another bad day, do you? I certainly don't want to write about it. Or maybe I should be writing it all down in minute detail, to prove just how horrible it was to be me. That sounds so pathetic, so self-pitying. It's not like I've been particularly unlucky — parents die all the time, don't they? Worse things happen… Why has this obliterated me, why has it been so hard for me to survive it? How do people survive worse?

When I was at University I went through a 'do-good' phase and volunteered to help out in a local school. I don't know why I'm writing about this. It was some kind of reading scheme, where you went in before the school day started to spend extra time reading with a child who was struggling. I always wondered why the children had to do this extra reading in school — wasn't there a parent or a grandparent who could sit down with them after their dinner? I was nervous to start with, had never done anything like it before.

After a training morning I was introduced to my 'reader', and my heart sank — his nervous eyes were hidden by thick smeary glasses, and his trousers were frayed at the bottoms. He was called Wayne — of all the names you could give a child like that. When I said, 'Hi,' he pretended not to notice me — I didn't know what to do with him. The teacher was hanging around watching me; I suppose she was offering support, but I felt like I was being judged. How could I get this ugly child to talk to me? But then he suddenly got up without looking at me and went straight to the bookshelf and pulled out a book about a doll. I remember thinking it was a girly choice. He put it down in front of us and then looked up at me, half breathing through his mouth, as his nose was a bit snotty. He looked right at me — Wayne, with his alcoholic father and his slightly retarded mother and his pregnant, thirteen-year-old sister — I learnt all of this later from my friend who lived in his street. He looked right at me, and I suddenly knew that I was one of the only good things in his life. A naïve, shy seventeen year old who would listen to him read for half an hour every Tuesday morning — that was as good as it got for Wayne.

I grew fond of Wayne, despite all my expectations. When he found a new word, he'd pronounce it extra clearly, then look up at me for the nod I gave him when he got things right. He never really smiled, but he was always sat waiting for me expectantly, and he always asked to read one more page when I said that our time was up. I knew he felt good after our reading sessions. I went there for a whole year, and he definitely got better at reading; I hope partly because of me. It wasn't a miracle, but it was enough that we both noticed it. It was important to both of us. And then the scheme ended, and on our last morning the teacher told me that he was ill, wouldn't be coming in. We never got to say goodbye. I suppose nobody thought a goodbye would be important, only a seventeen year old and a snotty little kid whose life was already written for him. I wonder where he is now. Hopefully not in prison or hospital. I haven't thought about him for years.

My eczema is really flaring up. It's on my legs, and around my elbows. Ugly. I lie in bed at night and all I can think about is the itch. Sometimes I give in to it and scratch for whole minutes, scraping the scaly skin off and getting down to hot, pink, weeping under-skin. It feels wonderful to scratch, even though I know I'm damaging myself. And I suppose I might as well tell you — it doesn't really make any difference, but it's still hard to say. I'm still cutting myself. But it's different this time, more often. It started the night that Red asked me out. I was so happy and scared that I needed to let some of it out before it forced me to explode or implode or something. I knew as soon as he asked me that it would happen later.

I'll tell you the rest another day. I'm tired now. I'm afraid that you've stopped reading already, that you've skipped the last couple of days. That you're looking ahead for some good news. Maybe you've already read the last page, deciding you'd only carry on reading if it were worth investing in me, if there was something to be saved at the end. What would be the point in caring about someone who wasn't going to be around? I hope that you're still listening to me. That's all.

Monday 3rd May

Red came round again tonight and banged on my door. He stayed for three- quarters of an hour. I huddled on the sofa again with my arms round my knees and my head down and just waited. Now I've been such an idiot, I can't see him again — it'd be too embarrassing. He calls every morning too, lets the phone ring until the answer-phone kicks in and then hangs up. I can imagine him holding the phone to his ear, tutting and rolling his eyes when I don't answer. I am stupid. I miss him. I miss his big hands and the kiss in his voice when he whispers 'Ruthie'. I miss being his.

I was glad of work today. It took my mind off the mess I'm making of my life. I could put my head down and do my strip tests for MRSA, examine my agar plates for rogue cultures, laugh with Jane about Mrs Thomas having a good night after Jane found sperm in her urine specimen. It's easier to leave it all at home and live like that. But it's not really living though, is it? Just forgetting... Unless that's what other people do too? I feel as if I should know more about how other people live their lives.

My photography class helped too. We were asked to do a street scene — to just go outside the college and see what we could find. I paired up with Sara, who was back this week. I tried to catch her eye and hang back from the others when people were pairing up, and she did the same. We had half an hour to go off and take some photos, and it was fun. Sara was quite brave about asking people to pose for us, so we got quite a few portraits — a businessman in a suit posing proudly like a four year-old for his mother, a Japanese couple and their huge camera who were surprised and pleased to be asked and grinned like Cheshire cats, a hippy mother with her little boy, tousled and cute as a kitten.

I'm feeling more and more at ease with my camera. I'm starting to see a shot without having to put it up to my face — I can look around as if I *am* the camera, including this but not that, using this filter... For the last few minutes we sat outside Covent Garden tube station and watched the street performers. There were five of them — four silver and one gold - balancing on posts or standing on boxes, most of them with a whistle inside their mouths, between their teeth, so they could make strange whooping and wheeling noises. After a while one stopped to smoke a cigarette and came over to strike up a conversation with Sara. He sounded Eastern European, and he had a dancer's body. He quite obviously fancied her but couldn't help looking ridiculous in his silver paint and suit, trying to be all macho. She teased him gently.

On the way back to the class, we talked about ourselves and I found out a bit more about Sara. She lives with her divorced mother in a big house in Kew — Sara said they didn't interfere with each others lives but ate dinner together a few times a week and caught up — an arrangement that suited them both. She'd split from her long-term boyfriend a few months ago, hence the classes — part of the 'new her'. She'd ended the relationship and was full of praise for him, so I wasn't really sure why they'd split up. She loves old black and white films and couldn't believe that I hadn't seen the ones she mentioned — a Welsh one, something about coronets... They had got her interested in photography, and when she's got more experience of taking photos she wants to try film. I told her about my photography books, and she said she'd love to see them. So I asked her round to tea after photography next week. She said yes. What am I doing? I shouldn't be making new starts with people; it isn't fair.

I spoke to Dad today. I thought I ought to call him to keep things moving after seeing him last week. It was a difficult conversation. At least before, I was able to talk to him about surface things and he'd let me… Now he keeps asking me silly questions like, 'How do you really feel about Julie?' or, 'Tell me the truth about what it's like to work at the hospital.' I kept taking the conversation back to where it should have been. Then out of the blue, he said that I should look after my own money if I want to. I said, 'No, I want you to,' and he said, 'Really? You're sure?' with a warm glow in his voice. I did want to look after it myself. But it was an important transaction between us, that he did it and that I was grateful. Like when a friend is known for making good soup, and everyone always says, 'Good old Pete and his amazing soup.' And the soup is good but not really amazing. But Pete likes to mention it himself every so often, and his friends really do care about him, soup or no soup, so the soup becomes the symbol. There's a place for that. We don't have to tell the truth all of the time.

Tuesday 4th May

Another shit day. I don't usually say shit. Shit shit shit. It's all shit. The only thing that's keeping me going is the cutting. How can that be, that the only thing I look forward to is hurting myself? It doesn't actually hurt much when I do it, only afterwards when it heals. It only hurts when it heals. I caught sight of myself the other day when I got out of the shower. I'm usually careful not to look, but a noise in the flat made me turn around, and my eyes swept over the mirror. What does it say about me that I'm not even comfortable holding eye contact with myself? I saw my legs — the red eczema, the black lines all over them.

OK. Here's my real reason for not being able to see Red again. How long before he wants to see my arms, my legs? How long before one of his hands slips in underneath my skirt, only to find me criss-crossed with scabs, dark against my pale skin, red around the edges? Would he still want me? Ugly. I know that's what he'd think, but I must admit to finding them quite beautiful in a way. They say something about me, they tell a story about how I manage to live. How different am I from people who pierce their belly-buttons — doesn't that hurt too? Or women who squeeze themselves into punishing high heels and then click about in them all day, dreaming of the moment they can sit down and kick them off? Or women who deny themselves food, cherishing the hunger pains that mean they're losing, losing. Why do we need to take up less space? Why are we so horrible to our bodies?

So yes — I'm cutting my legs now too. Arms and legs. And I've been looking at my stomach, thinking. It's so creamy and smooth; it feels naked now — it needs some decoration. There is something sacrosanct about it, and that makes me even more excited. I might start planning it. Putting the final moment off, just knowing that I can do it, whenever I want — having the equipment ready, the scalpels I got from an art shop, the gauze and the antiseptic from the chemist, all cleanly done, nothing unhygienic. Precise. Controlled.

What's it like to hear me talking like this? The strange thing is that I like to talk about it. It's like talking about an affair. It's *my* secret; it's something I do on my own, and I do it well. I feel alive when I do it. It keeps me alive. But I'm not so sure it does help, not really. Everything is still there underneath.

I had an argument with Maggie at work today, just to put the icing on the cake. She wanted me to speak to our manager about something for her, and I said I was tired of speaking for her like she was a child. It came out before I could stop it, my voice bitter, cruel. She was shocked, I'm usually a good girl; I keep all my bad thoughts inside. She stood there, searching my face. And then she left the room, didn't look back. I don't know what she was thinking. I don't feel that guilty about it. I should. Usually I would. Fuck it. I can't be bothered to write any more today. Red has stopped calling. Do I need to spell it out to you? Life is shit. I'm not cut out for it. Let me finish writing today. Red has stopped calling. Let me finish.

Wednesday 5th May

I had dinner with Abbie today — I was meant to be meeting Bill, but she made some excuse for him. She seemed nervous about something. I sat down at her kitchen table, we made small talk, she dished out dinner. And then she told me. She knew about my 'self-harming'. She had known ever since that night I got drunk and stayed over; she'd seen my arms when she put me to bed. She said she didn't want to interfere, but she'd been worried about me. She wanted to see if I'd seem better on my own now I had a boyfriend, now I was going to classes. But I seemed worse, quieter, more distant. She sighed, said she'd been kidding herself. She said she didn't want me to drift too far away from the world, and her voice strangled for a second.

She'd made proper moussaka, cooked from scratch, and a mound of steaming, fresh green beans. I'd been looking forward to it, but when I put a forkful in my mouth the aubergines seemed slimy, the beans tasteless. I chewed mechanically as she carried on speaking. She asked me about Red, whether I was still seeing him, whether he knew. I started saying, 'Yes, it's fine, he knows,' but I interrupted myself and said, 'No, Abbie, we've not spoken for ages. He doesn't know.' I didn't have the energy to lie to her. She was studying me the whole time, looking into my face as if there might be an answer there. And then she softened her voice and asked the worst question. 'Are you OK, Ruth?'

A fountain of sadness rose inside me under pressure, and a drop of it escaped and rolled down my cheek. I gripped my knife and fork hard, staring at my dinner. Staring straight at it, trying not to move a single muscle, because if I did, I wouldn't be able to stop crying, and I didn't want to dissolve even further; she already knew too much. 'I'm not hungry,' I squeaked, putting the cutlery on the plate and pushing it away from me. And as the sadness started to subside, I sighed a huge sigh — it was half-sadness, but also half-relief, at least now she knows, someone knows.

Abbie took my plate back into the kitchen and put cling-film over the plate. It comforted me that she would do such an ordinary thing in the middle of this. She asked me if I wanted a cup of ginger and lemon tea, said she could put a spoonful of honey in it. I smiled and nodded, tears streaming now; she was so kind, and I was aching — it was half pain and half love. I wanted her to know it all, and when we went into the other room with the tea, I said, 'Look, it's here too now,' and pulled up my skirt. She touched the skin right next to the scabs and stroked it gently. This made me hurt again inside, a wrenching feeling, like a part of me was trying to escape my body, pull itself away from my flesh, separate itself.

We talked about it for a little while. I told her what it was like to do it, and she listened to me calmly — she wasn't disgusted, she wasn't angry. She seemed sad, winced when I said about using the scalpels. And at the end, when there was nothing left to say, we just sat there next to each other in the silence. I got up and put some music on, and when I went back to the sofa, Abbie lifted an arm up and I crawled under it and leaned back onto her, all soft and smelling of lemons, and felt like I could stay there forever. She said, 'You know I love you, don't you Ruth?' and I just nodded, because my throat had seized up again, and if I tried to make a noise it would only get stuck. Later she said I should go and see a doctor, and I agreed — she said she'd come with me. She wanted me to tell my Dad too, but I said I'd think about it. And we talked about what I'd do about Red. 'You just need to let him in,' she said, 'and then see what happens.'

So when I got back tonight, at one in the morning, just before I started writing this, I called him. It was as soon as I got in the door, otherwise I would never have dared. It rang and rang, and I started feeling dizzy. It went into answer-phone, and it was so good to hear his voice. I didn't know what to say, and for a few seconds I just listened to the silence after the beep. And then I said, 'It's me, I'm just phoning to — I'm sorry. I've been so stupid. Sorry.' I said the last sorry quickly before I hung up on myself, so I wouldn't say anything else embarrassing. So now I'm on his phone, and it's up to him. Then I wrapped up the scalpels to make them safe and threw them all away. I'm going to sleep well tonight. Soon there will be people asking questions and prodding me, and it'll be harder to cut if I need to. That fills me with a fluttering panic. But in between the panic I feel tired, like after a long day walking. My body can rest now. I can rest.

Thursday 6th May

This morning there was a little knock on my door half an hour before my alarm was due to go off. I was still half asleep and opened the door without thinking. And there he was. I got ready to say something, but he just put a finger over my lips. He moved past me into the flat, took the door handle from me to shut the door, and lifted the duvet for me to get back under. And he got in next to me, fully clothed; he didn't even take off his shoes. I moved towards him, and one of his arms was up on the pillow for me to lie on. He touched my hair with his other hand as I burrowed my face into his jumper. The smell of him, oh, the beautiful smell of him. I kept my face buried, and he fiddled with bits of my hair. The fibres of his jumper tickled me, I wondered if he was leaving an impression on me, a knitted pattern of small dents on my cheek. And then, after a long time, I pulled my face up and snuck a look up at him — he was smiling, amused.

I pulled up the sleeves of my pyjama top and showed him. He'd find out soon enough; I needed to know if it would scare him off. At first he didn't understand. 'Ruth, how did this happen? Did you fall?' As he spoke, there was a growing awareness that he wasn't asking the right questions, that he was missing the point somehow. He squinted to see in the dark so I put on the bedside lamp. I showed him my legs too; they were uglier, the cuts more recent. They showed up more against the smooth white of my thighs. The skin puckered up around the wounds. And then I reached into the bin and pulled out a scalpel and gave it to him. I felt in a dream as I did it, like jumping off a high diving board and not thinking of the falling, only the jumping. He knew then, and he held the scalpel as if it were an earwig, disgusted. As his eyes moved from the scalpel to the marks on my body, his face melted somehow from disgust into grief — he wasn't angry, he wasn't angry. He put the scalpel down and gripped me by the arms, he hurt me, and I winced, and he winced too, as if he'd felt the pain as well. He loosened his grip and pulled me back in towards him, and it was a different silence then. It was a desolate silence.

With his arms around me so tightly, I couldn't help myself: I started crying, afraid I wouldn't be able to stop, but it was a sweet crying, the tears were sweet relief. After a few minutes, I heard a sniffing and looked up and saw that his cheeks were wet. And that made me laugh for some reason, through my tears, that he was crying because of me; it was ridiculous. And when I'd started I carried on, hiding my face from him again and shaking against him so he had to crane round to see if it was laughter or tears, and he was bemused, poor Red, and said, 'Crazy Ruth, my crazy Ruth.' I nodded through my laughter and carried on giggling, releasing the tension of him knowing, him knowing and not leaving me. I don't know why I ever thought he would. Maybe I was just as scared that he wouldn't leave me.

So then there was nothing left for us to do but lie there for a while as the emotion subsided. He kept hold of me. I listened to the ticking clock and his steady breathing. And eventually I said, 'I have to get up now,' and he nodded; we were smiling again, sheepish. There were things to be said, we both knew it, but there would be time for that later. He said he was worried about leaving me — he had someone coming to sit for him later, but he could cancel them if I wanted him to. I reassured him: I'd go to work and I'd be fine; I wouldn't do anything stupid. I was quite glad that I had another evening on my own to get used to being with him again before everything started happening. And I told him about Abbie knowing, that she'd told me I should see the doctor. He was glad and offered to come along, but I thanked him and said that Abbie was coming instead. Then he rubbed his forehead and said that on Saturday morning he would be back to take me away. He said it would be a surprise, to pack as if I were going to Russia. To remember a woolly hat and some long-johns.

After he'd gone, after I'd made him tea and got ready around him, after I chucked him out before I had to leave the house, I stood in the kitchen and absorbed what he'd left behind, more than just his smell, almost like bits of his soul had leaked out and been left behind in the air, his simplicity, his darkness, his solidity, his curiosity. I sniffed it all in and the molecules of it joined up with the blood in my lungs and moved all around my body, it made me stronger.

Friday 7th May

Abbie came with me to the doctor, straight after work. I felt the absence of Mother quite strongly and was surprised at it. It always surprises me. Even if she were alive, she probably wouldn't have been there with me. But I felt it, the mother-shaped hole where she should have been. Like I'd felt it when I got my A-level results. When Tom broke my heart at University. When I graduated. When I got my first job. I suppose her absence will accompany me to future events (if they happen) as well — births, weddings, significant birthdays, funerals. I nearly told Abbie, but I didn't want to hurt her feelings. It was good of her to come with me; I appreciated it.

I took Abbie into the consulting room with me. The doctor was a woman, and I was pleased about that. She asked me lots of questions, asked to see my arms and legs like I thought she would. She said a bit about Community Mental Health Teams which was a bit weird — 'mental health'. I don't see myself as mentally unhealthy. I'm just dealing with the reality of my life in a rational way. She also asked me if I'd ever thought about killing myself. That set off a strong urge to laugh, the giggles bubbling up inside me, but I tried to stay calm and look serious, act like a grown-up, told her what she wanted to hear. 'Sometimes I feel really down, but I'd never be able to do that; it's just not something I'd ever do.' I caught Abbie's eye after saying that, and she looked surprised by the question, as if she hadn't considered it herself. I'm fooling them so easily. They've got nothing to worry about for another few weeks. Maybe I'll give them some kind of warning when I get nearer. I don't want Abbie to get too much of a shock. But there's no point in making a fuss now.

This doctor said that she always felt counselling was a good idea. I could have six sessions free with the NHS, and when Abbie said that didn't sound like very long, the doctor said if I paid for it privately I could go for as long as I wanted. Abbie and the doctor had a quick conversation about this — it sounded like Abbie might have had experience of counselling herself. It was basically decided that Abbie and I would talk about it, and that I should get in touch with the doctor again if anything changed. Although I was pretending to be an adult, inside I was a naughty child being taken to see the headmistress. A child who was getting away with it.

I wasn't too sure about counselling. They'd tried to get me to go after Mother died, and I'd been reluctant; what would a stranger know about how I was feeling? How could they possibly help, when all I wanted was to have Mother back? In the end I agreed to see 'Dr. Hubbard' to keep Dad happy. He sat behind his desk, looking pompous and asked me stupid questions — how was I feeling? Was I angry with Mother for dying? He answered everything I said with a bland 'hmmm' and then wrote something on a form. I think I was quite rude to him, and I didn't go back. I asked Abbie to let me think about it on my own for a week. She's always keen to let me take control of my own life, so I knew she'd say yes. I think she's still feeling guilty about having to confront me in the first place. Maybe she won't mind me saying no if I tell her I'll do some other things instead, read a self-help book or something.

When I got home, after I'd called Red and told him what happened, I sat on the sofa and found some rubbish to watch. It was reality TV — people I didn't know and didn't care about being put through hell so I could watch them implode like a car crash. It annoyed me after a while, so I turned it off and sat there in silence, looking at the blank, grey glass of the screen. After a few minutes I noticed myself reflected and was surprised by how sad I looked. And once I'd seen myself, the sadness just welled up again from the huge reservoir inside me, leaked out, filled my body. I was too sad to cry, too sad to move. It scared me. I just sat there, not knowing what to do, perfectly still, filled to the absolute brim with grief.

And then I made a decision, almost as if a part of me had broken off and was watching, giving advice. Just sit with it. So I just sat. I didn't try to get rid of it, shake it off, think about something else. I even went inside it, it felt like I was swimming in it; it was thick and grey, silvery. After a while it seemed to ease off a little, loosened somehow. I still didn't cry. I'm still sad now, a deep kind of sad, right down into the core of me. It hasn't gone away, and I know the reservoir is still full. But I wasn't washed away. I'm still here.

Saturday 8th May

Red turned up at eight. He said he wanted to check my packing and make sure it would be OK for Russia. He looked at the clothes I'd chosen and said I would be very cold, but that was OK, because we weren't going to Russia after all. He also asked where my camera was, and what kind of a photographer would I be if I kept leaving my camera behind? We were going on the train — he made me close my eyes when we passed through the stations, so I couldn't see the signs. When the ticket inspector approached, Red met him at the top of the carriage before he got to our seat, showing our tickets and explaining his surprise. I had no idea where we were going — two tube trips and then a train ride, which went on for ages through beautiful countryside. I quite liked it when Red held his hands over my eyes when we went through stations, not trusting me to keep them tightly shut, and I got to feel the heat from his hands on my face and breathe in his earthy smell.

When I opened my eyes the last time, I could see the sea! We were in Brighton. We went straight to the B&B Red had booked; he'd organised it all himself, said one of his friends lived near Brighton and had recommended it. Red asked me what I wanted to do first, and I felt like a child on holiday with school. That reckless feeling when you pile off the coach with your friends (or *friend* in my case) and are given half an hour to spend your money in the gift-shop or collect stones from the beach. I haven't really been away for years, not since that awful time in the Lake District. I wanted to go to the beach straight away and eat fish and chips for elevenses, so we did. We sat on the wall with our polystyrene containers and our wooden forks, and the food was delicious — hot crunchy batter, steaming, salty chips.

Afterwards we walked down onto the pebbles, and when I got nearer to the sea I felt the urge to run towards it in a kind of backwards panic. I took off my socks and shoes and tiptoed into the water, the cold making me squeal. I waded up to my ankles and then a wave caught me and got my skirt all wet, but it didn't matter; actually, I was pleased. Red stood on the pebbles, shaking his head and calling me crazy again, smiling. When my feet started to feel numb I came out, and Red laid down his coat for me to sit on a bit further up the beach, so I could wait for my toes to dry. And then we went back to get my camera and I took a whole reel of film. I made Red wait for me in a café, as I was embarrassed about him watching me. I found some great seaweed next to a piece of driftwood and took a few photos of the old pier too. I think the bit I enjoy most is sweeping the landscape with my eyes and zooming in on things I want to try and capture — there are so many possibilities. There's also a baseline anxiety about how good the photos will be, but when I spoke to Red about that, he said it was natural for an artist to always 'feel afraid'. He said that when we stop feeling afraid, we know we have nothing left to say. Later we saw a film and then we went out for a pizza — all ordinary things that lots of people do every day. Wonderful, ordinary things.

I'm writing this on the beach. How wonderful is that? Our guesthouse is only five minutes' walk away, and when I told Red I wanted to write, he suggested I come here. To 'have space'. I liked him for saying that. So I'm sat on a bench looking out towards — France? All that water. I'm stopping every sentence or two to look at where the sea meets the sky, to watch people walking past me. Interesting people, with piercings and bright hair. And I'm feeling good, mostly. I don't want to write about the not good today; it's been wonderful, and I don't want to spoil it. But I don't want you to think I'm all better now, that a trip to the seaside and a paddle in the sea could fix me, wash out all the sadness. I'm not saying I'm not grateful. But the more others give me, the more I owe them. Abbie deserves to see me get 'better', Red deserves a 'good girlfriend'. I just hope I can hold up my side of the bargain.

It's getting cold. The sea is starting to look sinister. I wonder if any of the creatures who live in the sea ever get cold? I'm going to stop writing now and go back to the B&B. It's hard to stay here and write when I know he's back there, lying on the bed and reading the novel I'm going to read when he's finished. And Gretel Ehrlich is waiting for me too, in Greenland, with her icebergs and her loneliness. Her fierce, stubborn love of the beauty of impermanence. She's braver than I could ever be.

Sunday 9th May

I want to write about last night.

When I got back from writing on the beach, Red was already in bed, listening to a radio station on TV. I got changed into my pyjamas in the bathroom and got in with him. The bed was smaller than my bed at home. Red still had his jeans and T-shirt on. I'm practising telling Red how I feel — he's so good at it, makes it seem simple, and it seems like a good thing for me to do. So I told him I felt nervous. He did a pantomime shocked face and then started tickling me on my stomach and then grabbed an ankle and stroked the soles of my feet until I could hardly bear it and was shrieking from being tickled. I was sure our landlady would bang on the door at any moment — 'What's going on in there?' It did help my nerves, and when he'd finished, I lay there exhausted and relaxed but also ready to clench my muscles if he started it again, a pleasurable anxiousness. Maybe he's used it on girls before.

We lay next to each other on our backs for a while, looking at the ceiling, and then I got brave and walked one of my hands like a spider slowly from the right side of the bed over his stomach and onto his left arm. I landed on the fabric of his T-shirt and then skimmed it down his upper arm onto skin and over his wrist and towards his hand, slowly, slowly. And then, all of a sudden, he grasped my hand tightly and used it to pull me round to face him on the bed, making me squeak. We ended up lying on our sides, face to face. He's gentle most of the time, but then he'll surprise me and do something in a violent burst. It scares me, and I like it. He winked then — his usual wink where only his eyelid moves, as if it's a secret from the rest of his face. And I just grinned back at him. I hadn't grinned that 'just-happy-to-be-near-you' grin since Tom (unless you count the way I grinned at Dan in my fantasies). I want to remember these bits, wrap them up in pretty paper and ribbons and save them somewhere safe. And then he snuggled in closer and kissed me on the forehead, the nose, the mouth. He kissed me gently, gently, his lips soft and careful.

We played with each other for ages, touching each other's faces, lacing our fingers together, moving our fingertips over the parts of our bodies we'd already touched, our chests, legs, arms. He rested one of his hands on my breast, with his fingertip and thumb gently holding my nipple as he kissed me. I was hyper-aware of the pressure, and the way he could squeeze me hard if he wanted to. And then he started moving into new territory. He moved to my bottom, grabbing handfuls. He took off his T-shirt — his nipples were pale pink, a beautiful rosy colour. And then he gestured for me to take off my top, holding out his hands to help me, and then my bra (he managed the bra-strap a bit quicker and more expertly than I would have liked). We hugged skin to skin for the first time, cool, delicious. His fingertips lingered for a second over the scabs on my arms and then moved on; he didn't say anything. I played with his red, ringletty chest-hair, uncoiling small twirls of it and letting it ping back into shape. And then he took one of my breasts into his mouth and sucked, not hard; god, I was so turned on, it almost hurt. The ache of it. I pressed myself up against his leg, arching, breathing short, quick breaths. He was breathing deeply, husky, low in his throat. And he put his hand between my legs, on the outside of my pyjama bottoms, and just held it there. I wanted to touch him. I wasn't sure what to do next. Felt a bit scared. So I pulled back and stopped for a second and told him.

He took a deep breath and gave my whole body a tight hug, and then moved away so we weren't touching, not anywhere. We talked for a while. And then we started again, and went as far as we'd gone before and a little bit further, and he slipped his hand inside my pyjamas, outside my knickers, and pressed a finger down the centre. I almost thought I might come. And I felt him through his jeans, one of my hands circled him. And then panic buzzed inside me again. I felt like a virgin. I kissed him and held him away from me at arms length. Red screwed up his face and starting a low humming that got louder and higher until he made a loud explosion noise and opened his eyes wide. We laughed; he was making it OK for me to say 'not yet'; I felt so lucky to be with him. It was late, and we were tired. And so we slept, the length of his body cupping mine.

In the morning I woke up on my back, and his arm was draped over my waist. I lifted it and put his hand on my cheek where it rested for a while until I couldn't wait any longer and got up to go the toilet. He was up just behind me, rattling the door, laughing at me for locking him out and not letting him in until I'd finished. And then it was time for breakfast, our stomachs pulling us downstairs. The woman at the B&B cooked us the most amazing breakfast. I love breakfast when you're away — the luxury of it all being laid out for you, little packets of jam, toast cut into triangles. We both had scrambled eggs, and they were the best I've ever had — I'm not exaggerating. Red asked the woman how she made them — he's brave about talking to strangers, braver than me. She said she used three eggs each and lots of cream and butter. Cream! Red said he'll cook them for me when we get home.

We didn't do anything after that; we just lay on our bed and read until it was time to be kicked out. We didn't want to go. And Red said to 'wait' and disappeared for five minutes, and then he came back and said we could have another hour. I would never have dreamt of asking. That extra hour was a gift. We lay back on the pile of pillows and carried on reading. I finished my book about Greenland. On the last page an old traditional hunter is speaking to Gretel about the dangers of new ice. It's so clear and smooth that it's sometimes difficult to tell it apart from naked water. Hunters often go under with their sleds and never come up. You have to pay extra attention, look more closely. He said, '...the ice comes to teach us how to see.'

Monday 10th May

I felt a bit nervous before my photography class today, as I'd rashly invited Sara to come round afterwards. I wasn't sure how I felt about her any more. But then we smiled at each other during the class, and I 'fell in like' with her again. The class was fun — we did a still life. There were lots of odd objects in a big box at the front of the room, and we were asked to choose some and put them together into a good composition. It felt like when you had to choose a card at school to help you to write a story. Sometimes it was the first few words of the story, 'When I got up this morning, I couldn't believe my eyes when…' or it was a little scenario — 'Mrs Waterman, the lady detective, has a cat called Marmalade. Tell the story of a murder through the cat's eyes.' There was such excitement in rifling through the cards. You could take your imagination to all these beginnings and let it leap off in whatever direction it wanted. For my still life I chose some dried flowers and a battered old hat. I liked the colours of them, all washed out.

It was odd walking home with Sara, being with her outside of the class, out of context. I talked about rubbish to fill up the silences, stuff on TV, work. I'm not sure if it was very interesting for her. She didn't say anything about my flat and plonked herself on my sofa as if she'd lived there for years. I didn't know what she liked to drink, so had bought Coke, lemonade, orange, apple and cranberry juice and mixed fruit squash for her just in case. She wanted juice, so I could offer her three types; we both drank sharp cranberry with clinking ice. She'd brought along an old 'femme fatale' video she wanted me to see, *Detour*, and we put it on straight away. It took the pressure off our conversation.

A few seconds after the film started, she asked me how my day at work had been, and we ended up talking through the whole thing. I told her about the weekend with Red — I felt good to tell someone about it, and she said she was jealous. I ended up telling her things that I haven't even told Abbie or Zoë, which made me feel a bit guilty, but it felt like she was really listening, and I don't know her very well yet, and it just felt easy to talk. We talked about my mother a bit, and I even told her about Dan and my seven-year 'thing'. I'm still not sure what to call it; the word crush doesn't do it justice. She told me things about herself as well, so it wasn't just me spilling my guts. She'd had a pretty tough life — she'd been ill when she was little, seriously ill, and had spent most of her school years in hospital. Then when she came home, her father had a breakdown and went into a different type of hospital. I admired her in a new way when I knew all that about her.

She said that she was happy now, and I believed her. She glowed in a contented way, as if nothing could ruffle her. Although when I said she seemed really happy, she laughed and said, 'You should see me when I'm not feeling so good.' She said that she'd been 'in therapy' for years and that her therapist had saved her life; it sounded a bit over-dramatic to me. I asked her lots of questions about it, what the therapist expected her to say when they first met, whether she had a couch, what she told her she should do... When she commented that I seemed very interested, I told her I was thinking of going. I even told her why I was going, in a roundabout way. She didn't seem very shocked, which was a relief, but I also felt bit disappointed, I don't know why. Eventually we talked ourselves out, and she asked me if I had anything sweet, so I made chocolate sauce to go on ice cream: golden syrup and cocoa like Mother used to do it; you just put it in a saucepan and bubble it up a bit. If you get it right, it changes into chocolate toffee. We laughed about silly things while I was cooking. And then when we'd eaten our ice cream, I walked her to the tube. When we said goodbye it felt awkward suddenly, like the end of a first date. I went to kiss her goodbye on the cheek, and she went to hug me instead, so we did a strange kiss/hug.

I called Red when I got home — he asked me to; I think he's still keeping an eye on me. We told each other about our days. And now I'm lying in bed thinking about my weekend in Brighton. If my fairy godmother meets me outside work one day, with fat rosy cheeks and a white puffball dress, and she says she can grant me a wish, I'd ask her to flick her silver wand and give me my weekend in Brighton all over again, exactly as it was. Maybe I'd have longer in bed with Red on Sunday morning. No — I wouldn't want to change anything. It couldn't get any better than that.

Tuesday 11th May

I woke up early today and decided to walk all the way to work. The sky seemed a little bluer than usual. If I believed in God, I'd say that he'd added a few extra drops of colour with a giant pipette. The air smelt cleaner, as if it were rich with tiny crystals of ice that melted into pure water inside me. I felt shiny, like polished metal. Cold. I walked fast, until I was out of breath. I smiled to myself every so often, when I thought about scrambled eggs or black and white films or syrup chocolate sauce. I felt full of life. I bumped into Mary in the corridor on the way to the lab. We talked as we walked, dodging the endless stream of hospital porters pushing bits of equipment or patients on trolleys from one end of the hospital to another. She was smiling — told me she'd found a place to live and had moved in at the weekend. She was sharing with a student doctor, a Christian — they had lots in common and were getting on really well. She seemed happy; I was glad.

This morning there was a postcard waiting for me on the mat. It featured four stunningly tacky photos of Brighton. I turned it over; it said, 'Here are some photos for you to learn from. Sorry you are not here… oh yes, you are. Love, Red'. There were twelve kisses underneath. He must have sent it on Saturday night when I was writing. I called him to say thank you. There always seems to be something to talk to him about these days. I keep thinking of things to tell him, I make a list in my head as things happen. I pay more attention.

Today we arranged for me to finish modelling for the second painting. We'll start again next week. I'm seeing him this Thursday for my birthday; we're going out for a meal I think — there's a place he wants to take me to. He got his new mobile last week and texts me quite a lot. Not normal texts like, 'Could you buy some milk,' or, 'Nice to see you yesterday.' They're like little pieces of poetry. Last week I had, 'The sun is sitting on my lap today,' and, 'You are not here, and I am not there, but we are together in my head.'

Abbie called tonight — she said she didn't want to push me, but she's found a counsellor I could get in touch with if that's what I decide to do. One of her friends had recommended her; she's called Rachel. So now I have her number. I wouldn't know what to say if I called her. I returned Zoë's calls too; I haven't talked to her for more than a week. I don't want her to feel left out of all this. Told her that I'd been feeling down, that I'd been having some problems and had seen a doctor about it. I didn't give her any details. She wanted to come round right away to talk to me about it properly, but I persuaded her not to, and she sounded a bit rejected. She didn't push me for any answers, just wanted me to reassure her that I'd be OK. I said I'd tell her about it when I saw her and that she shouldn't worry. She was pleased that me and Red had made up after the party, said, 'About time.' She seems to be getting on alright, and is still settling into her new life. She'd put another bookshelf together yesterday evening on her own and felt proud, even though she'd put the back bit on back to front. She said she'd missed me and her words were like sunlight.

Tonight I looked properly at one of my own photos for the first time. It was a print from the class, from when we went out onto the street. Sara was fooling about with that silver street performer, and I'd taken a couple of quick snaps, not really knowing what to expect. And one of them has come out just wonderfully. It's a close-up of both of their faces, and the look between them is just perfect. He'd been flirting with her outrageously, bravely trying to disregard the fact of his silverness, and she was keeping him back. But the photo has caught a moment when her face has just begun melting towards being amused, towards letting him in, sharing a joke with him. I looked at her face for ages; it was a wonderful thing to have captured, and it made me feel a bit emotional — I'm not sure why. I feel emotional all over the place these days; yesterday I cried at a baked bean advert because of the sweet, choral background music. A baked bean advert!

Sara was wearing such a private expression in my photo that I felt like a voyeur. It revealed things about her — that she wants to be loved like everyone else, that she's a bit scared to let people in. It was strange to look so closely at a scene I'd been present at, a scene I'd captured myself. I liked it. I had an extra layer of knowledge about what was going on. I felt a part of the photo — I felt a part of the world.

Wednesday 12th May

It's late and Zoë is here, in her usual place on the sofa. I can hear when she slides between being awake and being asleep — her breathing becomes slower and deeper. I like listening to it. Like the quiet distracted purring when good old Oscar used to sit on my lap. I like to be the one who's awake, the one who's watching out for danger. If anything happened, if there were a fire or if her mother suddenly got ill, I'd be able to wake her up gently, take her where she needed to go, be in charge. It feels good to have her here again, and it'll be lovely to not be alone tomorrow morning on my birthday. The first time for years. I'm going to be thirty-three. It feels like a good age, still young-ish. Not as old as Red — I call him 'old man' sometimes. Still some time to change the direction of my life. Still some time to become a new person. I'm not sure if I really think that's possible, if I really believe it could happen. But I don't want to get all philosophical today.

I wasn't sure how I was going to tell Zoë about the things that have been happening, but once I'd started it wasn't too bad. I sounded very casual to try to reduce the impact, but when I told her about the cutting, she looked away from me. She didn't ask to see my arms or legs. I ended up telling her pretty much everything — the way Abbie had found out that night, the time we watched that TV programme together and I was terrified she'd guess. I told her a white lie about having booked an appointment with a counsellor, as I wanted to reassure her. I've almost decided that I'll give it a go, anyway. She was quiet, didn't ask any questions. I don't know if she was able to take it in properly. I hope it's not too much of a burden for her to carry. I hope she'll still want to know me now.

Afterwards, later, she said some things that really surprised me. I've always thought of Zoë as pretty sorted — even when she broke up with Jules, it seemed as if she had a core of strength running through her. Even when she was shaky, I never thought for a second that she wouldn't get through it. I thought she must have had a pretty solid base behind her, a happy, normal childhood. But it turns out it wasn't that solid, after all. Nothing dramatic happened — there weren't any beatings, and she didn't get locked in any cupboards. But she told me she used to be fat, until she was thirteen; she said she'd show me some pictures when I went to hers next. We were eating while she was telling me this, macaroni cheese I'd made in the oven with masses of cheese and crunchy breadcrumbs on top and tomato and cucumber salad — it was delicious. She said she'd always had a thing with food. She didn't know where it had come from.

A long time ago she'd been so desperate to be thinner that she'd made herself sick a few times after binging, and she also went through phases of eating strange things or at strange times. Once at University she'd lived on noodles and tinned sweetcorn for six weeks. Six weeks! I have noticed her being a bit funny around food, saying she shouldn't be eating whatever it is we're eating or mentioning her weight a lot, but I didn't realise how serious it was for her. How serious it IS for her — she said she's much better these days, but sometimes she still has difficult weeks and can only face eating the same meal every night. Jules used to tease her about it, said it was because she only knew how to cook one meal. She'd never had a proper conversation with him about it, had never even tried to explain. It seems like the more I tell other people about the odd things I do or feel, the more they share their own dark secrets with me. Can everyone really be so screwed up? I suppose at least I'm not the only one. Is that a good thing or a bad thing? If they're all screwed up too, how do they manage to get up every morning and go to work? How do they bear it?

But I said I didn't want to get philosophical. And I don't — I do enough of that. I think enough about it. And it's my birthday tomorrow; I should be looking forward to it. My last birthday? I think that's why my thoughts keep getting drawn into the darkness. The dark wood of confusion and doubt and monsters and dead people and dead ends. My last birthday… it could be. Let me think some happy thoughts instead. Happy thoughts for my birthday. Fluffy baby rabbits hopping about in fields, friendly sheep jumping picket fences. Abbie's kitchen. My camera sitting up on its shelf. Red in his charcoal grey jumper, me snuggling in, his warm smell… sleepy now. Going to climb into my dreams…

Thursday 13th May

Happy birthday to me, happy birthday to me, happy birthday dear Ruth… Happy birthday to me! It's been a great day. I got lovely presents — a new handbag from Zoë, a cookbook from Abbie, book tokens from Maggie at work. A special breakfast of croissants and home-made blackcurrant jam from Abbie. She told me that blackcurrant was Mother's favourite jam. A bit of morning TV with Zoë, both of us still in our pyjamas, like the old days. A day off work, the morning shopping for clothes, lunch with Maggie. She got on well with Zoë. A quick visit to a gallery. The afternoon at a girly film, with popcorn.

And then Zoë went home and Red took me to a restaurant he'd chosen, Lebanese. The food was fantastic. He said he hadn't had time to get me my present; he didn't even apologise, and I was worried by that — what did it mean? That I wasn't important to him? But then he slipped into a bookshop on the way home. He made me wait in the bathroom in my flat while he wrapped up my present. It was a beautiful 'how-to' book about photography, a kind of encyclopaedia for photographers, and I said I forgave him, but only this once. The nagging, worried feeling left me, and I filed the incident away with the other 'possible causes for concern'; I could get them all out and look at them another time.

And then we kissed on the sofa for a while. We talked about stuff too, nice, dreamy, future stuff: where we'd like to live, how many children we'd have, what we'd call them.

After Red recited all of the Russian names he could think of, we decided on Gregory for the boy (he pronounced it gree-GOH-reey) and Darya for the girl. I practised my pronunciation so I could get it exactly right; Red said it would be very confusing for them if I said it wrong. All silly fantasy, but it was still fun to talk about. A lot of the things we want from life seem to be the same. It's late, and as a present to myself, I'm not going to write any more. If I did I might start thinking about the last birthday I had with Mother or something else that would totally ruin my mood. I can stop writing if I want to. It was a good day. That's enough!

Friday 14th May

After Red left this morning, I lay in his warm spot and drifted off again. I really didn't want to go to work. I felt 'full up' after yesterday. I'd bought a print in the morning when I was out with Zoë — I saw it as soon as we walked into the gallery and fell in love with it. It was quite expensive; I told Zoë I'll have to stop going out with her, as she makes money haemorrhage from me. I can see it from where I'm lying now. It's the first Ansel Adams print I've ever bought — everything else is in books, hidden away. It's called "Dunes, Hazy Sun, White Sands" and I love the title as much as the picture. I say it over and over in my head when I'm looking at it. It's a single plant growing out of the desert, with a hat of flowers or seeds and a few straggly grasses around it. I know it's growing up through sand because of the title, but it could just as easily be snow. I love that it's able to take in food from the desolate-looking ground — it's thriving. It makes me happy to look at it.

I called the counsellor today. Rachel. I think I'm doing it for Abbie, mainly; I know she's probably more worried about me than anyone. I feel a responsibility towards her, even though she's careful not to expect anything from me. Funny that. It feels good — like I've chosen to take her into consideration. I wasn't sure what I thought about the counsellor on the phone; she sounded quite brusque. It was all business-like — what times she worked, how much it costs. It's quite a lot of money, but I can afford it really; it just feels a bit weird to be spending all that money on myself and not getting anything in return. I've booked an appointment to see her; she said the first one is so we can decide whether or not we want to work together. That made me nervous — maybe I'll say something wrong, and she won't want to see me again.

I thought about not telling her about the cutting at all in the first session; counsellors can't enjoy seeing people like me, who have lots wrong with them; it must be a real pain. I might write down a list of some things I could say in the first session. Or maybe she'll ask me lots of questions. The session is fifty minutes — a weird length of time; I feel short changed by it — why not an hour? Anyway, I'm booked in to see her at one on Wednesday. I'm going to book at extra long lunch. I'll pretend I've got some other kind of regular appointment, or maybe I'll tell my line manager the truth — I'll decide on Monday. I'm not sure what it'll be like going back to work afterwards; maybe she'll make me cry. I'm a bit scared. But also sort of looking forward to it.

I talked to Abbie about Dad tonight, I popped round for coffee. I said I felt empty about it — a tinge of sadness, but mostly just nothing. She seemed to get a bit sad when I talked about it. When people care about you, you make them sad without even meaning to. Anyway, I'm not sure what to do about Dad, or even if there's anything I could do. Maybe it's just one of those things. Maybe I could meet up with Julie on her own; see what she thinks. At least I'd be trying something. We talked about my 'career' too; I've been thinking a bit about my future. I was telling her I'm not sure if I'm in the right place. There's nothing wrong with my job, but I'm just not sure it'll be enough forever. I hardly even dare write this down, but I wonder if there's anything I could do that would involve photography. It's silly to even think about it; there are probably thousands of people out there with better qualifications and experience. But I wonder if it might be possible in the long term — maybe as a part time job with something else. I'd be so scared of failing, it'd be easier not to try.

There are lots of things that it'd be easier not to try, I suppose. I didn't say anything about the photography to Abbie. She talked to me about how her work was going, too. She'd finished the story about Malcolm and his Bubbles, and her publisher was really happy with it. She'd been put forward for some more work for a couple of books by the same author; she was really pleased. I was pleased for her too. She said things were still going well with Bill, and that she'd still like me to meet him, said I should come round with Red. Said it wasn't fair of me to keep him all to myself. As we spoke, she dished out triangles of lemon tart with single cream on the side. She'd baked it herself and it was sharp and creamy and sweet. We had two slices each, with strong black coffee. I asked her for the recipe and she wrote it down for me on a scrap of paper, pleased to have been asked. I don't want to puncture this bubble of happiness I'm sitting in. I'm holding my breath.

Saturday 15th May

I called Julie quite early this morning, when I knew Dad would be out playing golf. He started playing as soon as he could after his accident, even though he could only do one slow hole before he got tired. I've always thought it an odd kind of sport, so solitary. Why would anyone choose to be on their own? She sounded surprised to hear from me and asked me if anything were wrong. Said that Dad wasn't there. I said I knew, that I wanted to talk to her, asked her if she was free to see me later. I said I wanted to get her opinion on how I could handle Dad. After she stopped being worried, she sounded pleased. She said she was just off to see her son (I haven't told you about her grown-up son — believe me, there's nothing much to tell) and that she'd be free after that. She even offered to see him another time if it were urgent. She likes to be needed. Maybe it's OK to feel good when someone needs you.

We went for coffee at Portobello Market. I got off the tube at Notting Hill and tried to pull some English words out of the cloud of sound coming from the throngs of tourists — lovey-dovey couples, older women in unflattering clothes, gaggles of teenagers. I couldn't hear a single person speaking my language and felt out of sync with everything. I knew a place that Maggie had taken me to once — you step off the busy street and suddenly you're in a womb — it's quieter, darker, you can sit on battered leather sofas and order good food. I met Julie outside, I hate walking into places on my own. She looked healthy, had put on weight. She told me later that they hadn't eaten vanilla ice-cream or apple pie since the accident, but that Dad was still making up for having to eat hospital food. It was good to see her; maybe I'm fonder of her than I realised.

We both ordered apple juice, and small-talked for a while before getting down to business. I said I didn't really know what I was expecting from seeing her. Then I told her how I was feeling about Dad. I told her how things didn't feel the same since I'd lost my temper at him. Said that I wasn't sure how to deal with the questions he asked me now, that I wanted to answer them truthfully but didn't think he'd be able to deal with the answers. That I feel angry and that he's let me down, but I don't really have any good reasons, or any recent reasons. I told her about the time he forgot to pick me up from Debbie's house, and she nodded sympathetically, even though it sounded stupid when I said it out loud. And I told her that I do worry about him, especially about his health.

She listened carefully; I was impressed — listening isn't usually her style. Then she told me how she saw the situation between us. That he just didn't know how to deal with emotion. That I reminded him of Mother (she called her 'his late wife'). That she knew that he loved me more than anything — she squeezed my hand as she said this, and tears came to my eyes. And that it was difficult to know what to suggest to make things any easier between us. That maybe I could start by saying some of what I said to her to him, maybe in a letter. She also shrugged and said maybe it would never get any easier, and I liked her for saying that, for being realistic.

By the time we'd finished, I think we knew each other a little better. We ordered risotto and talked about normal stuff again. I told her about my birthday; she told me how her Beanie site was going. When she said goodbye, she hugged me again, and I luxuriated in it for a few seconds; she was like a huge marshmallow. I'm glad I saw her. It's a step.

I saw Red in the evening, and we watched an arty film that Red had chosen. It was depressing. When he asked me afterwards, I pretended to like it at first, but I suddenly thought, 'What's the point in lying?' and told him the truth. I don't know why I'm not honest with people more often. It's so tiring to always do what I think other people want me to do, to make sure that my face exactly matches what I'm saying. To keep the frustration packed away. It made no difference to him anyway — if it were the other way round, I'd feel guilty about dragging him along, but Red doesn't do stupid stuff like that. He's sleeping next to me now; he starts to snore when he's on his back — he told me to push him over to his side or wake him up, but I don't like to disturb him. We almost went all the way tonight (it feels funny to be writing with him so close, he might wake up and see) — if I didn't have my period, maybe we would have. I had to tell him, was embarrassed. He didn't seem to be. I wonder if he ever is? Things are going well with him, but there are still things he doesn't know about me. Things you don't know.

Sunday 16th May

Red was in a bad mood this morning; it must have been something I did, but I'm not sure what. He said it wasn't, said he was just tired. I asked him what he wanted on TV, and he snapped at me that I should choose for myself 'once in a year'. He said, 'Who are you?' and I wasn't sure what he meant. I went quiet, and usually he hugs me then, says it's OK. Today he didn't — he just carried on buttering his toast in the kitchen and then came in and ate it, taking great crunching mouthfuls. He was cold, quiet. I wasn't sure how to handle it and thought it best to keep quiet as well. So we read the papers in total silence with the TV on the first channel I put it on. I actually wanted to watch a programme about bees, but I didn't want to change it again, in case it might annoy him even more. And I didn't want to ask him if he minded, in case that was annoying too. He kissed me on the forehead when he left, squeezed my arm, smiled a sad kind of smile. I don't know what he meant by that smile.

It feels hard to write today. It's easy when I've got something to report on, something to describe to you. Today there's just blank white space. Where are you, next thing to write about? Where are you in the mist?

A hat. A red woollen hat, one with a bobble on top, the bobbles you used to make at school by winding wool round and round two cardboard donut shapes until the magic moment when you tied it, cut around the edges and fluffed it all up. Like magic. It's an old hat, a favourite hat. It's mine. I can see it lying on the grass, the grass frosty as if it's been dipped in icing sugar. We're at the park near my old house in Maida Vale, and if I look round I can see Mother sitting a little way away on a bench, reading a magazine like always. If I look down at myself, I'm wearing my red coat and my sheepskin gloves. I loved those gloves; they were so thick and soft. I loved knowing they came from a real animal — I never understood at the time that they were made of skin as well as fur. I used to dream about a whole outfit made of it, all furry inside, so I could be sealed up into it like a spacesuit.

I'm with a little boy. I can't remember his name now, but I remember he had pale blond hair, almost white, and small eyes. We used to play together. He's a bit bigger than me; I must be about five. His mother doesn't seem to be there — maybe he came with us; I think he lived on our street. I don't like him — there's something odd about him, sinister. I couldn't explain it. I don't like playing with him and would rather be with Mother. He's asking me to do something I don't want to do — something naughty… I can't quite make out the words, but I can feel in my stomach that I shouldn't do it, and that he might make me.

I look round at Mother; she's still reading. It's odd — she's there, but I know that I'm all alone. I know with a cold certainty that she wouldn't help me, that she's concentrating on what she's reading. There's no space for me in her head. I'm alone with this strange, naughty boy who's bigger than me, who wants me to do things that I shouldn't.

I don't like it, this memory. Why not? I think it's because Mother doesn't come out looking like a super-mum. I don't have many memories where she isn't perfect, where I don't see her as perfect. I feel guilty — I shouldn't be thinking bad things about her. Now that she's dead? No — it's not that — I'm confused about this. I think there was something about her that made it hard to criticise her, that put her beyond reproach. If she wanted to read her magazine, then she should be allowed to, and if I had interrupted her and she had brushed me off like a fly, then it was because she worked so hard at her job and because she deserved some time of her own. There were always such good excuses for her to not do the things she didn't want to. She was always right. We always owed her something.

I wonder what it was like for Dad? To live with a perfect wife. To be the one who's still alive at the end of it. Mother's been pretty absent from these pages so far. It's like she's lost, stuck in the middle of the myth of her life. I can't find the real her, the real woman. I think I felt let down by her when I was little, when I wanted her to look after me and she wasn't there. Even when she was there, she wasn't. Does that make sense? I think I've blocked that out, and maybe other things too. All that's left of her in my mind is larger than life, loving, glamorous, colourful. Who was she really?

Monday 17th May

I met Zoë for lunch today, and it was a bit like the old days. We went to the restaurant where that first tear escaped and rolled down her cheek; it seems like so long ago now. She's like a different version of Zoë now. Version 2.0. The 'fake-strong' front that always had me pretty fooled has started wearing through in places, and you can see some of her raw pink bits inside.

She was talking today about how pathetic she is about being on her own in the dark. The first thing she bought after she moved in was a night-light you plug into the wall, the ones that throw out a continuous soft glow into the blackness. She says she often wakes up in the middle of the night and lies there listening for strange noises, frozen, and turns her head slowly round towards the night-light, as if any sudden movement would scare a monster out from under her bed. She was laughing as she told me this; we laughed together. Why not have a night-light? It's a simple solution — maybe we should stop feeling so ashamed of our little quirks; maybe we should just do what we need to do to make things easier.

I told her about Red being in a bad mood yesterday. She said maybe I shouldn't worry so much, that worrying too much might make it worse. Maybe she's right, but if I stopped worrying, then who would be on the look-out for cracks in the relationship? Someone has to keep an eye on these things.

Sara came home for tea again after our photography class. I told her I was seeing the counsellor on Wednesday. We didn't talk about anything deep today; I don't know why. It was still nice to have her round. We talked about photography a bit, and I showed her some of my books. She doesn't seem to be into it the same way I am, seemed to get bored of certain photos I showed her quite quickly and flicked the pages onto something else. It didn't feel like she was looking at them properly, and I almost said she should slow down but thought she might think I was rude. There are lots of things I want to say that still end up getting pushed to the back of my throat. I'm not sure I used to be so aware of wanting to say them. Is that progress? Or will it make my life harder?

Writing about my day today feels like a waste of precious time. Here I am with a couple of weeks to go. Nobody knows anything about my deadline at the end of the month. It's coming too fast; I need more time. I haven't started thinking seriously about what I'm doing. I should be. Maybe the decision will be easy when it comes down to it — maybe I'll just know. What do you think? What do you think of me? There's a part of me that wants to avoid making the decision. Just give myself another three months to decide, or put it off indefinitely. But that doesn't seem like any way to live. If it's always a serious option, then what motivation will I have to get better at this thing called living? It'd be like going out with someone and deciding to just 'see where it goes' even after you've been together for twenty-nine years. Making it easy to leave if things got difficult.

That's no basis to form a relationship on. Is it? I need to make a decision. I'm feeling more and more confused. I've been looking back at what I wrote at the beginning; it feels like years ago. I keep reading the bit where I said that this journal would be undeniable proof of how terrible my life is and how I tried everything I could before I decided. I haven't been concentrating. I worry that people will read this and think 'she has a new boyfriend, she's made up with her aunt…' and find ten new reasons for me not to give up on it all. In a way I don't recognise myself from what I read. There are terrible things about being me that I don't seem to have captured at all. Because I haven't had the energy, because they're difficult to say. As if they sit so deep inside me, if I wanted to say them, I'd have to plunge my hands in up to my elbows to pull them out. And these things are all entwined with other things that pull and rip, that hurt, that bleed. I've failed to say those things.

It also worries me that I've written down private things about Red, about my family. I'm not sure I want anyone to read that. Who am I doing this for, anyway? It's stupid, this whole project. Stupid. Never mind what other people would think, I thought that at least it would give me some solid evidence, some reasons one way or the other. Some clues. I feel even more confused than I was at the beginning. How will I ever be able to make the right decision? Is there such a thing as a 'right' decision? What should I do if there isn't? What will I do?

Tuesday 18th May

I went to sit for Red today. He seemed OK after being grumpy on Sunday — maybe a bit quieter than usual. I wasn't sure if I should ask him about it or not, but I decided not to. It was odd to be back in that chair; I hadn't been in his studio for weeks. I realised that we didn't spend any time there at all as a couple (as a couple!); he always came to mine. I asked him why, and he said he didn't know, that it was better for him to come into my world, easier. I didn't like his answer. He was happy for me to move over and make room for him on my sofa and in my bed, but he didn't want me in the way in his house, his life. I went quiet after he said it, but he didn't seem to notice, maybe because he was concentrating on his painting. Or maybe he did notice and didn't want to talk about it. It felt different between us. I looked over at him standing there, and I didn't know who he was any more.

As I travelled home after work, the knowledge of what I was going to do was there for a while before I recognised it for what it was. Does that make sense? Like when you find yourself in a room in your house, and you know you're there for a reason, but you can't remember what it was. Or you look down and see a teaspoon in your hand and can't remember picking it up. Before I knew what I was doing, I was looking under the bed for the scalpel I hadn't thrown away with the others. I'd tucked it into a sheaf of papers just in case I needed it for something arty (OK — I'm not fooling myself either). I felt suddenly Zen-like, sitting naked on the bed, on a dark red towel, just in case, and it made me realise how tight and panicky I've felt inside for a while. As I pierced my skin, the pressure eased and fizzed out into the air like steam, filling the room. Drifted away. Like a huge sigh. There was sadness in it; I got a little teary. Usually I don't feel guilty or bad until the day afterwards. When the rush of feelings have faded away, and I look at what I've done in the cold light of day. But this time I tasted regret as soon as I saw blood.

I feel good now. Clear-headed. I'm drinking a cup of peppermint tea as I write, and every sip is cleansing me inside, wiping out the last remnants of the pressure, the stuff that builds up. I'm not sure what it's made of, the panicky pressure. It's not the same as the oily sadness, but maybe it's related. I don't seem to be aware of it building up until it's too late. I don't know how to stop it from getting inside me. And I don't know of any other ways to let it out. Maybe this is what people smoke for, or get drunk. It'd be OK for me to do that — society says it is. Not OK to do drugs. Not OK to hurt other people. OK to do some stupid, dangerous sport. OK to be horrible to myself inside my head. Not OK to hurt myself physically.

Stupid, stupid rules. I suppose it makes people feel better. "I might get drunk every so often, but I would never cut myself — that's for wierdos." I just felt a tiny lick of panic inside me as I remembered I'm meant to be talking to that counsellor tomorrow. I don't want to go. She might make me stop. I don't want to stop. I'm not doing myself any lasting damage, am I? I'll just have to be more careful about hiding it, that's all. If I have any chance at all of surviving past the end of this month, I have to keep it; it's my only way of coping. It's all I have. Nothing else is certain. No-one else is certain.

It's only appropriate that I should look at this photo today. It's of a Hutu man, a close-up profile. He's turned to the right and looking forward and slightly down. His curled hand is resting on his neck, as if he's protecting himself. His mouth is open wide — he might be saying 'ah', he might be in pain. And there are four slashes on his face. They are healed, but they still look raw. They're deep. One of them has stopped his shorn hair from growing back; the next one slashes straight across the top of his ear (what happened to the sliver of ear, did it fall onto the ground? Did someone pick it up?). The next cuts across his cheekbone, and the last joins the line of his jaw to the corner of his mouth. There are smaller scars above and below each line where he was stitched, where somebody stitched his skin together again to keep his face in one piece. His eye — I look at his eye again, and it is wide, there is too much white above his pupil. It is as if his whole face is straining to contain the horror, the horror that another person, a human being, one of his own people who suspected him of being an informant, cut his face into these pieces. I want to touch him gently on the cheek, soothe him, sing him to sleep. Sing quietly, gently, sing him gently to sleep.

Wednesday 19th May

My first appointment with the counsellor was at lunchtime today. This morning at work, as I collected my Petri dishes and peered down my microscope, the weight of anxiety bore down on me, crushed me. What would I say? What would she ask me? What would she think of me? What if she couldn't help me? And suddenly — snap — I knew I had no other option. I wasn't going. I wanted to let her know, but I thought she might answer the phone if I called. I couldn't face speaking to her. I feel like the worst kind of person. I just didn't go. Told my line manager my lunchtime 'classes' had been postponed to next week. Worked through my lunch. I didn't go.

Abbie called this evening to ask me how it went. Red didn't call; he'd probably forgotten. More important things on his mind. I lied to her, said it was fine, fine. She didn't press me; I don't know if she knew I was lying or not. She told me how things were going for her — things with Bill are still good. She sounded girly, giggly. Very unlike her. She enjoyed telling me about him. I feel like even more of a bitch, knowing that I'm lying to her. I'm letting her down, letting the counsellor down. That's what happens when you care about me — I kick you in the teeth. I'm warning you. Don't feel sorry for me; I'll snarl at you, bite you on the hand.

Dad called too. Yesterday, I would have been pleased. I thought that things might have been better between us after I saw Julie; I'm not sure why. That she might have been able to speak to him, to make him listen. He was his usual self and talked about nothing — it reminded me of how he was before the accident. He'd called me because he'd had some information about one of my investments and wanted to warn me. I wanted to say to him that I couldn't give a shit about the financial health of Hoggett and Sons or whoever the fuck they were. What difference would a couple of hundred pounds more or less make to anything? I was polite, put on my happy-Ruth voice as I pinched into the skin on my wrist with my nails; he didn't notice. I wanted to say 'Dad! I'm unhappy!' I wanted to put the phone down on him. I wanted to smash the phone against the wall. I'm scaring myself a little. What am I capable of?

I thought about Dan all evening. For a few weeks after he left work, people would still mention his name — they'd talk about a project he'd started off, or someone would impersonate him and say, 'Need nicotine now!' when they went to have a cigarette. He doesn't get mentioned so often any more. Even my brain is mentioning him less. I used to think of him constantly and everything reminded me of him. I'd look at daffodils in the park in springtime and think, 'I'll buy him a bunch of daffodils on the way home, and he can put it them in my blue vase.' I'd read a story in the paper and imagine telling him about it over morning coffee.

You might think I'm really crazy if I tell you this. He had his own side of the bed. The left side. I was (am) aware of lying towards the right during the night in preparation for when he gets home late and slides in beside me. I was (am) always aware of the absence of him when I slept, a cold expanse of bed-sheet that was going to be warmed by his tired body at any moment. Sometimes in the night I'd reach out a hand to see if he were home yet. Don't worry, I didn't do anything really crazy, I didn't set a place for him at the table or have conversations with him out loud. But he was there with me all the time. I don't want to give him up, I don't know what it would mean if I did. Without the chance of it becoming real, however small a chance that was, what point is there any more? Have I wasted my life for seven years? For longer?

Does it really matter if anyone reads this or not? What am I trying to prove? That I've fought bravely, like when they say someone has fought a brave fight against cancer? What's so wrong with giving in gracefully? Welcoming death with open arms? She got cancer and received it gratefully. She died as soon as she could. Why the fuck not? What's to be gained by living in that much pain for as long as you can? Is it that you'd be letting the rest of the human race down by abandoning them? Why shouldn't you if you want to? What is it that keeps me here?

I have death in me like an embryo. It keeps growing. I can't ignore it kicking. But we all have death inside us. It's growing in all of us, right now, getting bigger and bigger and sucking away more of our life until we give birth to it, our own dead bodies, a huge, horrible, bloody mess. Fuck it. Fuck it all.

Thursday 20th May

I saw Red. I tried to put on a front, but he saw through it. He was painting me, he had to look carefully. I wonder if he would have noticed if he weren't painting. He stopped and looked sad. He put his brush down. Came over. Touched me on the cheek. Looked into me. I felt like I was going to throw up — got up, ran to the door. I left my jacket behind. Travelled home on automatic. Called Maggie, told her to tell work I'd been taken ill. I am ill. You don't know how ill.

I can hardly write tonight. Short sentences feel easier. It's such an effort, moving the pen against the paper. It rubs, it pains me. A tense, uncomfortable feeling. I get it in my hands sometimes when I'm typing, need to shake them, release them. I can't get enough breath inside me, keep finding myself sucking it in, slow sigh after slow sigh. Like Mother near the end. I want to curl up so tight that I disappear into myself. This isn't nice to read, is it? Reminding you of anyone? How honest are you with yourself? You think you have a nice life? Comfortable, suburban… nice husband, nice wife, nice children, comfortable job… it doesn't mean shit. None of it. How happy are you? Really? That dead bit inside, you manage to forget it for most of the time, don't you? It's real. It's real and it's going to eat you. Can't write any more. Can't. Write. Any. More.

Friday 21st May

I woke up early and left a message on my supervisor's answer-phone before she got in so I didn't have to speak to her. All day I've been thinking again about how I'm going to do it. I've been doing some more research. This time I typed in 'kill myself'. I got some lyrics by a band I've never heard of, "Ken's Last Ever Radio Extravaganza: I'm Going To Kill Myself ..." Then a chat room where an eleven year old had posted that they wanted to kill themselves, and a reply — 'You'll eventually understand but right now you wont because your too young to realize the repricusion of suicide.. just know that when the times right you'll do it... if thats whut u really need to do..'. What kind of a thing is that to say to an eleven year old? How can an eleven year old want to die?

And then I read further back, and the original post by the eleven year old was a joke, a sick joke, but people have replied sincerely — 'Please don't do it, life will get better, go to your doctor.' Kind people. This makes me feel — I don't know how it makes me feel.

Next I typed in suicide. And the first site that comes up on the list is 'Suicide, read this first.' So I do, like a good girl. The person who wrote the site said that it would only take me five minutes to read, and that they don't want to talk me out of my pain. It told me that you want to kill yourself when the pain that you're feeling outstrips the resources you have available to cope with it. That made sense. It told me that I should wait a bit, even if it's just twenty-four hours.

That bit didn't help — I've been waiting for so long already. It told me that I'm looking for relief and that relief is a feeling and I wouldn't feel it if I were dead. I don't know— I still think absence of pain is better than pain.

And then the last thing it told me to do was to call someone. To call someone right away. As I read this I let out a low groan, like I was something wild. I got off the chair and sat on the floor, curled myself up like a foetus, and made a small hurting noise over and over, rocking. I don't know how long I was there. The feeling slowly subsided, there were longer gaps between the noises, they were quieter, softer. I sat there and my eyes glazed, and I didn't really feel anything any more. I could see my mobile from where I was sitting. So I pulled it over and dialled Red's number. When he answered, it sounded like he was in a pub; there was a general hubbub around him. I couldn't say anything for a couple of seconds, and he said, 'Hello?' and paused, and then a louder, 'Hello?' I thought, 'It's now or never, Ruth — *speak*.' And said, 'It's me,' and my voice was all choked up; I had to clear my throat to carry on. But he didn't need to hear anything else. He said, 'You are at home?' and I said, 'Yes,' and he said, 'I will be there. Wait.'

So I waited. Mostly on the floor, but then my embarrassment overtook my misery and I felt silly sitting there, melodramatic. I cleaned myself up in the bathroom, trying not to look at my red eyes, puffy cheeks. When he got here he hugged me, and the crying came again. I didn't know what I should tell him when the crying finished and he wanted to hear some words. I wanted him there, but I didn't want the burden of him caring. When he eventually said, 'Something has happened?' I just shook my head, said, 'It's nothing, it's… I don't really understand. I can't talk about it yet.'

He nodded, let go of me and walked away over to the window. He stood with his back to me. I thought he was angry. But when I went over to him, his face was a stone and there were tears on his cheeks. I was exhausted. I wanted to get under the duvet with my clothes on and watch TV, something funny, something I didn't have to think about. I said I was sorry. For a second I wanted to tell him the truth, but I'd let him see too much of the truth already; it had hurt him — that's what happens when you tell the truth. Instead I told him I would be OK, told him I was just being silly, told him not to worry. He shook his head slightly, still not looking at me. He said, 'I am here again. Again! You are not here. I can't help you. I am tired of it.' I stood on my tiptoes and kissed his tears away, one, two, three. Tasted the salt on the tip of my tongue. He took my face in his hands and pulled it back to where he could look at me, then kissed me on the forehead and sighed a big sigh. I took his hand and led him to the bed, brought us both some juice. Held one of his hands in both of mine, tight. We were quiet. We watched TV together and eventually his breathing slowed and he fell asleep. And now I'm writing this. I'm not sure what I've done now, what this means.

Saturday 22nd May

I did it. We've done it.

I woke up late this morning, when I heard Red moving around in the bathroom. I still had all my clothes on, and my face felt tight, as if it had shrunken in the night, my bones straining to be out. I could hear the high-pitched hollow back-and-forth of a toothbrush and went in to stand next to him and do the same. We looked at each other as if we'd had an argument. And when he'd gargled and spat, he said, 'I take you back to bed now'. He picked me up and folded me in two, so my bottom hung down between his two arms, and carried me through and dumped me onto the bed. He made a gesture with his hand out flat, his palm pushing towards me, his face stern. Stay there.

He put a CD on, one that I've played for him before, a band called Insides. The music is sparse and electronic, short bursts of notes repeat like birdsong. The drums pull my heartbeat towards them. The singer's voice is rich, breathy. I closed my eyes to wait for the first few words she sings. "Thanks for waiting. I'll start now." I know the insides of these songs — I have heard them over and over, paying attention to the different layers, different melodies, different beats. The way I know photographs. And I felt Red's lips on the tip of my nose, then moving across my cheek in a string of tiny kisses, and down to my earlobe, which he took gently in his mouth and sucked. I suddenly wanted him inside me. I kept my eyes shut. And all of a sudden we were pushing against each other hard, the whole lengths of us; there was an urgency, a violence. Red stopped, and when I opened my eyes, he'd pushed his arms out straight and was looking at me. He said, 'It is OK today? You are ready?' and I nodded, grabbing him by his T-shirt and pulling him back towards me.

It hurt. It's been a long time since anyone has been that far inside me. It got easier towards the end, but I was glad it was quick. I liked afterwards best, when he caught his breath and I watched his face above me, his eyes still screwed shut. And then he opened his eyes and looked straight into me and cocked his head onto one side. He smiled at me with his eyes, kissed me on the lips, gently, and lay down on top of me. I loved the weight of him, crushing the breath out of me, squashing me. I wanted to keep him there forever, joined to me, quiet, spent.

We ate toast in bed, from plates balanced on the duvet. He was still naked and I'd put a T-shirt on, shy. The things we needed to say were still hanging above us, like a balloon full of water, but that was OK. And when we'd eaten, I reached out for him again, ran my fingers up his thighs, nuzzled my head into his neck, feeling the heat of him against me, spreading inside me, melting me. And we made love again (made love… had sex… fucked… nothing sounds right) and this time was better; he was slower, paid more attention to me — I got what I needed. Something shifted inside me, low creaking shudders, deep ice on a lake. He said to me afterwards that now it had happened, I was more beautiful than I had been before, and that he wanted to paint me right away. He joked about me getting my clothes on and hurrying to his studio. He said my face had 'become new'.

He had to go to a sitting but he was worried about me again and said he wouldn't leave me until I called Zoë or

Abbie and asked someone round to keep me company. He said he'd be back later to stay the night. I called Zoë, and he took the phone from me when I was speaking to her and said to her that I was feeling down and that she had to look after me. He waited until she got here and spoke to her out in the corridor. I was in the bath and could hear their low murmuring. I was reluctant to wash so much of Red away. I felt a little better afterwards. Like the end of the flu when you get out of bed and eat something, feeling shaky, thinking about going out into the world again. I wondered if Zoë would guess what had happened with Red. They always make a joke of it on TV — people always get caught out by their colleagues the morning after. But she didn't notice, so I had to tell her — we giggled about it all afternoon, talking about sex, sometimes embarrassing ourselves at the intimate things we were telling each other. Then Red came back and Zoë left, and we still didn't talk about what had happened. We stayed up late and watched an old film. One part of me enjoyed watching the film with Red. Another part of me watched this part and knew it wasn't the whole story. Waited. Bided its time.

Sunday 23rd May

When I woke up this morning, I looked over at Red sleeping and I knew what I had to do. His face was squashed by the pillow on one side, and his mouth was open. His freckled feet stuck out the bottom of my duvet, hanging over the end of the bed. He looked too big for my bed, for my flat. I wasn't sure I had the strength to tell him. We stayed in bed most of the morning, watching TV, and I got ready to say it a few times, but the words kept sticking in my throat. I decided to leave it for another day — no point in saying it just yet. Red didn't seem to know how to treat me after Friday. He alternated between being normal and joking around, and treating me as if I were ill, offering to fetch me drinks and cardigans, glancing over at me when I went quiet.

He touched me a lot more than usual — stroking my hair, lacing his fingers into mine, putting an arm around my shoulders. As if he were trying to make up for the drought of conversation. I let him do what he wanted, putting on my best 'normal Ruth' act, making occasional comments about my week ahead, arranging my face into the right shapes — contentment, relief, gratitude. Sanity. He was all around me like an octopus, and I felt hot, claustrophobic. I wanted to be on my own, with no-one except myself to worry about.

By Mid-afternoon we both felt hungry, and went to a small Italian restaurant near my flat. We ate the same meal. Mozzarella, avocado and tomato salad to start with, the flakes of salt making little explosions of flavour. Homemade pasta for our main course, with aubergines and mushrooms and soft yellow peppers. And tiramisu — sweet, boozy, dreamy. I told Red I needed an espresso before I could possibly move and we lingered over it, taking tiny sips until the coffee was stone cold and tasted earthy. The whole meal was pregnant with unsaid words. I felt like I'd given Red enough of a chance to see I was 'OK', but I didn't know if he'd be happy to leave me on my own. So I lied and said I'd arranged to see Abbie that afternoon. After the meal we both walked to the tube station and parted awkwardly. I pretended to get on a train and instead went straight back home.

When I got home I started to make preparations. It suddenly seemed simple — I had to get away from all these people to make a proper decision. I couldn't decide where to go and got down a couple of my books for inspiration. I came across a photo of a beach and remembered Mother telling me a story about her favourite place when she was a child — a small place by the sea called... something beginning with an A... I couldn't remember. She had just turned thirteen the first time they went, and she was allowed to walk down the beach on her own for a while, much to Abbie's annoyance. It was one of her first tastes of true freedom. One day she sat near a fisherman who was making repairs to his boat on the beach. His teenage son had come along to help — he was sun-bleached, wiry and gorgeous. She sat quietly behind them and watched this boy for nearly an hour, revelling in the luxury of being alone without her parents watching her. I remembered Dad rolling his eyes and saying, 'Not this story again!' when she told it, jealous of an oblivious fifteen-year-old boy twenty years ago.

I nearly called Abbie to ask her what beach it was before realising what a bad idea that would have been. I wouldn't have made a very good murderer — calling up a friend to ask them to recommend a hotel in Morocco before fleeing the country. So I got out a map and looked at the whole coast of England. I thought I could rule out tiny places like Atwick and Allonby. That left Avonmouth, Aldeburgh, Ashington… none of them rang any bells. Maybe it didn't start with an 'A'. I remembered her saying it was a couple of hours drive from London. And also that she sat on pebbles, because when she went back to where they were staying she'd found red dents on her bottom where she'd sat still for too long, lost in admiration. I looked on the internet and decided on Aldeburgh — it had pebbles, and was about the right distance away from London. It was on the Suffolk coast. I found a photograph of it I liked called 'A Winter Walk'. The whole photo was grainy, misty, in deep cornflower blues. The beach stretched out ahead of you, with the sea on the left and big craggy buildings on the right. Two figures were walking near the sea, not touching. That was the place. Aldeburgh.

It's the 23rd of May. I have eight days left. I need to clear my mind now, get some perspective on all of this. I need to get away.

Monday 24th May

Tonight was our last photography class. Milly had asked us to bring in our favourite photos from the course so we could spend the lesson discussing what we'd learnt. We spread them on our tables and spent time with each person as they talked through their experience of the course. I brought the one of Susan from the first week, the one of Sara and the silver man, and the still life with flowers and a hat. It was good to see them there together in a group, I was proud of them. It was amazing how different the groups of photos were, even though the subjects were the same — you could see embryonic styles developing. We'd got to know each other a bit better over the course, but it was still nerve-racking to talk in front of them all. When it was Susan's turn, I could see her hands shaking. I wasn't sure what I was going to say, and found myself talking about the way I looked at the world a bit differently now, as if I were a camera. Before I only trusted other people to show me things, to arrange things into a frame and present them to me as the truth. Now I was interested in what I could see for myself. Milly nodded a lot as I was speaking; I felt encouraged.

We'd all planned to go for a drink in the college bar afterwards. It was OK; it was good to have Sara there — we didn't spend much time talking to each other, but we looked at each other across the room every so often, and she'd raise an eyebrow or I'd smile, and it made me feel at home, safer.

Sara and I had arranged to have a meal afterwards, and as we were saying our goodbyes, Milly asked if she could have a quick word with me. She took me round to the other side of the bar and suggested I should carry on studying, that I had an 'eye'. She asked me to come to her next series of classes that started in a few weeks time. I wasn't sure what to say, so just said thank you over and over, nodding like an idiot. I said I'd think about it; I didn't want to promise her anything. I didn't tell Sara or anyone else; I don't think I even want to tell Red, he might get his expectations up. I still get an excited swelling feeling in my stomach whenever I think about it. She thought I had an eye!

I didn't really want to see Sara, as I've got lots to do, and I resented the extra time it took. We made it through the meal quite painlessly; she didn't guess that anything was wrong. I almost enjoyed it — being old, fake Ruth is less tiring as well as less risky. When I got home I looked at the list I'd made before I went to work —

Find somewhere to stay
Letters for Red, Dad etc.
Tell Red what I need to tell him
Packing
Travel
Decide if/what to tell Dad, Abbie etc.
Sort out work — how will I get the holiday?
Decide on method and make preparations

All I had time to do tonight was find somewhere to stay. I found a hotel that looked big enough for me to be anonymous in it. The rooms were expensive — £80 a night — but it felt a bit silly to be worrying about money if it might be the last I ever spent. In the end I threw the boat out (ha ha — staying near the sea, throwing the boat out...) and spent £11 a night extra for a room with a sea view. I thought I'd leave here on Thursday morning, which would give me time to see Red on Tuesday and then get all the letters written so I could leave them here in the flat. I booked the room until Tuesday, the 1st of June. I won't need to be there longer than that either way.

I'm really not sure what to do about work. If I ask for emergency holiday, they might say no, and then I couldn't pretend I was ill without them finding out. Maybe I could get that doctor I saw with Abbie to sign me off with stress. But I'd rather not have that kind of thing on my record. Or maybe I could lie — tell them Dad has got ill again, or that I've got a bad back... What I really want to do is just not turn up, but if people got worried about me too quickly maybe they'd come looking and find me too early? So much to think about. I've found myself slipping in to thinking of Dan again; it's easier than thinking about Red. I want Dan to come with me. But I need to leave him behind as well. They all need to stay behind.

Tuesday 25th May

I sat for Red today, and he asked me to move in with him. Talk about timing! It was at the beginning of our sitting. He threw it in casually, saying that then he could paint me any time he wanted. Last week I think I would have felt awful, or wonderful, or both. Today I felt strangely unmoved. I laughed it off, saying he could never bear my tidiness or my cooking. He didn't say any more, went a bit quiet.

It felt odd to be with him back in his territory. I was aware of how little time I'd actually spent there. I wanted to make more of a mark, leave a toothbrush in the bathroom, an extra mug on the mug tree. I realised with a jump of shock that I'd never even been upstairs. I got up right then and said to Red that I wanted to see his bedroom. He followed me, joke-pinching my bottom every other step. Upstairs was less chaotic, cleaner, it didn't smell of turps. His bedroom was nice and cosy, actually; I was surprised. Full of rich colours, a soft carpet, a big, velvety armchair. He had a big, solid, wooden bed, and the duvet was a patchwork of reds and browns, different types of material, satin, cotton, fake fur… I lay down on it and stretched out my arms and legs like a starfish. It was like sinking into deep moss on a sun-dappled forest floor. He took off his shoes and jumped on me. We didn't get any more painting done.

Afterwards, I knew I couldn't put it off any longer. I stared up at the ceiling, said I had something important to say. 'You are leaving me?' he said. I turned to look at him and saw that he was serious. I can't fool him as easily as I fool the others. There's nowhere to hide; I feel naked. And so I told him I needed to think about what I wanted from my life before we carried on. That it wasn't fair on him for me not to be there for him, for me to be so confused. I didn't expect him to wait for me. My voice broke there, shuddered to a stop. He said the things I expected him to say — he didn't mind me being confused, he wanted me to find out with him. He also said things I hadn't expected him too. He was angry that he had found himself here again with a woman who wasn't able to commit to him. He said maybe he couldn't bear it either, being with someone who wasn't really there. Maybe I was right. We talked ourselves into silence and lay there for a while and held each other. And then I put my clothes on, got my things together and left.

At work, I picked up the stuff as planned. I won't tell you what I took or how I got it, in case someone might read this and do it themselves. I don't want to be responsible for anything like that. Then I took a deep breath and asked my line manager if I could talk to her privately. I lied to her. I said something shameful. I told her I'd had a miscarriage. That it was early, that I was just about starting to show. That I'd been trying for years with my partner. That we'd already named her, Morden, after Mother. I even cried a little. An Oscar-winning performance. My manager wasn't sure where to look; she's never been very good at tea and sympathy. When Maggie burst into tears once, my manager went over and patted her on the back and said, 'There, there,' before going to get someone else to deal with it. I didn't get any, 'There, there's, but she did offer to give me some time off work if that would help me. I was very grateful, told her we were having a funeral in a few days' time, that a week or two would help me to get myself together again. She bought it all. It was a horrible thing to tell her. I hate that people believe me.

I thought a lot about cutting today. It's a comforting thought but it doesn't have the same effect as before, a coolness smoothing my brow, a hand pressed tight across my back, a loosening of the tightness in my stomach. Since I told Red and Abbie, it's not my secret any more. It's one of the things that I'll have to commit to giving up. I haven't given it up yet, not if I'm going to be honest with you. I haven't actually done anything since last Tuesday. But it's with me constantly, in some of the space that Dan used to take up. If I truly want to live, I have to start saying no to death, even if it's just in small pieces, a few drops of blood, a taste of pain. It's one of the things that makes my life bearable — maybe I could keep it? Keep it under control, be careful, make sure I don't give myself an infection? No. I'm kidding myself. I know in my gut that I need to say goodbye to it. I don't expect that I'll stop straight away. I don't expect the feelings to disappear over night, for the fantasies to drift away. But I would be changing direction.

Wednesday 26th May

I woke up remembering that I would have been seeing my counsellor today, if I hadn't run away the first time. It might sound stupid, but I missed her. I know I haven't even met her yet. I got a letter from her a few days ago, saying she was sorry not to have seen me on Wednesday and that she'll wait to hear from me — I got it out and looked at it again. And I decided to call her before I even got dressed, hoping to get her answer-phone. She picked up, and after a second's silence I said I was sorry to call her so early. Apologised for not coming the first time, said I'd pay for it. Asked if she'd see me again. She said she could see me next Wednesday at the same time, would that be OK? I was relieved that she was still willing to see me. She said she looked forward to meeting me and to just give me a ring if I couldn't make it. I can't stand her up a second time. The only reason I won't be seeing her on Wednesday is if I'm not here any more. The thought of the appointment waiting for me on the other side of this week is strangely comforting, like being at work all day and knowing I have a new book of photographs waiting for me at home.

I wrote a note for everyone today. To Abbie and Dad and Red and Zoë and Sara and even Dan… one each, so I can say the different things I wanted to say. I wasn't sure how to do it, and in the end I went out and bought cards for them — a different one for each person. I was in the shop for an hour. I know how long it can take me to put things into words, so I thought I'd limit myself to a couple of sentences — I tried to make them simple, honest. I put a couple of standard sentences into each one — 'I'm doing this because I'm not very good at living — I've really tried, but I know this is the right decision. I want you to know that you are not to blame in ANY way and that you wouldn't have been able to change anything if you'd known.' I finished them all with, 'Sorry,' and, 'All my love, Ruth.' Here they are.

Abbie: I can't tell you how much I appreciated you being there for me when Mother died, and for confronting me about my cutting. I know it was hard for you to do, but you did it anyway. For everything you've done, thank you.

Zoë: I'm really proud of you and everything you've achieved over the last couple of months. I loved you coming to stay with me, I loved that you trusted me. Thank you.

Sara: I feel privileged that you shared what you shared with me, and listened so carefully to me. And thank you for all the fun we had at photography class.

Dan: You might not even remember me, but I was always aware of you at work, and you gave me comfort for a long time. I'm grateful for that. Thank you.

Julie: Thank you for meeting me that day and for being honest with me. Thank you for looking after Dad all these years — I'm glad he's got you.

Milly: Thank you for teaching me. Thank you for encouraging me, it felt wonderful.

Dad and Red were much harder. I wondered if I should write them longer letters; there was more I wanted to say. But then I thought maybe they should be the ones who see this journal. Warts and all. It might help them to understand. So in the end, I just wrote a card for both of them with all of my love in it and told them to read the journal if they wanted to look for answers. I don't know if they'll find any here, but at least there are more words. You know I love you, don't you, Dad? You know I love you, Red? Don't ever doubt that. Don't ever think that if I'd only loved you a bit more, I wouldn't have done it. That's just not true. I know that I need to make a decision for myself. It's not fair to live just because you'd be upset if I didn't. You'll all get over it. You can live without me. You'll survive; you'll be happy again. Surely it's better to live because I want to live, or die because I want to die, rather than stick around for someone else.

I spent my last (?) evening in my flat looking at photographs. Whatever happens next, this feels like the end of the something. I put on some music and got all of my books off the shelves, twenty or thirty of them. I looked through all of them, paying more attention to the photos I've spent time on, the ones that asked me in and let me live in them for a while. People. Things. Places. Moments. Stories. All moving past in a blur of beautiful colours, as if my whole life were flashing before me. And then, last of all, Charlotte Marie Bradley Miller, hanging on to life with her beautiful fingertips.

Thursday 27th May

This morning before I left for Aldeburgh, the postman dropped a letter onto the mat. I recognise Red's handwriting now - he'd taken to leaving little notes around the flat for me — 'I'm happy in here,' in my underwear drawer, and, 'Save some for Red,' in the biscuit packet. I could feel a square shape inside, like a big credit card. I was about to open it and felt suddenly nervous — maybe he never wanted to see me again, whatever I decide? Or he might say something that would persuade me not to go? So instead I put it with the other things I was bringing along — the turpentine-y rag he gave me to blow my nose on, a pebble from the beach in Brighton, the postcard.

I also took a few of my favourite birthday cards from Abbie, the recipe for lemon tart she'd written down for me (she'd drawn little pictures of lemons round the borders), and the old, blurry photo of Oscar she'd given me. The only photo I have of Dan. A card Zoë had bought me to say thanks for having her, and the necklace I bought on our first shopping trip. And finally a photo of the three of us at the beach when I was little, Mother squinting into the sun, Dad with his arm around her, stiff, proud.

I set off mid-morning with my case, feeling like Paddington Bear. Please look after this bear. Before I left the flat, I went around and touched everything — my computer, my pillows, the clothes left in my cupboard, my kettle, the rug in front of the sofa... silently letting go of each thing.

As I drew my fingers away from the TV, from the bed, I cut ties with each thing and it sank, leaving me lighter. By the time I'd finished, I was floating. I shut my front door behind me and then touched that too, and the whole flat slipped away from underneath me.

I looked through the train window at the grass and trees gliding past and saw a heron stood by a lake doing tai chi like an old man. Crows took off from the tops of trees suddenly, like warnings. Where was I going?

The hotel had a good feeling to it, the art was tasteful, modern, there were comfortable sofas downstairs; it was clean, new. The staff were professionally distant — the woman who checked me in said, 'Here on a holiday?' and when I said a short, 'Yes,' she didn't push it; she left me alone. I wanted to be left alone.

I ordered a late lunch in my room (oh, the wonders of room service) and then noticed a voicemail on my phone. It was Mary. It was the first time she'd ever called me on my mobile — I'd given her my number weeks ago when she was still living at home with her mum. She said on the message that her mum had caught her boyfriend cheating on her with a much younger woman and had kicked him out. Mary was going to stay where she was — she was enjoying her new independence — but she'd plucked up her courage to confess to her mum what had happened. Her mum had been upset, said she was sorry for not noticing, told her she shouldn't blame herself. Mary was calling to say that she was grateful to me for telling her it wasn't her fault, and for listening. She had heard I was off work for personal reasons, and she hoped everything was OK. I put on the burden of her caring for me like a heavy overcoat.

I needed some air, went for a walk on the beach. The hotel backed onto the shingle — from inside you couldn't see the beach, and it looked like the whole place, with its identical lamps and bed linen and full English breakfasts, was adrift on the ocean. It was a blustery day and felt more like autumn than spring. A few hundred of the billions of pebbles crunched underneath my feet. The smell of salt reminded me of Brighton, and I had a pang of missing Red. I walked until I reached the Maggi Hambling sculpture I'd read about when I was looking for a hotel. It was installed in honour of Benjamin Britten, who'd spent most of his life here. There are two giant, severed scallop shells rearing up out of the beach in an explosion of steel, four tonnes of it, twelve feet high. A lot of the people around here hate it — there's been a petition to get it moved. I thought it was wonderful — solid, silvery, a shipwreck, a spaceship. Along the top rim, a phrase from one of Britten's operas is pierced through the steel so you can read it against the sky — 'I hear those voices that will not be drowned'.

Apart from an old woman walking her dog, the beach was deserted. I looked for a place to sit on the massive structure and found a spot where I could rest my back. It was cool to the touch. I sat and looked out at the sea. I looked and thought. The wind blew through me. The sea listened to me. By the time I got back to my room, I was exhausted. When I've finished writing I'm going to fall straight into a dreamless sleep.

Friday 28th May

This morning I got up early, and after a proper breakfast with toast and eggs and beans and bacon, I took photos of Aldeburgh. I wanted to make something special to give to Red and Abbie and the others. I also wanted to take photos. I wanted to find a good angle for the scallop, and the perfect square of pebbles. In the end, I used up three films. While they were being developed, I chose some good photo frames — there are lots of arty shops along the main street, so there were plenty to choose from. I picked a few with wooden edges, some with metal, some with glass. I didn't even look at the prices.

I still had time to kill, and it didn't seem worth walking all the way back to the hotel. After eating some chips, I walked past a hairdresser's, turned round and went inside. I looked at myself in the mirror when the woman asked me what I wanted. Long, black, straight, boring hair. I wanted rid of it. I asked her to cut it all off. I was tempted to ask her to shave it off, but I was too embarrassed, so instead she shaved it into the nape of my neck and cropped it short on top, with some wax in it to shape it into short soft spikes. I felt naked when I walked out into the cold, seaside air. Lighter. I'm dropping ballast. I kept catching sight of myself in shop windows and wondering who that person was. She looked confident, independent. All afternoon I ran my fingers up the back of my neck against the grain of the hair. Like stroking a mole, if a mole would ever let you stroke it. Velvety. Wonderful. I closed my eyes and imagined my hand was Red's, imagined his voice. 'Crazy Ruth.'

When the photos were ready, I took them back to my room and spread them out on the bed. I'm getting better, I really am. There are a more photos now that seem to 'work'. I don't know if it's because I'm better at using the camera or just that I've learnt to see differently. Most of them were easy to choose — one of the whole beach from a black and white reel for Sara, a close-up of pink, rosy-grey and pale blue pebbles for Abbie. A wooden fishing boat with a spidery fishing net for Dad. A neat length of pastel coloured houses for Zoë, any one of which I could imagine her living in. None of them seemed quite good enough for Red. In the end I chose one of the scallop. An elderly couple were stood behind it with their backs to me, looking up to read the blue words. 'I hear those voices that will not be drowned'. You couldn't see their faces, and they weren't holding hands, but from the way they were standing, I imagined they were in love. I put the photos in the frames that suited them, wood for the pebbles, metal for the boat... and wrapped them up in paper covered in silver starfish. Labelled them carefully. Left them all in the cupboard by my bed.

My phone rang twice this evening. The first time it was Abbie — she left a message to say she'd tried me at home last night and tonight and hadn't had an answer; she was worried about me, could I just give her a ring to let her know I was OK. The second time it was Red. He didn't leave a message. It made me cry to hear Abbie's voice. It made me cry to not hear Red. I wanted to text them over and over, 'I love you.' 'I love you.' What I should really text, if I'm going to be honest, is, 'I'll hurt you.' 'Stay away from me.' I put my phone under my pillow and waited for it to ring again, for Red to leave me a message. Maybe if I don't answer, they'll get worried, will come looking. How would they know where to start? Would they be able to trace me by looking at my bank account? Would they break down the door of my flat? Would they find the letters too early? Do I want them to look for me?

I thought about Dan today. I know now that whatever I had with him (or didn't have) is in the past — there isn't a place for him in my life any more. I've been mourning him. And I've been worrying about the person who'll find me. Ambulance men (do they still send for an ambulance if you're already dead?) are used to seeing things like that; it's part of their job. But what if it's a baby-faced seventeen-year-old cleaner with the whole of her life before her? I don't want to put anyone through that. I think I'll put a notice on my door just before midnight on the 31st. The envelope could say, 'Please read this before you come in.' I'll address it to the manager; I can warn him about what he'll find inside. Maybe I should apologise to him as well, tell him I've enjoyed my stay and that it was nothing to do with the horrible pork chop I was served at dinner last night. Does it disturb you that I'm finding things to laugh about in all of this? Are you angry at me?

Saturday 29th May

Red rang again last night, much later, past midnight. I was watching a film on TV. I nearly picked it up. He didn't leave a message. I couldn't bear not to hear his voice. I put my clothes back on and left my room and went down onto the beach. I checked, and there was no-one around. I walked up to the very edge of the waves and threw my mobile into the sea as far as I could. It landed with a quiet plop and sank. I stood there until I got so cold I had to come back inside. When I got back to my room, the grey liquid was waiting for me. I haven't been feeling sad at all recently. I've been feeling strangely detached, with short spikes of longing or fear. And there was my grief again, waiting for me under the covers.

I suppose it never really leaves me. Maybe we all carry our pain around, and our happiness depends on how we carry it. Maybe we need to find out the best kind of hold for it, carrying it in front of us with our arms around it, or on our backs, in a pain-papoose. Maybe we need to take it out and take a proper look at it, a bit at a time, in small pieces that we can manage. At the moment, mine is covering me like a shroud.

I've got two days left. Today after breakfast, I put my 'do not disturb' sign on the door and went back inside to be with my journal. I stayed there most of the day, getting up to have a hot bath and then getting back into bed, eating expensive room-service sandwiches. The sadness was with me, but I could feel other things too. Some of the bits of paper had become crinkled or smudged — the ones I'd written at Red's house, or on the beach in Brighton. I re-wrote these ones so they looked perfect, like the others. It felt weird to say the things I'd already said once. I wondered about the person who had written them. When I'd finished, I stacked them up in front of me in order and took the first page from the top of the pile. I started reading.

I remembered how mean I was to be out of touch with Abbie for all these years, all of those cards. She never gave up hope. I read each of the hundred 'nothing's I'd written, they echoed in my head like bullets shot into a canyon. I smiled at my description of Red before anything had happened between us, how when the sun shone on him he lit up like a match. About the liquid oily stuff, about meeting Abbie for the first time, how nervous I felt. Mother in the bath. It chilled me to read it; I pulled the blankets around me. The blank spaces when it was too hard to write. Dad's accident. Zoë moving in. Telling you more and more all the time. Telling you just how bad it was. Just how bad I was.

It felt at times as if I were reading the same thing over and over. Poor Ruth. Poor Ruth. The photography classes, more sittings, getting to know Red. Starting to wonder how he felt about me. I looked for clues as I read, as if it were a mystery. Not 'who is the murderer', but 'should there be a death?' The argument with Zoë, the awful fight with Dad. I could hardly read what I had said to him. All I wrote on Sunday, the 11th was, "I want it to come early. I want it to just finish now." I cried here and there, tears of pain or tears of gratitude, careful not to splash tears onto the ink, catching them in the free hotel tissues. I put pieces of paper down and rocked, waiting for the hurt to wear off a little like a physical pain that throbs and then eases.

I read on. Red asking me out on April 15th — only six

weeks ago — it feels like we've known each other forever. And it feels like we hardly know each other at all. Zoë's new flat. My pink cardigan. The first time he held my hand. Starting photography. Getting drunk with Abbie. That awful party. Our trip to Brighton… so many things. What does it all add up to?

This evening I sat on the scallop and listened to my Insides album on headphones three times as I looked out at the sea. I could hardly bear the beauty of it. "I hate lovers. I hate the way they go to the bathroom in shifts after they've fucked. What do you think about when you're lonely?" The water moved towards me and then away. I couldn't hear it shaking the pebbles. "This is as close as I can bear." I fell so deep inside her voice, I was afraid I wouldn't be able to climb back out. My body was carried along on the river of drums, melodies rising and falling. "I'm not going to shout just to get hold of your attention. I don't care for fighting to get possession." "I don't know if I can let you back inside again." "God knows it's hard enough to keep my chin up, harder still to keep afloat." "How long could I hold your attention? Would you wait another hour? A week? A year? Five years?"

Sunday 30th May

My time is running out. It's time to tell you about the third thing that happened when Mother was dying. The third thing I was a witness to. Have I built up the tension enough? You're probably expecting something gory, something horrifying, something that will stay with you as it's stayed with me all this time. A story so ugly that you'll need to tell it to a couple of people to dilute it. A story that will teach you something new about what it is to die. You'll be disappointed.

It was the night that Mother died. She was in hospital. We were there, Dad and me — she hadn't been awake for a while; she'd already said her goodbyes. It didn't feel like she was hanging on to life, more that she was waiting for death, like waiting for a bus. Getting impatient. We both sat there in silence for hours on end and listened to her breathe. There was too much time between each breath. I waited for each one, like when someone is snoring, and it's not the snoring that keeps you awake, but the waiting-for-the-next-snore. It started to feel as though I were keeping her alive by making sure of each new intake of air.

We only spoke to each other when we fetched coffee or went to the toilet. Dad was too deep in his grief to look after me, to worry about me. And I was fine with that — I wanted to be left alone. I don't know what I thought about, those last hours. I didn't even look at Mother much, just sat in her room, reading, doing puzzles in a puzzle-book. Dad just looked at her, his eyes glazed. And then, just when I was wondering if she might go on forever, she took a big breath and then her breath left her, but it was different, like it was leaving of its own accord, not being blown out. It went on for a long time. I wondered how she could have so much air in her. There was a silence then, stretching on and on.

How long did we sit like that? After a while, I realised that I was holding my own breath and let it out suddenly. Dad was looking at her face, waiting. He took one of his hands and held it flat over her chest, not touching her. I don't know what he was trying to do, what he was thinking. And he said, 'No.' So quietly, so quietly I could hardly hear. No. No. No. They didn't join up into a string, each 'no' was separate, all on its own. Utterly final. No. No. No. I wanted to leave the room. I wanted someone else to be there. It was too much, the three of us together in this small room. The two of us. One of us gone. Dad got louder, slowly. No. No! No! NO! NO! I felt embarrassed. I felt embarrassed that someone would hear us, that someone would hear my dad grieving for his dead wife. I said 'Dad!' quietly. He didn't hear me. I was stuck to my seat. There was no room for me to be sad. He was taking up all of the space, all of the space. And then people came in, lots of people, and started doing things to my mum. Not Mother. My mum. My mummy. One of the nurses went over to my dad and put her hand on his back. And he just kept on. NO! NO! NO! His face distorted. No-one was with me. I got up. I left the room.

And none of this, none of this is the third worst thing. The third worst thing was this: I walked out of that room, that room where my mum was dead and my dad was screaming. I shut the door behind me. I walked out into the corridor. I didn't know where I was. And I walked out in front of a woman, all dressed up in a business suit, a bunch of flowers in her hand. She was in a hurry. She bumped into me, she dropped the flowers. I opened my mouth to say sorry, but before it came out, she looked right at me and said, 'Get out of my way.' She said it quietly; her eyes were cold. And she picked up the flowers and walked off. She says it to me in my dreams, night after night. Get out of my way. Get out of my way. And I stood there, thinking, 'My mum has just died! Don't you care? Can't you even stop for a minute to let me tell you?'

And then I wondered why she should care. I thought about how Mum's death was going to affect the world. It would rip into me and Dad, of course. Her family and close friends would be left with huge holes in their lives. But her acquaintances — would there be more sadness that she'd gone, or more fear about how this could happen to them? And the people she used to know — her best friend at primary school, her third boyfriend — would they ever find out? And the people she passed on the street in her lifetime? And all the people she'd never met, who never even knew she existed — that anonymous woman in her business suit — the shockwaves wouldn't even touch them. When we die, it'll be the same.

Monday 31st May

Just now I decided to open the letter that Red had sent me. It was a single piece of notepaper wrapped around a Polaroid. The notepaper said, 'Maybe this will help you with your decision,' that was all. It was a Polaroid of a painting. The painting was of me. The first thing I noticed was that the colours were very different. The first canvas had red-grey tones — muted, warm. This one had a huge splash of fuchsia across the bottom — he'd painted me in my new cardigan! I looked at the colours in it, the whites, the deep crimsons, the electric pinks. And it was beautiful, that cardigan — it was even more beautiful than it was in real life. I slowly looked up from the cardigan and looked into my eyes. They were small on the photo, it was difficult to see, but they answered me. They had fire in them. I don't know if he'd painted it that way on purpose, but I swear I could see flames. Not big flames, not raging, but gently burning. Giving out heat. My face was looser, somehow. It looked like it could move. There was still sadness and pain. But there was more than that. And I liked it. I liked myself.

It's early evening. Monday, 31st May.

I didn't sleep for a single second last night. I didn't want to waste it. I wasn't tired, anyway. I looked out of my window at the sea. I listened to the waves. I talked to the sea; I was heard. My mind whirred.

Tomorrow is June. Have you guessed? Would you want to live if you were me? Is it worth all the trouble? All the pain of what's already happened, all the fear of what might or might not happen next? I've made up my mind. I'm not saying it was an easy decision. But my time has run out. It was a decision that had to be made. Would you want to live if you were me?

I've seen so much; I've learnt so much.
There's still more for me to learn. I'm just beginning.

I've told you so much. All these words.
I've still got more to say.

It still hurts. It still hurts.
Sometimes it hurts too much. Sometimes it's unbearable.

There are things I want to do.

I might fail. I might want things, really try to do them, really try, and fail.

I'm so grateful you've listened to me. I hope you believe that, whatever else you believe.

Tomorrow is June. I'm going to get up in a minute, put this journal somewhere safe. I'll wash what's left of my hair. I'll smooth cream into my skin, being careful with my scabs.

I'll put on my pink cardigan and my new strawberry lip-gloss. I'll treat myself to a good meal in a posh restaurant around the corner.

Then I'll pack some warm clothes, a blanket and pillows from my room, the pebble from Brighton, the photo of my painting. I'll walk down to the scallop, make myself comfortable, lie back and look up. I'll let it cradle me. The waves will listen to me.

I'll watch the stars until just before midnight. And then I'll get up, and go towards what's next.

Acknowledgements

Thanks to Anna Torborg, Emma Barnes and Rob Jones for looking after me.

Thanks to Harry Hall for telling me to read more slowly.

Thanks to Simon Brett for being my first (careful, encouraging and gracious) reader.

Thanks to Fraser Dyer for keeping me going when I needed it.

Thanks to Kit Harding, Maggi Fletcher, Alison Baker, Irina Ignatova, Alison Hill and Tamara Everington for important details.

Thanks to Joanna Devereux for shaping Thaw and for believing in my writing.

Thanks to Susan Utting, Jo Brogan, Esther Morgan, Sarah Utting and Ian House for caring about Ruth.

Thanks to Steve, always.

About the Author

Fiona Robyn was born in 1974 in Surrey and grew up in Sarawak. Her website is at www.fionarobyn.com, and she keeps a blog about being a writer at www.plantingwords.com. She lives happily in rural Hampshire, with her partner, her cats Silver and Fatty, and her vegetable patch.

Also by Fiona Robyn...

The Blue Handbag

Available Now

Chapter 1: A Posy of Painted Ladies

Leonard is feeding the dusty, battered suitcase into the mouth of the wheelie-bin when he catches a flash of azure blue shining from inside. He judders to a complete stop and holds himself perfectly still to give his eyes a chance to focus. There's something in there. His heart speeds up. He pulls the suitcase back out and opens the jaws of the zips wide, letting in light. It's a handbag. It must have been one of Rose's. Rose, his dear, dear wife. His body softly crumples in on itself. He presses his forehead with his left palm. It's been nearly three years now. Three years since that last migraine that wasn't a migraine at all, but a clot of blood that had detached itself from one of her arteries and travelled up to her brain. Setting off an explosion of pain, filling her with a beating, rising fear. His Rose. Three years. It seems like yesterday. It seems like a lifetime ago.

He hunkers down on the pavement, his sixty-two-year-old knees reminding him to move carefully. He lifts the handbag out, brushing away cobwebs from the material as if he were stroking his daughter's cheek. He places it on the step beside him, wiping dust from the cold bricks before he sets it down, and checks the inside of the suitcase, sliding a flat hand inside the pockets. A biro lid, a sweetie wrapper, nothing else. He pushes the suitcase back into the wheelie-bin - it just fits and the sides of it scrape the plastic. He looks around nervously to see if anyone has seen him, not knowing why it matters if they have. His heart is slowing down. He sucks in two lungfuls of late October air and turns away from the road and towards his house. He carries the handbag as if it were a baby. As if it were alive.

He's on his way to the kitchen when the phone rings and forces him back into the hall. He rests the handbag up against a green glass vase full of pink-spattered lilies on the telephone table. As he picks up the receiver, all thoughts of his wife leave him as if he's flicked a switch.

"Hello?"

All he can hear is a faint squealing noise. His daughter comes onto the line just before his second hello.

"Hi, Dad, is that you?"

"No, it's the Viscount of Prussia. How may I be of assistance to you?" he says, disguising his usual Berkshire accent with his best aristocratic voice, which despite his efforts comes out a little Welsh.

Raine makes a harrumphing noise. Leonard feels a little sad for the giggling girl in pigtails who got lost – when? When did he lose her? He used to love making her laugh. He seems to have lost the knack.

"Dad, for goodness sakes. How are you?" He can hear the familiar edge of brusqueness in her voice and guesses she's only asking from a sense of duty.

"Tickety-boo, darling. How are the twins?"

"Oh, fine, fine. Rory has a bit of a temperature. He's playing up something rotten; I can't get him to eat anything, the bugger." She breathes a quick sharp sigh. "I'm sure he'll survive. He's annoyed with me right now – I tried to force some bread and marmite down him just before I called you."

Leonard already feels a rising impatience with the conversation.

"Mh hmm," he says, to encourage her to carry on. She pauses, waiting. There's a small fluttering in his stomach.

"Is everything OK, darling?"

"Oh, yes, all fine." She pauses again. "Yes, everything's fine. I'm just tired, I suppose. Are you still coming down this weekend?"

"Yes, of course."

"Great." The squealing noise starts up in the background again – it sounds as if it's coming from a trapped animal. They both listen.

"Look, Dad, I'm sorry but Rory is making a fuss. I better go and check on him. You'd think I'd been starving him, the way he carries on. I don't know what to... well – anyway – I'll call you in a couple of days to arrange things."

"Yes darling, talk to you then. I'll let you know what train I'll be on."

"Bye Dad."

"Bye."

Just as he's pulling the phone away from his ear he hears her say "Oh – wait! Dad?"

"I'm still here."

"I forgot – the whole reason I rang was to ask you if you liked turkey. Rory, wait a minute! I can't remember if you said something about... last time I... RORY! We're... Dad? Turkey?"

She rushes him into answering. He wonders how she ended up like this, never stopping for long enough to catch her breath. So unlike him, so unlike Rose. He slows his voice down, willing some of his calm to infuse into her, to infect her.

"Yes, that'll be lovely, darling. You're sure you're OK now? Is Ed helping you with the boys?"

"Yes, Dad. Speak soon. Bye! Oh, Ed's fine! Bye!"

By the time he gets his goodbye out she's already hung up.

He stands with the empty phone against his ear for a few seconds until his eyes catch on something blue. The handbag! The colour reminds him of Rose's wedding dress. They were so young - she was seventeen, still a child. He pictures her now, grinning at her friends from work in the congregation, her arm linked through his. The dress was plain, full-skirted and the colour of cornflowers. She told him it was a tradition in their family to wear blue rather than white. She looked so pretty with her painted lips and her dark hair cropped close to her scalp. He'd loved to run his flat fingers against the grain of her softly prickly hair. He gave it a quick skim most days, while teasing her about her temper, or when coming into a room and finding her there. She wanted sweet peas for her wedding bouquet - they'd always been her favourites. They got married in May so he grew her 'Painted Ladies', pale pink with a deep pink nose. She held them in a fat posy at her waist and ticked him off for crushing the petals when he kissed her with too much enthusiasm. He'd whispered into her ear that now they were married he'd grow her bucketfuls and bucketfuls until she was sick of them. And he had - year after year, until she really did get fed up of the sight of them. She finally spat it out one night during an argument, and it had pierced him in his chest. He didn't blame her, really. He always did go a bit over the top with things.

He leaves the handbag on his chair and goes into the kitchen to click on his shiny silver kettle. He can take his time - nothing is going anywhere. One of the advantages of living on your own – nobody will be bursting in to ask him if he can fix the Hoover or get a child a drink. He unhooks his favourite mug from the mug tree, winter-berry red on the outside and glossy green on the inside. Raine bought it for him a few Christmas ago. He readies it with a Yorkshire teabag and turns the lid off the milk. He's been drinking Yorkshire tea for twenty-five years, since a trip to a National Trust property up North. He doesn't enjoy tea at other people's houses; it always tastes insipid. He flicks his eyes around his tiny kitchen as he waits for the water to boil. There are bright crayon scribbles from the twins taped up on the fridge. According to Raine the blocks in the middle are tanks – 'They're utterly obsessed with the bloody things,' but they have bright yellow suns above them and sit on solid green grass spotted with purple flowers. There's a single glass, plate, knife and fork on the washing up drainer. He can see his face reflected, ghost-like, in the white kitchen tiles above the work surface. He notices a smear of something greasy and gets out a cloth to disappear it. He's kept the place clean since Rose died; he prides himself on that. Rose would be impressed. She always kept things neat and tidy.

As the kettle gathers steam and clicks itself off, Pickles jerks his head up and looks at Leonard, startled. He lets out a small wake-up growl. His eyes are button black and shiny, perfect rounds. He's looking scruffy again, his fur choppy as a rough sea, old mud clinging to tufts of hair on his belly. Leonard makes a mental note to tackle bathing him at the weekend. It's always a messy affair. As soon as Pickles sees there's nothing to worry about he drops his chin back onto the well-worn fur of his basket and goes back to his doggy dreams. He's always liked to sleep in the kitchen, even at their old house. Maybe he likes to stay close to his food bowl at all times just in case there are any ad-hoc doggy snacks. Leonard fills his mug and gives the bag a good squeeze, encouraging it to release its dark flavour. Rose used to say it looked like he was milking a cow in there. Finally he jolts in a small splash of milk to stop the horrible floating film that comes with black tea. 'I like it dark and sweet, just how I like my women,' he used to tease Rose – she'd always come back with, 'And I like mine weak and lukewarm, just like you, darling.' He holds the spoon under the tap to help wash away this memory so he can return to the job at hand.

He sets down his tea on the small table next to his chair, resting it on top of a rickety pile of crossword books, and lifts the handbag into his hands. It feels silky against his fingertips and reminds him of the silvery leaves of the canary clover, *Dorycnium hirsutum.* He laughs at the memory of sneaking away from his digging in the middle of the afternoon so he could crouch beside a new batch of them and stroke them. They'd have him carted off if they knew. Leonard lets his mind rest on what he's holding. One of Rose's handbags. What was it doing in their old suitcase? He can't remember ever seeing it before. Is it definitely hers? He lifts it to his face and sniffs, tentatively at first, then great, sucking-in breaths. It's only an echo now, but he remembers the original scent so well - a hint of jasmine, sandalwood, and then something underneath... what is that Indian spice called? Cardamom? The handbag was hers alright. He'll never forget that perfume until the day he dies. She must have kept one of her little bottles in here, where it spilt a golden drop or three. This scent is as familiar to him as her face is – no – more familiar. It's more of an effort now to remember exactly what she looked like, and this worries him. But that smell. Mmm. He feels his eyes prickling and allows a single tear to escape from each one, warming his cheeks, before taking a sharp breath and blowing his nose. He's done his crying.

He studies the material close-up for a moment. It's woven, and has lots of tiny hairs like the hide of a strange blue animal. Maybe one with six legs and purple eyes and a huge mane like a lion. He places a flat palm on one side and moves it across and back, across and back. He's aware of taking his time with it, as if he's choosing the perfect chocolate from the box. The clasp is one of those old-fashioned metal ones where the metal prongs push hard against each other before finally snapping free. He un-clicks it, and then clicks it shut and un-clicks it absentmindedly a few times more before pulling it open and peering inside.

Nothing. Empty. His heart sinks – and then he laughs at himself – what exactly was he expecting to find? A new photograph of her? A bright burst of her laugh? The things she left behind are all souvenirs now – her wedding ring, the favourite cardigan he keeps in his top drawer in the bedroom. He puts his hand inside to feel the silk lining, already thinking about putting it back into the bin outside, and as he slips a thumb under the piece of silk-covered cardboard at the bottom he encounters something sharp. It's the edge of something. A small piece of paper. He checks first to make sure there's nothing else there, and then pulls it out and holds it in front of him so he can see it properly. It's a return train ticket from Pangbourne, where Rose worked as a nurse for many years, to Didcot. It's dated the 15th of December 1998. Nearly seven years ago. On the back she's written '*decide about next Tues??? L's on hol*' in blue felt tip. She'd never been to Didcot. He never went to Didcot with her. He pauses to search his memories more carefully. Did they ever go shopping there? No. To see the railway centre, or friends? No. Had she cried off when he'd suggested it, saying something about not liking the town, something about a bad memory? He can't remember. Why would she go there? What is it she needed to think about next Tuesday? Why would it make a difference that he was on holiday?

These busy thoughts fade away and he sits and points his eyes in the general direction of the window for five whole minutes, not thinking of anything in particular. He's noticed that he 'phases out' like this sometimes – if someone else were in the room they might ask him what he was thinking about. No-one asks him. He rouses himself with a shake. He used to growl like Pickles when he did this, to make Rose, and then later Raine, laugh. He does it now anyway – grrreeowwwwWWW-HUH! – and makes himself laugh instead. He puts the ticket back where he found it and goes outside to throw the handbag in the wheelie-bin. He comes back into the sitting room and considers rolling a cigarette. Instead he turns on a programme about ancient Rome and picks up his hot cup of tea and a crossword book. He flicks the pages, gulps his tea, and tries to ignore the ichneumon wasps who have laid their eggs inside him.